My good friends gather around the campfire with me. We will share our stories and sing songs of praise. Testimonies of God's grace will inspire us to live closer to Him. Our best friend, Jesus will walk among us, touching our lives, giving us strength for the day's journey, and giving us the blessed assurance that He will never leave or forsake us.

The words of praise continue as each person uses his or her talents to glorify God. I would like to take a few minutes of your time to express my hearts desire.

I love to write; God has blessed me with this special gift to help others along the pathway of life. I pray each day for Him to bless and use me in His own special way.

I know that words rightly spoken will be as medicine to the soul, healing the broken hearted and restoring faith in God above.

My hearts desire is to show kindness; give a lot of love, and help others know Jesus Christ as Lord and Savior before the midnight hour. My desire is for souls to be saved.

Daily

Inspiration

Daily Inspiration

Micro Stories

Daily Devotion

David L. Hurst

Published by David L. Hurst

Cover Design copyright © 2012 by David L. Hurst.   All rights   reserved.

Interior Design copyright © 2014 by David L. Hurst

Published in the United States of America

ISBN: 978-0-9855779-2-6

1. Micro Stories/ Inspirational & religious
2. Religion / Christian Life / Devotional

Dedication

There are some wonderful people in my life whom I would like to honor and show my love and appreciation: my mother, Agnes L. Hurst, and there is a special place in my heart for my son, Kris M. Hurst.

It is my privilege and honor to dedicate "Daily Inspiration, Micro Stories" to the Hurst family. My brothers and sisters, I pray that the Lord will bless each of you and keep you in his love and care. This book is in loving memory of my father, Roy L. Hurst.

Acknowledgements

It is my pleasure to recognize and honor my brothers and sisters, Gordon, Marie, Gene, and Sherry, for the many words of encouragement. All of my friends and family are greatly appreciated for their kind words and their loyal support. I am thankful for the prayers that ascended to heaven.

With heartfelt gratitude from a sincere heart, I give thanks unto God for inspiring me to write Daily Inspiration and blessing me with a spiritual thought for each micro story.

January

1 The Old Year Is Past
2. From the Miry Clay
3. Plenty of Time
4. The Midnight Hour
5. The Hourglass
6. Look Up, My Friend
7. A Little While
8. Take the Time
9. It is Later than you think
10. Here Today, Gone Tomorrow
11.Surely Goodness and Mercy
12. The Last Page
13. A Time to Fast
14. A New Life in Christ
15. It is Suppertime
16. A Time to Rejoice
17. To Stay or Go
18. It Is Time
19. The Train Is Coming
20. The Journey's End
21. Solid Rock Foundation
22. When does life begin?
23. The Last Amen
24. Today Is Borrowed
25. Clouds Pass Away
26. Heaven or Hell
27. King's Palace, Poor Man's Home
28. The Chief Cornerstone
29. Where will He find us?
30. My Hearts Desire
31. Where is Jesus?

February

1. God is never too busy
2. Tomorrow May be too late
3. Waiting for the Day
4. White as Snow
5. Melt the Ice
6. When the Path Is Hard to See
7. The Pure in Heart
8. Open the Window
9. Righteous Living
10. Nothing but the Blood
11. As I Have Loved You
12. Bread for a Stranger
13. Heaven's Gold Mine
14. He is worthy of the Honor
15. Please Forgive Me
16. No Looking Back
17. Run with the Son
18. Talents Used, Souls Forgiven
19. I Can't Do It
20. Deep Desire
21. A Light on a Dark Path
22. When Jesus Comes Again
23. The Trumpet Sound
24. Our Home in glory
25 Great Expectations
26. A City in the Sky
27. A Prodigal Son Returns
28. Walk by Faith, not by sight
29.Treasure in Heaven

March

1. Asleep at the Midnight Hour
2. Restore to Life Eternal
3. A Safe Passageway
4. Open the Gates
5. Passing Through
6. Higher Ground
7. Memories of the Past
8. Calendar of Regret
9. Patiently Wait
10. Run to Win
11. A Place in Glory
12. Christ our Best Friend
13. This Same Jesus
14. Stranded on a Highway
15. Keep the Faith Alive
16. Ready or not
17. Names Called in Glory
18. A Refreshing Rain
19. A Stranger in the Camp
20. Thanks Again, Jesus
21. No Grapes on the Vine
22. High Calling of God
23. Gold in the Hills
24. Break up the Fallow Ground
25. Carry the Torch
26. Build a Bigger Barn
27. Never Thirst Again
28. Change the Track
29. Saved by Grace
30. The Calmness of Nature
31. Shadow of Death

April

1. He Is the Son of God
2. Where will We Find Him
3. Walk on
4. No Time to Waste
5. Crucify all Over Again
6. Walk with Jesus
7. He Didn't Send an Angel
8. He Didn't Come Down
9. Anyone Need a Ride Home
10. The Third Day
11. No Flowers on the Grave
12. Faith Is Alive
13. Faith Barriers Removed
14. No Excuse This Time
15. Jesus Saves
16. We are Va. Tech. Let's Go Hokies
17. Paid in Full
18. Pure Sweet Honey
19. Meet Jesus at the Crossroads
20. Life in Christ
21. Security Breach
22. It Is Finished
23. Be Alert, Stay Alive
24. He Has the Key
25. Faith to See Christ
26. Faith Never Quits
27. He Died for an Enemy
28. If in This Life Only
29. He Gave His Life
30. Partners in Crime

May

1. Come from Behind
2. Dusts on the Bible
3. The Choice Is Mine
4. Class for Sins Dismissed
5. A Pen in God's Mighty Hand
6. The Cross and beyond
7. A Sharp Axe
8. flames of Faith
9. Detour Turn Right
10. No Talents Left
11. Mother's Day
12. A Flickering Flame
13. Train Wreck
14. Fear no Evil
15. Gather in the Grain
16. Work in the Harvest Field
17. Strawberry Pie
18. A Fresh Refilling of Faith
19. Weeds in the Garden
20. A Porch of an Idle Life
21. Silver and Gold
22. Allegiance to God
23. The Battle is not ours
24. Rich in Spirit
25. His Search Is Endless
26. Memorial Day
27. The Potter and the Clay
28. Get Out Now
29. Endure to the End
30. Astray from the Fold
31. Red Flag Warning

June

1. Lost and Found
2. In the Miry Clay
3. Follow the Son
4. He Paid the Price
5. Asleep on our Watch
6. Not Guilty
7. He Is a Friend
8. Be of Good Cheer; It Is I
9. One Day with Jesus
10. The World or Jesus
11. Faith Is Believing
12. Greater Is He
13. The Right Path
14. Spiritual Rain
15. Father's Day
16. Neglect our Salvation
17. My Good Friends
18. His Visitation Hours
19. A Personal Visit
20. Grace Always Abounds
21. Led by the Holy Spirit
22. Come and Dine
23. Life Saving Responders
24. Storm Chasers
25. Safe and Secure
26. Under the Radar
27. Sins will find us
28. Jesus, the Only Way
29. Come unto Me
30. Bind Us Together

July

1. Debt is paid
2. Final Review
3. Only by Permission
4. God Bless America
5. The Master of the Clay
6. Behold, the Man, Jesus
7. Life or Death
8. Shelter in the Rock
9. The Fire Escape
10. Pardon Me
11. Stagnant Life
12. Light in Darkness
13. Keep Holding on
14. The Stain of Sin
15. The Worth of a Soul
16. Blind Spots of Faith
17. Race for Life
18. Transformed Lives
19. A Decision for Life
20. Too Faraway to Focus
21. Bread for a Beggar
22. All Have Sinned
23. Garden of Sin
24. One Lost Lamb
25. No Doubt in Faith
26. Runaway Train
27. God's Housekeepers
28. A Personal Delivery
29. A Blind Beggar
30. Lies of Deceit
31. A Decision for Christ

August

1. Left Town, No Regrets
2. One Word Assignment
3. Heaven is Real
4. Keep the Fire Burning
5. Almost Persuaded
6. Ten Commandments
7. Sins Miry Clay
8. The Verdict
9. Temptation Trap
10. Tomorrow
11. Bad Apples
12. The Reality of Life
13. One Image Equals Two
14. Enticed by Sin
15. Restore to Life
16. Faith in a Storm
17. Never Give Up
18. High Security
19. Thorns and Nails
20. The Wrestling Match
21. In the Line of Duty
22. The Right Road
23. Glory Land Road
24. Deceivers Among Us
25. River of God's Love
26. A Crack in the Frame
27. Revisit Old Sins
28. God will make a Way
29. Keep the Stream Flowing
30. One Day Shy of Eternity
31. Entangled in Sin

September

1. Keys of Faith
2. Salvation's exit
3. House of Neglect
4. Drifted Away
5. An Old Fire Escape
6. Fiery Furnace
7. Keep Running
8. Oil for the Lantern
9. Throw out the Lifeline
10. A Thief in the Home
11. Foxes Spoil the Grapes
12. Search for God
13. Walk Away
14. Our Best is not a Fraction
15. Walk in the Dark
16. A Fall From Grace
17. In the Lions' Den
18. Adopted into the Family
19. Oil in the Lamp
20. The Rails of Faith
21. Lion on the Prowl
22. Thin Ice
23. God Never Abandons
24. Too Close to the Edge
25. Self-Inflicted Wound
26. Open the Floodgates
27. Escape Sparks of Sin
28. Drifting on Waves of Sin
29. Unexpected Grace
30. Never Castaway

October

1. SOS, Help is on the Way
2. Abundance of Grace
3. A Reflection of Christ
4. Tear the Old Fence Down
5. Prepare to Meet Thy God
6. Search Diligently
7. Break the Bonds of Sin
8. A Runner has fallen
9. In God We Trust
10. Unbreakable Cords of Love
11. Home Fires Burning
12. A Shortcut to Heaven
13. Glory Land Express
14. Fervent Prayer
15. Stir Up the Coals
16. Unload the Wagon
17. Slippery Slopes of Sin
18. Wait on the Lord
19. Stay on Course
20. Don't Give Up
21. Cougar Attack
22. Grounded in Jesus
23. Force the Door Open
24. Flames in the Night
25. Fresh Supply of Grace
26. Big I and Little u
27. Self-Sufficient
28. Faith Lines Open
29. Meet Me at the Cross
30. Follow Jesus
31. Fox in the Hen House

November

1. Wet Matches Burning
2. Sneak out the Backdoor
3. One Call for a Bailout
4. Life Expectancy
5. Shelter of His Love
6. See You in the Morning
7. No Turning Back
8. Tragedy at the Circus
9. A Wild Man's New Life
10. Old Sins and Divine Grace
11. God Bless the Veterans
12. How much do you love me?
13. Closer to Home
14. When We Fail to Pray
15. Exalted Above Humility
16. Jesus is too far Away
17. Strong Current of Sin
18. Earthly Riches
19. Locked in the Past
20. Water is contaminated
21. An Empty Bucket
22. A Divine Connection
23. Bloodhound on the Trail
24. God's Power Over Sin
25. Faith's Battery Recharged
26. Second Chance
27. Thanksgiving Day
28. Too Late to Pack
29. Overcoming Hurdles
30. Arise from the Shadows

December

1. The Wagon Trail of Sin
2. The Candle of Faith
3. Keep Our Eyes on Jesus
4. Fearful of Deep Water
5. Faith Comes by Hearing
6. Personal Response Required
7. Trapped in the Mine
8. Daily Inspiration
9. Special Moments of Prayer
10. Jesus gives us Peace
11. Peace with God
12. The Choice is ours
13. Blank Page of Sin
14. Little Sins and Giant Waves
15. The Blood Trail
16. God's Gift to Mankind
17. Give Him our Hearts
18. Doorbell is Ringing
19. Joy Comes in the Morning
20. God's Best Gift
21. Countdown for Christ
22. Ten, Another Opportunity
23. Nine, Your Choice
24. Eight, Christmas Eve
25. Seven, Christmas Day
26. Six, No Excuses
27. Five, except we Repent
28. Four, Unexpected Visit
29. Three, Turn the Herd
30. Two, the Fear of Death
31. Then There Was One

The Old Year is Past
January 1

A new year has begun. There is no turning back to the days of the past. The days are gone. They will not return. We would like very much to reclaim some of them. It is too late, now. The calendar page has already been turned. The only way back is by the memory trail.

The days are gone, but they are not forgotten. December 31st was the last. It is time for us to move into a new year. Please don't worry about the days that have faded into the past. Let us hold onto the kind words and gentle affection of each person's heart.

The blessings of God will be many as we walk the straight and narrow way. Let us continue to follow Jesus with love sincere and faith unwavering. Obey His commandments and love one another, our relationship with God will grow stronger as we show a little kindness and help each other along the way. A word of encouragement will revive a perishing soul. Use us Lord in your own special way.

Look ahead, my friend; this is a new year. Take one step, one day at a time. Trust Jesus all the way.

Love Him with heart, soul, and mind. The glory-land is in sight and very soon the gates of heaven will open and we will forever be with the Lord. The old year is passed; the new one has begun. Faith in God's Son, a crown of life will be won.

From The Miry Clay
January 2

Deep in the miry clay and sinking more every day. A faithless sinner whose life is filled with corruptible things will soon find a resting place in a shallow grave. Everyone is welcome, no one is denied. The grave is not bashful, even the pure in heart and the faithful will abide.

We must realize that all have sinned and the miry clay of sin will separate us from a kind and loving God. If there is no repentance, there will be no hope of going to heaven or walking the streets of glory. Sinking deeper every day, closer to the grave, I don't intend to stay.

One day when I was sinking in the clay, Jesus was walking by. He heard my heartfelt pleas. He reached way down to save a wretch like me. From the miry clay to the rock of ages, Jesus lifted me.

When my time on earth has ended, if the rapture has not taken place, I will be laid to rest in a shallow grave. I will be there for just a little while. The trumpet will sound and the King of glory will appear in the clouds of heaven and the dead in Christ shall rise first, then those who are alive will be caught up together in the clouds to be forever with the Lord.

God's grace is sufficient for a poor wretched sinner. He knows those who are repentant and He will not hesitate to deliver. God is deeply touched by the sincere emotions of the heart. I am sorry, was my heart's plea. Jesus came into my heart and saved me. "Thank you, Jesus.

Plenty of Time
January 3

I have plenty of time to give my life to God. There's no need to be in a hurry. God will wait another day. Live for today, eat, drink, and be merry. These are the thoughts of a careless mind.

No one knows how long life will last. The shadows of death will cross each one's path. There will be no room in the grave for rejected grace.

"Plenty of time," the words echo through the ages. There is a time for dying, no more time to live. The departed will not sing the heavenly hymns. No one can escape deaths dark hour.

There is coming a time when it will be too late to pray, to seek after God. Plenty of time is a false commitment that fades away when life comes to an end.

Hope shines brighter still when the heart is receptive to God's will. Don't put off tomorrow the things you could have done today. Jesus is walking by, salvation to impart. Do not hesitate or the hour of salvation will pass.

Thoughts from the grave, "I wish I had time. But the days are gone. I would like to change my mind and believe in God's Son." "Choose you this day, whom you will serve." (Joshua24:15). Many cries from the grave, where is God's grace? It all depends my friend, if Jesus was rejected or accepted in the time allowed. It's not too late to pray.

The Midnight Hour
January 4

The day is approaching when Jesus will come in the clouds of glory. There is still time to repent. Ask Jesus to come into your heart and forgive your sins. It is time to get ready! Jesus is waiting to hear your hearts plea.

Salvation is granted the moment you believe. All those who are washed in the blood will be allowed to enter the kingdom of heaven.

But just suppose your love for God has faded and you are no longer following Jesus, please don't despair; the call from heaven is the same, "Repent."

When Jesus comes again, the sweet harmony of hallelujah will rise and the gates of heaven will open for all the faithful believers. This could be the day when you meet the Lord in the skies. No one knows the day or hour He will split the eastern sky.

Keep looking for His return. Will He find you spiritually asleep or wide-awake to rejoice in the resurrection power? The coming of the Lord is near. Some of the sleepers are unaware that Jesus will soon appear and the kingdom of God they will forfeit.

Hear the Masters call, "Repent!" Join with the saints and martyrs of old and be ready to meet Jesus in the clouds. Prepare to meet thy God. It is getting very close to the midnight hour.

This could be the hour when the saints take flight and stand before the throne greeted by the King. "Enter into the glories of the Lord."

The Hourglass
January 5

Particles of sand in an hourglass move ever so slowly to record the time. They are not in a hurry. There will not be an alarm when the final grain falls into the bottom of the chamber. The hourglass will certainly lose its power if the glass is not turned every hour.

Watch the sand as it falls. It only takes a few minutes for the eyes to close in a life of boredom. Time is so precious. No one knows the day or hour our Lord is coming in the clouds of heaven.

No one knows the final hour of life. Make sure your soul is ready. The grains of sand will fall until the last. Life will be no more when the earthly hour is past. No one is promised another day.

Jesus told us all to watch and pray. This will not be a life of boredom, but of the glorious hope of meeting Jesus in the sky. There will be joy unspeakable and full of glory when Jesus comes again. The particles of sand in an hourglass slowly pass. Soon they will be gone. If our eyes have not closed in death, there is still time to repent. Call upon the Lord. He is not very far from all of us. Sins need to be confessed. God will hear all the cries of a repentant heart.

Sand in an hourglass is only for an hour. Peace with God is for eternity. The day is coming to an end. A strong ticking heart grows fainter. Soon it will be time to meet the Master.

Look Up, My Friend
January 6

From that first emotional prayer when our sins were washed away. Jesus came into our hearts and forgave our sins. "Thank you Jesus for the life you gave so we could be saved." Oh, blessed is the day when a person calls upon the Lord.

No need to look back at the old sins of a corruptible life. They are all forgiven. We are told the angels rejoice in heaven when a sinner repents. Truly it is a wonderful life to live for Jesus. The things of earth have lost all their enchanting power. Gods grace abounds and His love is from everlasting to everlasting.

A new vision was created with our hope and expectation of meeting the Lord in the air. He is coming in power and great glory. We don't know when He will return, morning, evening or night, but if we remain faithful, Jesus will take us home to be forever with Him.

The day of His appearing will not be for me alone, but to all those who love Him with heart, soul, and mind. Look up, my friend, the day of redemption draws near. The time of our departure is at hand.

We do not know the day our Lord will descend. When He comes, the graves will open and the dead and the living shall rise to meet Jesus in the skies.

A Little While
January 7

In Just a little while Christ would go away. His time on earth was coming to an end. Jesus had just been beaten with a whip, thirty-nine lashes cut deep into His back. Many of the victims died from the beating alone. He carried that heavy cross until He was too weak to carry it any more. A man called Simmon was compelled to carry the cross the rest of the way.

This was a time of extreme sadness and sorrow for all those who loved Jesus. Many people were crying as Jesus was nailed to the cross.

Soon they would be rejoicing in the mighty working power of God. In a little while, Sorrow would be turned into praise. Grief and mourning replaced with a smile. "Weeping may endure for a night, but joy cometh in the morning" (Psalm 30:5). Jesus was taken down from the cross and laid in a grave. On the third day Jesus arose from the dead; Glory, Hallelujah, Jesus is alive!

He was no longer in the tomb. The grave could not hold Him. A few days later He had ascended to the throne room above. He was at the right hand of the Father, embraced with His love. In just a little while Christ is coming back to earth. Keep holding on, we are almost home.

Take the Time
January 8

The weather station announced the coming of a severe winter storm. "Snow, freezing rain, and sleet will cover the highways. Driving conditions will be very hazardous! Stay off the roads if at all possible."

This announcement was made so we could make preparation for the storm. State trucks are loaded with gravel and chemicals have been applied to the roads.

Many travelers do not have the choice of staying at home. Before the storm comes there are a few things that we need to do. A good blanket in the car will keep us warm. An emergency kit, flashlight, and even a signal alarm could save our lives.

The sleet has started coming down. Roads are slick. The car slides into the bank. The driver and family are left alone in a remote part of the country, no other cars passing by. This family was prepared with all the safety equipment for survival. They were rescued just in time.

We see how necessary it is to prepare for a storm. There is something far more important. Prepare to meet thy God. I know you have heard the warning, in church, by a friend or loved one. This warning was given by many people who love and care for you. Take the time to be ready. Invite Jesus into your heart before it is too late.

It Is Later than You Think
January 9

The final hour is approaching. It will be a wonderful time for those who are watching and praying. Those who love Jesus have a blessed hope of meeting Him in the skies. No one knows the day or hour He will come back to earth.

Will you be ready when He comes? Do you think He will come today, tomorrow, or some other time in the near future? It would be a very costly mistake if you were looking for Him later in life and He came today. You might hear Jesus say, "Depart from me, I know you not."

I have a watch and it keeps very good time. Every once in a while the battery dies and the time is very deceiving. The hands stop moving, but the hours keep passing by. The watch shows one thing; it is really telling a lie.

According to the time of a stopped watch, all is not well with your soul. The sun begins to set and dark shadows covers the earth. A decision for Christ will be made in the morning. Death came in the middle of the night without a sin confession and Christ was not accepted into the heart.

The coming of the Lord is near. Is it later than you think? It may be time to reset the timepiece, restore the spiritual battery of the heart. Jesus is coming on time. He will not be late. If you put off tomorrow what can be done today, will it be too late?

Here Today, Gone Tomorrow
January 10

Let us take a walk through the seasons of time. At the end of our journey we will discover they all have one thing in common. A good place to start is the season of spring. The birds sing sweet melodies and the flowers in the garden are beautiful with their array of colors. Refreshing showers come from above. This season comes to an end; another one will begin.

The long hot days of summer are warmer, I'm sure you will agree. Families are going on picnics and walking by the riverside. Have you noticed the leaves on the trees, changing color? Summer comes to an end.

In autumn there is always a colorful display. This is really a good time to see God's beautiful creation. The earth is His canvas. He paints the colors of life with a gentle touch. This is a beautiful picture; enjoy it while you can. This season will soon be past. Look out across the land.

Snow is beginning to fall. I hope you are ready for the strong winter winds. A snow scene is a picture of pure delight. Tree limbs sparkle bright with a glaze of ice on each limb and the snow covers the ground. Just like all the seasons, here today, gone tomorrow.

Just a little while to stay and then they are gone. So are our lives. We are here for a little while and then we will be gone. We are just passing through. Live for Christ today; tomorrow may never come.

Surely Goodness and Mercy
January 11

In the dark days of depression when our lives are burdened-down with grief and sorrow, joy cannot be found. The enemy would try to rob us of our peace and lead us down a path of corruption. He stands in the shadows just waiting for an opportunity to over power us.

I have good news, my friend. Our heavenly Father loves us and He can see the danger. He has appointed two of His best character representatives to follow us and keep us safe from the enemy. These two characters are well trained for they have fought the enemy many times. Because of their vigilance and devotion to God, souls have been reclaimed and peace restored.

I don't know if you have personally met these two courageous warriors. Allow me a few seconds of your time and I will introduce them. "Goodness and mercy," remember their names for they will follow you all through life. The virtue of goodness is honesty and righteousness and it helps to keep the heart pure, undefiled. Mercy is divine favor when Christ paid the price for our sins. He gave His life for ours. Compassion forgives.

These are the character representatives of a holy and righteous God. Surely goodness and mercy will follow us all the days of our lives.

The Last Page
January 12

There is only one page left in the book and this is it. This will be your last opportunity to share with friends and loved ones your final thoughts on life. This page is reserved just for you.

I don't believe you would be very happy if a crook stole your last page. It looks like some of your last words have already been taken. There is not much space left. You will not be able to tell your innermost feelings.

The writing space on this page is gradually disappearing and you have not even spoken the first word. It seems a crook is already here.

Take a few minutes and gather your thoughts. We are all listening. We know your last words will be of great wisdom and they will help us through life.

The crook is feeling guilty and he comes forward with a confession. He did not mean to steal the last page. He is really sorry and hopes you will forgive him. We would expect rage for stealing your last words. It looks like there is more than one thief. A whole page has been taken from your life.

There is only enough room for two words. What will they be? The answer is: "I forgive!" Surely this is a good way to end in the Lord.

A Time to Fast
January 13

The table is spread with plenty of food to spare. It is always good to sit at the table and enjoy the meal of the day. Three meals a day is really sufficient. There is always more than enough food to satisfy our appetites. We receive nourishment for our bodies with the benefit of good health for the task of each day.

The bounty of God's goodness supplies all of our needs according to His riches in glory. We have food, water, clothes, and even shelter to keep us safe from the storms. Our lives are truly blessed.

Let us take a good look at our spiritual relationship with God to examine our spiritual health and well-being. God's blessings are truly bountiful in our lives. Every day we sit down for a meal, but there are times when our spiritual lives suffer because we do not take the time to be with God.

A time to fast is a really good time to get in touch with our heavenly Father and to draw close to Him. The body will become weak for lack of food. We will be stronger spiritually and the Holy Spirit will touch us. God will bless us abundantly with grace. Give up a little food, walk away from the table. Receive an extra helping of God's loving kindness and mercy. A plate left empty can lead to a life full of grace and unwavering love

A New Life in Christ
January 14

A very important visitor is coming by today. He has a special agreement that will change your life if you accept His terms and conditions. He is not coming with a life insurance policy that would be paid at death. If everything is in complete agreement, a life changing transformation will take place the moment you believe.

Please don't keep Him waiting; He is standing at the door. He made a special trip from the throne room above. There's not much time. A decision needs to be made today. There is no promise of tomorrow.

Please don't turn Jesus away; it only takes a few minutes of your time to receive a new life. Perhaps you would like to review the contract and see if you are eligible for all the benefits of a transformed life.

One of the qualifications is for you to be a sinner. That's not a problem, Jesus can forgive sins and He will if you invite Him into your life. Some of your requirements are to believe, repent, and accept Jesus into your heart.

What did Jesus do for you? He was nailed to an old rugged cross. His blood was spilled for your sins. He was buried and He arose from the dead. He was resurrected by the mighty power of God. Jesus is standing at the door, waiting for your decision. "Jesus, come into my heart."

It Is Suppertime
January 15

Go with me to a small country home where a family is preparing for the evening meal. This is a special time for the family to gather around the table and have the final meal of the day. Mom has cooked a wonderful supper. She labored over the stove and made sure everything was just right.

The family members wait patiently for her invitation to come to the table. All things are ready; she calls for her husband, sons and daughters. They commented her on the delicious food that was served to them.

The best part of the evening meal was the family meeting together, laughing and talking, sharing the events of the day. This fellowship bound them together with a love that would never fail.

It's only a matter of time when the Lord of glory will call to the saints of God. "It's suppertime." All those who received an invitation and responded with faithfulness to the Master's call will be in the presence of the King. All things are ready.

Can you just imagine for a moment sitting at the table, knowing that you have entered into the kingdom of heaven and Jesus is beginning to serve.

Listen to the angels sing; join in the heavenly choir with words of "Glory, Glory." The voice of praise is a sweet melody that will be heard throughout eternity. The songs of mercy will be from everlasting to everlasting.

Now is a good time to accept the invitation of salvation. Believe on the Lord Jesus and you will be saved. "It is suppertime." Are you ready?

A Time to Rejoice
January 16

There are some things that money cannot buy, happiness, joy, and peace. These gifts are from a kind and loving God.

The orchard is bare of fruit, no grapes on the vines. The cupboard is bare and there is no money to spare. Whether we are rich or poor, hungry or full, God wants us to cast all of our cares upon Him for He cares for us.

We do not live according to the abundance of the things we posses. A rich sinner or a poor one, their need of salvation is the same. No money or too much money will not bring peace with God.

A humble spirit God will not deny. The blessed assurance of life eternal is promised when we confess our sins and believe on the Lord Jesus.

There is coming a day, I don't know when, Jesus will descend. This will truly be a glorious time in our lives. Rejoice for He is coming back to earth. He is coming for those whose sins have been purged by His precious blood.

Regardless of life's situation, it is time to rejoice. Jesus is coming in great power and glory. Praise and love Him with all thy heart, mind, and soul. Wait patiently for His coming. It is only a matter of time from earth to glory we shall ascend.

To Stay or Go
January 17

The sun begins to set on the twilight days of life. It is not my choice to leave today. I have come to the end of my journey. I would very much like to stay with my family and friends to enjoy life a little while longer.

My hopes of living will descend into the darkness of the night. Please don't worry! I will be here just a short while. Just long enough for the Lord to prepare my room in glory. Everything has to be just right.

I like to think of my room as having a really big window so I can see all my friends and loved ones as they walk through the gate. Truly it will be a time of rejoicing as we gather around the throne and sing praises unto our Lord.

I want to go to the place the Lord has prepared for me. There will be no more pain; all tears will be wiped away. I want to hear the angels sing and join in heaven's choir. My greatest joy of all will be to see

Jesus and thank Him for His amazing grace that saved a wretch like me. To stay or go, the choice is not mine. "My time of departure is at hand.

Please don't ask me to stay. I have to leave now, my Lord and Savior is here. I will miss you, but I will be looking for you in glory. Good-bye, I love you!"

Called up to heaven to be forever with the Lord, truly this is our heart's desire. Help us Lord to press onward, to keep the faith, we are almost home. Just a little while longer, we will meet our good friend who is looking out the window of his brand new home and singing in heaven's choir.

It Is Time
January 18

Through the years of countless ages, the faithful followers of Christ have been looking to the sky for His return. They know He will come without warning. The expectation of meeting Jesus in the clouds of glory is our present hope.

No one knows the day or hour He will return to earth. We of the Christian faith know He is coming. Our prayers for the lost are to repent and invite Jesus into their hearts as Lord and Savior. We want everyone to know of His great love and we want each person to have that blessed hope of going to heaven.

When Jesus ascended into heaven, two messengers of God said to the people, "Why stand ye gazing into heaven? This same Jesus, which is taken up from you into heaven, shall so come in like manner." (Acts.1:11).

This is a promise that we can hold close to our hearts for we know it will come to pass. It is written in the Holy Bible and we believe it.

Now is the time to draw closer to God, dedicate our lives to Him and walk the straight and narrow path that leads unto life. We need to hold our cross high for the glory of God. Jesus is coming! The trumpet will sound and when it does, we will be heavenward bound.

The Train Is Coming
January 19

Family members wait at the old train station for a journey into eternity. A family of seven has planned for this trip for many years. Some of the members have passed away, but they are all together now, except for one son. The conductor shouts "All aboard!"

The train begins to move slowly down the track. Dark clouds of smoke roll from the smoke stack. A person is seen a short distance behind the old train. He is running with all of his might and shouting "Stop the train; don't leave without me." If he is unable to get on the train, he will have to forfeit his time in eternity.

The old steam engine continues to move toward the eternal sunset. The father heard the heartfelt cries of his long lost son and he moves quickly to the caboose. He tries desperately to save him by reaching out his hand to the young man. The father's final attempt was successful and his son was rescued just in time.

I told this imaginary story to help us understand that one day Jesus is coming back to earth. He will be coming for those who are saved by grace and they will have eternal life.

At the cross sinners are saved. God the Father is reaching down His hand. He is not willing that any should perish but that all would repent. "Please don't leave without me."

The Journeys End
January 20

The end of a life is only hours away. A precious soul will be departing in the evening hour. A faithful servant of the Lord will die. The sun will set for the last time. This beloved family member will not rise with the morning light.

Friends and loved ones gather around his bed. Each person comes forward to tell him how much he is loved and that he will truly be missed.

The dying man lived a good Christian life and will leave behind many wonderful memories. He knew his life was about to expire and he would soon be at home in heaven.

A good friend stood at his bedside and asked him for advice on living the Christian life so that we too would have the blessed hope of going to heaven.

This would be his last opportunity to tell his family about the love of God. He told them to believe on the Lord Jesus that God would save them by grace. He said that God wants us to love Him with heart, soul, and mind. His eyes began to close and his voice was fading away, but his last words brought tears of joy into each person's heart. "Jesus arose!"

In those two words we can have the hope of life eternal of one day passing through the valley of death to our home in glory.

Solid Rock Foundation
January 21

On a dark stormy night, one family lived in a house built on sand, the other family in a house on solid rock.

Build on the sand; strong winds and rain will come with a vengeance. Huge waves will wash the sand from underneath the house and it will fall.

A house of the same design built on a rock foundation will still be standing when the storm is over. Gigantic swells of water splash against the rocks, but to no avail. The house remains steadfast, unmovable.

Jesus as the rock of ages withstood the most violent storm when He was crucified on an old rugged cross. Nails were driven into His hands and feet; a crown of thorns forced upon His brow. He had to endure the pain and suffering that was unbearable. The only way Jesus would come down from the cross was by death. Even then He was not defeated for He arose from the dead.

One family built on the earthly sand of sinful living without faith or hope and soon their house fell when the torrents of rain came. The other family whose house was built on the solid rock withstood the storm.

Christ in our lives is a foundation that will never fail. He is our solid rock foundation that will keep us safe and secure in the storms of life. Let us yield our lives to Him. He has all power in heaven and earth.

It is beginning to rain. Do you have a good solid rock foundation?

When Does Life Begin
January 22

At birth a baby is born. In a hospital room a child takes its first breath. I would like to know if this is when life begins? The child's birth certificate has the day and year of the baby's birth. This is the beginning of a new life.

How wonderful it is for the parents to hold the little one in their arms. They watch the child as it grows. Their love grows stronger as the years pass.

Our hearts are broken when the journey of life comes to an end and that child who was loved so much, takes its last breath.

The wonder of the creation goes beyond the grave. Please let me explain. Life comes into existence at birth. A child is born. But somewhere along the pathway of life that child needs to be born again.

This would be a spiritual birth. When our hearts are made right with God. This happens when our sins are confessed and we believe on the Lord Jesus Christ. He forgives us and from that day forward, we have a new life in Christ.

We were born on a certain day and saved by grace. Our death will also be recorded, but our hope of life goes beyond the grave. When does life eternal begin? It begins at birth when we are born again. A glorified life will ascend from earth to heaven when Jesus comes. Have you been born again?

The Last Amen
January 23

All through life a friend's Bible was read with love and devotion. Tears for lost loved ones stain the pages. Many prayers ascended to heaven on behalf of friends and family. Now she is gone; she had spoken her last amen.

Recently she was called away to glory. Her precious Bible closed for a little while in silent memory of a loyal companion. The highest honor of respect was given to her.

She found joy and peace in God's holy Word and the words in red were a comfort as they helped her to live a faithful life.

The Bible is not dead as some people might think. If we could only ask the woman who was called up to glory or the multiplied millions whose lives have been changed by the Holy Bible, they would all tell us: "It is the book of life."

The Bible was closed in honor of a friend. Her hearts desire was for all to be saved. Open the sacred book, read its holy pages. Life will be found in a caring, loving God. Peace and joy will abound in each person's life as they come to know Jesus Christ as Lord and Savior.

The Holy Bible is the inspired Word of God. When life comes to an end, the last amen has been spoken. In just a little while the gates of heaven will open.

Today Is Borrowed
January 24

The days of our lives quickly pass with no promise of tomorrow. Today is borrowed. A Payment will not be made in the near future. If life ends today there is no way we could repay our debt that is due tomorrow.

Today is the day of salvation. Hear the Master's call, "Come unto me." Please don't wait too long as the sun is beginning to set. You may need to walk a little faster. A day of delay could be a costly mistake. A decision to let Jesus come into your life will not be made from the grave.

Today is a good day to be saved. God is patiently waiting, but soon the heart will stop beating and tomorrow's delay will not bring peace today.

Call upon the Lord; He is near. Salvation He will impart. He will respond quickly to a repentant heart. Sins confessed, salvation is granted. The time is now to Ask Jesus to come into your life. Tell Him you are sorry for your sins and He will forgive you.

Tomorrow's debt is paid today when you believe on the Son of God. There may be no tomorrow. If you are not yet saved, don't you think it is time to move a little faster? Pray with me, "Jesus, I'm sorry for my sins, come into my heart. I believe that you died and rose again. Thank you, Jesus for saving me."

Clouds Pass Away
January 25

Clouds gather in the morning at the beginning of the day. They move according to the wind current. Occasionally they stop for a visit and just hang around for a while.

If there is a fire emergency, they might be found hovering above the flames waiting for an opportunity to release the rain. Dark storm clouds with rain to spare have saved many a forest or homes from being burnt to the ground. Winter clouds will not be satisfied until there is a fresh coating of snow on the ground.

There is a type of cloud that I believe is worse than all the rest. This type of cloud cannot be distinguished from the others, sunshine or storm, winter or spring. Lives have been taken when these clouds pass through.

These clouds represent the time of a person's life. No one knows how long life will last. Whether we are here a few days or many years, life will come to an end.

The time clouds follow us everywhere we go. The danger comes when they fade away. These clouds are not really harmful. They just represent our lives. Here for a little while and then they are gone.

Our lives are the same. We are just passing through. Here today, gone tomorrow. Soon the clouds will fade away and we will not live another day.

Heaven or Hell
January 26

When I met Jesus at the altar, I was a sinner of disgrace. He came into my heart and forgave my sins and now I am saved by grace.

Go with me a few years back in time to the days before Christ came into my life. I attended church and went to Sunday school class. The teacher told us about Jesus and the life He lived. We heard about His death, burial, and resurrection. Jesus was at the church; however, none of us saw Him. I did not know Jesus personally.

Later when I graduated from high school and went to work, my good friends told me about Jesus and His sacrifice on the cross for my sins. I started thinking about Jesus dying for me, dying in my place. I felt conviction of the Holy Spirit.

I started going to Sunday school again. One Sunday I decided to stay for the church service. I am really glad I went to church that day. The service was just about over when the evangelist said he was going to have a countdown for Christ. He started counting from sixty back to zero and then he was going to dismiss the service. As he counted, he continued to preach: "God loves you, Jesus died for you, heaven or hell, it's your choice."

I walked down the aisle to the altar and Jesus came into my heart. I met Him personally and now I know Him as Lord and Savior. "Thank you, Jesus!"

King's Palace, Poor Man's Home
January 27

Travel with me back in time to the king's palace. We will visit for a while. I know it is a long journey. Our mission is to find a spiritual treasure.

We are not looking for gold or silver, or any of the precious metals that are found in the earth. We are looking for things that money cannot buy. According to the treasure map, the palace will be a good place to search.

Peace, joy, happiness, these valuable treasures are found in a person's life. The king is on our list and we will search diligently to find any Godly gifts.

He has an abundance of wealth. The king talks about all of his earthly treasures. He is very selfish and speaks with an arrogance of pride that all the riches in the palace are his. He had no time to live and serve God. We knew the heavenly treasure would not be found here.

There is one other place we need to search. The map shows a poor beggar's home. As we entered his little shack, we saw a poor man sitting at the table with just a morsel of bread for his dinner. He said grace, gave thanks, and spoke of God's love and mercy as he held his worn-out Bible. There was no gold or silver, but we knew this man loved God.

We found the treasure we were looking for in the heart of a poor beggar. He had peace, joy, and happiness. When grace is found, peace abounds.

The Chief Cornerstone
January 28

Many years has gone by, civilization was still young. There was no modern equipment for heavy construction. Bulldozers, cranes and backhoes had not yet been invented.

When a structure was built, huge rocks were rolled up a steep incline. They were carefully designed and each one had a special place in the pyramid. A cornerstone was the main part of the structure. All of the other stones were locked together and held fast by the chief cornerstone.

My imagination shows that the craftsmen worked continuously, but for this special project, their years of labor would be in vain. The chief cornerstone was rejected and this project was doomed to ruin.

We do not have time to see the drastic results. Please return with me to the future. No equipment is needed for our next project.

This will be a personal adventure in the formation of a new life and Jesus will be the chief cornerstone. If this stone is accepted then there will be perfect peace. A life will be developed into the fullness of

God's grace and mercy with holiness as the end result.

If He is rejected, the formation of life will be incomplete and will end in a terrible ruin. Please accept Him for life.

Where Will He Find Us?
January 29

When Jesus comes back to earth, where will He find us? Now this is a question that we need to give some serious thought. If He finds us in a corruptible place, living a sinner's life, He will not be very pleased.

The place is important, but our spiritual well-being is God's main concern. He knows the condition of each heart, whether it is sinful or full of grace.

I'm so glad the Lord followed me when I was living a sinful life. He didn't give up on me. When I was away from God and I did not know Jesus as my Savior, God loved me still and He did not want me to perish. His love is the same for us all.

The Lord walks the dark hills and the desolate valleys in search of sinners whom He loves with all of His heart and soul. Many fine folks would say He found them in a place of disgrace. He brought them out with love and mercy.

He has gone to many places in search of the lost. His heart is very heavy with grief for those who would not repent and invite Him into their lives. When He comes again, where will He find us?

I like to think in church would be a wonderful place. Down at the altar praying and worshiping God or at home reading the Bible with the family and talking about Jesus, His great love for us.

He is coming back to earth, whether we are in church or in a corruptible place. He will be coming for those who have repented of their sins and for those who love Him with heart, soul, and mind. Where will He find us? I hope at the cross with Him as our Lord and Savior.

My Hearts Desire
January 30

My good friends gather around the campfire with me. We will share our stories and sing songs of praise. Testimonies of God's grace will inspire us to live closer to Him. Our best friend, Jesus will walk among us, touching our lives, giving us strength for the day's journey, and giving us the blessed assurance that He will never leave or forsake us.

The words of praise continue as each person uses his or her talents to glorify God. I would like to take a few minutes of your time to express my hearts desire.

I love to write; God has blessed me with this special gift to help others along the pathway of life. I pray each day for Him to bless and use me in His own special way.

I know that words rightly spoken will be as medicine to the soul, healing the broken hearted and restoring faith in God above. Songs and books have been written down through the ages and words like "amazing grace" still bring tears to our eyes and joy unspeakable in our hearts.

My hearts desire is to show kindness; give a lot of love, and help others know Jesus Christ as Lord and Savior before the midnight hour. My desire is for souls to be saved.

Where is Jesus
January 31

In just a little while the sun will set and time will be no more. We are searching for a Savior who died on a cross for the sins of the world. He was buried and rose again.

The death hour is approaching and it is only a matter of time before each of us takes our final breath. We must search diligently as this will be our last opportunity to make things right with God. We must find Jesus before it is too late.

There is just not enough time to travel overseas and search for Him there. There is talk that He was at a certain church in our community. The sun begins to set a little more and the shadows of death move us closer to the grave.

The little church in the valley is a few miles away, but too far for our life's expectancy. The word spreads quickly of our impending doom. Deep sorrow begins to fill our lives as we think about departing this life without Jesus in our hearts.

I am very happy to say that our Lord is not confined to any certain place. Anywhere there are repentant hearts; Jesus will be there too with grace that is able to save to the uttermost. Where is Jesus? He is here with salvation to impart. We found Him just in time.

God Is never too Busy
February 1

Our heavenly Father is never too busy to hear our heart's pleas. He is not on a journey, or taking a vacation. He is on the throne listening attentively to all the request of His adopted children. While we are yet speaking, the answers to our prayers are being delivered from above.

We don't have to stand in line and wait hours for Him to hear us. We are all familiar with the telephone system. The answering machine will put us on hold and keep us there until we get tired of waiting and then in frustration we hang up.

Our God is ever present to help in time of need. He will bless abundantly when we cast all of our cares upon Him. We are not left on hold and kept in a waiting room with a number to be called. His love is great towards us and He takes the time to hear each of our heart-felt prayers.

As a father loves his children, so does our heavenly Father love us. His love for us goes back to the time when we were sinners, before we were adopted into His family. At that time we did not know of His great love, but God heard the pleas of our hearts and grace was found when Jesus came into our lives.

Whether we have a need or we just want to praise Him, our God is never too busy to hear our hearts pleas.

Tomorrow may be too late
February 2

Many years have passed since I heard this story. I cannot remember a lot of the things that happened or the words that were spoken. If you don't mind I would like to tell it in my own words.

A man who worked in the mines went to church one night. He was not a Christian, but he was caring a heavy burden in his heart that only Jesus could help him.

Whatever was bothering him had to be settled that night. After the sermon the preacher gave an altar call. This young man walked down the aisle to the altar. Some of the church members went with him and they prayed together for a really long time.

It was getting late; everyone had left except the pastor and the miner. This person's problem had to be settled that night. He had to make things right with God.

He prayed into the early hours of the morning and finally his faith brought peace as he believed in the Lord Jesus Christ. He was saved just in time; his sins were forgiven.

The next day he went to work in the mine and there was a terrible accident. The shaft had caved in and this young man was killed. "Thank God, it was settled last night." A decision for Christ may be too late tomorrow.

Waiting for the day
February 3

Hurry up and wait I can remember this from my Army days. Rise early in the morning and rush off to a special place. We had to be there on time or face the consequences of a mad drill sergeant. I don't believe anyone liked doing pushups or KP.

It did not take us long to learn the basic skills of being on time. Army discipline also taught us to wait. When the time had finally arrived, we saw that waiting had some very good benefits.

I remember waiting for my time to go home from Vietnam. The flight was on time and soon I would be with my family. Truly it was a wonderful blessing when I walked into my parent's home and they received me with a loving embrace.

I cannot emphasize enough the importance of waiting. One day Jesus is coming back to earth. He will be coming for those who have learned the discipline of watching and praying.

We know that we are to patiently wait and be prepared for our heavenly flight. Jesus is coming; He will not be late. There is still a little while to get ready, but we had better hurry for he will not wait beyond the expected time.

White as Snow
February 4

Just imagine God painting a winter scene. It all started last night with the clouds moving slowly across the sky. With a few brush strokes from His hand, beautiful snowflakes began to appear. After a while they became larger and soon the ground was covered with pure white snow.

In the dark hours of night the snow continued to fall. The beauty of this picture could not be seen in the darkness. After a while the sun began to rise on the horizon.

All across the land as the people began to wake and look outside for the first time. They were simply amazed at this beautiful winter scene that God had created.

The mountains were glazed over with crystal snowflakes that glistened in the morning light. This snow was not polluted with impure substances; everything was pure white.

God painted a masterpiece in nature. He was not quite finished. Some of those fine folks who looked out their windows were impure and living corruptible lives.

They had to be changed by grace. God began to touch them and draw them by the Holy Spirit. They knelt in prayer and asked Jesus to forgive them of their sins.

Behold, God's winter scene of nature, sinners washed in the blood, the impure and defiled are now white as snow.

Melt the Ice
February 5

A sparkling glaze of ice covers the frozen lake. Many days of frigid temperatures have brought extremely cold weather to the region. The snow continues to fall; Icicles hang on the trees. A strong north wind has created blizzard conditions. It is not safe to be outside for any length of time. Frostbite and the bitter cold can be fatal.

There are many farmers who have to go outside and break up the ice on the ponds for their livestock. Fresh water is sometimes transported to the fields to keep the animals alive. Survival for these creatures can also be found in the snow to satisfy their thirst.

I have to believe that the winter season is not the favorite time of year for the farmers. They can hardly wait for the first signs of spring when the ice begins to thaw and the grass turns green.

Life is entirely different when the sun shines upon the earth. Some people have cold frigid hearts unresponsive to the warmth and care of a loving God.

Stay out in the bitter cold or come inside to the shelter of His love. The choice is an easy one to make. Living conditions of life have created a cold hard heart.

Believe in the Lord Jesus and immediately the ice melts. It is a blessed day when the Son shines in our lives and our hearts are thawed by grace.

When the Path Is Hard to See
February 6

Stranded in the desert with only a set of footprints to follow. The guide was unaware of a small family that was left behind in the windstorm. They were just a few hours away from their destination when they were separated from the group.

It would be very easy to get lost and perish in the sandy dry land. Their only hope was to follow the footprints. Canteens were nearly empty. It would be a terrible thing to die of thirst in the desert.

This family continued on their survival route. They were so close to home and yet so far away.

Visibility was very poor. The swirling sand from the windstorm caused the footprints to gradually fade until they were completely gone. The sun began to set on the horizon. Their chances of survival were slim in the darkness of night.

Instead of giving up and calling it quits, this brave family pressed onward with unwavering faith that they would be united with their group and make it safely to their home.

When there seems to be no way, God will make a way. A glimmer of light was seen in the distance and a voice was heard. It was the guide, he had returned and the family was rescued.

On the pathway of life when the storms come and the path is hard to see, don't give up or quit. We are almost home. Jesus is calling, "Follow Me."

The Pure in Heart
February 7

A good friend of mine will be visiting you today. A lot of chores need to be done before He comes. A good place to start would be the living room. This will be a good place to entertain your guest. Oh, by the way His name is Jesus.

After several hours of hard work the house is finally clean. Floors are swept and all the dirt has been removed. All of the unsanitary items are kept out of sight. You don't want Him to see the corruptible things of your life.

Jesus is at the door; please invite Him inside. There is a brief moment of hesitation and then the door is opened. This is a very special meeting.

It's not everyday that you have a chance to be with the Son of God. I know you are probably a little nervous about the conversation; it will be personal.

Jesus thanks him for opening the door and allowing Him to come inside. He makes a nice comment about the clean house. The talk becomes very serious as Jesus inquires about his souls salvation of having a clean and pure heart.

This young man was feeling guilty and under conviction. There was no hiding the unsanitary things in his life. Finally he realized that peace would come if he would believe and invite Jesus into his heart.

Right there in that room on his knees in prayer, he was saved and his corruptible heart was cleansed of all ungodly things. Peace at last. "Thank you, Jesus."

Open the Window
February 8

The sun sets in the evening and the rays of light fade into darkness. Windows are closed and the latches are fastened for the night. This will help stop intruders and prowlers from breaking in and hurting the family. The curtains are pulled tight, blinds are closed and the doors are locked.

It is really peaceful on the inside with the lights on. There is no fear of anyone breaking into the house. A thief will not usually approach a dwelling where life can be seen in the home.

All is well and the family settles in for the night. They wake in the morning hours and pull back the curtains to let the rays of light fill the room.

There is a tranquility of peace in each person's life as they begin the day. When dark storm clouds appear in the sky, there seems to be an overcast of gloom that touches us and removes some of our joy.

Let's open a new window today. This one will let the light from heaven shine upon us and we will have peace for evermore. This window cannot be found in a house or any other type of structure.

Jesus is the light of life and I believe it shines bright when we open the window of our hearts.

Righteous Living
February 9

After a peaceful nights rest, It's time to get up and get ready for the tasks of the day. Sometimes it is good to start the morning with a cup of fresh coffee. Some of us are more satisfied with a breakfast of bacon and eggs.

Whatever our choice, the activities for the day will not wait any longer. Let's get moving. Time spent in prayer will help us to be faithful to God and He will give us grace for the day's journey.

"Help us, Oh Lord, as we begin our daily routine to go through life with the purpose of living a holy, righteous life."

We know this will be very pleasing to you. I heard this morning in our worship service that the first recorded words of Jesus were for us to live righteously.

Living a godly life would certainly bring glory and honor to your name. It would be a wonderful blessing for us to have our lives cleansed of all ungodliness and living Christian lives. Jesus said we could and we believe it; that settles it.

We also learned that we should hide your Word in our hearts so we would not sin against you. "Just one more thing Lord before we begin our chores. May our worship of you be of praise and love all the days of our lives."

Nothing but the Blood
February 10

Down through the ages, sacrifices were given for various reasons. Sometimes a calf or a lamb would be slain and placed upon the altar. I believe the blood was applied in a special way and it represented the atonement of sins.

I am sure it would have been a real emotional time, especially for a family whose child raised the animal and nourished it to good health.

Now this chosen sacrifice would not be very old and sometimes it would be the favorite pet of a small child. The families were told to bring the very best for this blood offering. It was to be without spot or blemish.

Truly it must have been a really hard thing to do, go out in the field and catch the small animal while the little child watches with tears in his or her eyes.

Since they were going to sacrifice the animal anyway, why couldn't they use one of the poor stock, maybe a sick one and leave the child's pet alone? The law was written and they lived by it.

We think about how cruel it was to take a child's pet and slaughter it for a sacrifice, but we see Jesus who was crucified on an old rugged cross for our sins. He was the only one who could die in our place as a sacrifice for us.

But what about the unholy, unrighteous, I believe that would be us. If we died for our own sins, we would still be sinners.

God who is rich in mercy gave His only begotten Son to die on a cross and give His life a ransom for us so we could be saved. Neither the blood of bulls or calves or our own lives would bring forgiveness of sins. Nothing but the blood of Jesus, God's beloved Son would suffice.

As I Have Loved You
February 11

Our story is told of a Fathers great love for His Son and the love of Jesus for us. Now that is something to really think about.

Remember when a baby boy was born in a stable and laid in a manger. Oh, how everyone adored Him and brought gifts. This was our heavenly Father's Son.

When God saw the newborn infant wrapped in swaddling clothes, His heart was overflowing with love as He saw His baby boy.

Tears probably ran down His cheek as he thought about His Son becoming a man and dying on a cross for us. These two were bound together with such a great love that nothing could separate them, not even death on a cross.

Before the death of Jesus, He gave us something to hold on to that would keep us all through life. Notice what He said: "As the Father hath loved me, so have I loved you: continue ye in my love." (John, 15:9). Glory, Glory, Glory, Hallelujah!

Think about His great love and what He had to endure on the cross for our salvation. A crown of thorns forced upon His brow; spikes were driven into His hands and feet. He was spit on, humiliated, and He suffered with unbearable pain.

God's love is great towards us in that He gave His Son. His Son gave His life. "Continue ye in my love."

Bread for a Stranger
February 12

Find a little bread, feed a hungry soul. Living in dark alleys and sleeping on park benches. The homeless live in unbearable conditions. They have to sleep in cardboard boxes and other self-made materials to escape the bitter cold. Some of them have no shoes and they have to walk in the snow.

They did not choose to live homeless lives. Their place of employment may have closed down or they might have been cast out into the streets for some other reason. I don't think any of them wants to be beggars.

Life would be so much better if they had a nice home, a stove to keep them warm, shoes and good clothes to wear. They would really be blessed with food on the table and fresh water to drink.

It would be good if we could supply all their needs and help them along the pathway of life. If a beggar happens to come our way, hungry and thirsty, please don't turn him or her away. A good meal and fresh water would be a beggars delight.

Our hearts desire should be to help others along the way. It should not matter if it is a homeless person, a neighbor, or anyone who is in need.

When we help them, it is the same as helping Jesus. "For I was an hungered and ye gave me meat; I was thirsty and ye gave me drink: I was a stranger and ye took me in: Naked and ye clothed me: I was sick and ye visited me: I was in prison, and ye came unto me." (Matthew 25:35,36). If we had a chance to help others as if it were Jesus, our lives would be blessed beyond measure. "In as much as ye have done it unto one of the least of these.... ye have done it unto me." (Matthew 25:40).

Heaven's Gold Mine
February 13

It looks like a good day for prospecting. There's not a cloud in the sky. The weather forecast is excellent. It will be sunny all day.

Our search will be for a gold mine, now this treasure will not be found in the hills or deep in the earth. Picks and shovels are not required. No mules are needed to carry our valuable assets back home.

We all know that earthly gold is valuable and some people will search all of their lives to find it. Many of them have labored many hours in a mine in search of this precious ore. Their final results ended in a shallow grave on a hill.

Our search will be for heaven's gold mine, this precious gem of life will be easier to find and the joy it brings will last forever. There is one thing that will be needed in order to find this godly treasure. There is no need to search the backpack for this special tool.

Before we started on our journey, God gave each of us a measure of faith. The use of it will determine our final fate. The blood flows from the veins of Jesus. We are not far from heaven's gold mine. Strike it rich with joy, peace, and love for eternity. "Jesus come into my heart, I believe." Welcome to heaven's gold mine.

He is Worthy of the Honor
February 14

Give honor where it is due. There are many special events where people are recognized and honored for their distinct qualities of life.

The military is a good place to show respect for those who are obedient in service. Those who obey orders and live honorable lives will be rewarded in the end when they leave for civilian life.

If they have done all the things that were required of them and they did it to the best of their ability, they will receive an honorable discharge from active duty.

It is really a wonderful time for all military personal that has served our country with loyalty, bravery, and heroism. They stand united in battle, even to die for our freedom. Give honor to them for they are worthy.

Our honor today goes to one man who was obedient, even to His death on the cross. His name is Jesus, God's beloved Son.

He was faithful all through life. His loving kindness still touches lives today. We all know Him by His love for us in that He would not come down from the cross, no matter how severe the pain.

He died in our place for our sins so we could be free. He gave us an Honorable Discharge, but it cost His life. Give Him the glory, honor, and praise for He is worthy.

Please Forgive Me
February 15

There is a time of guilt in our lives when we have hurt someone, accidently or on purpose. The emotional pain we caused will not go away unless we go to the person and tell them we are sorry. This is the healing process for them and us. An apology is offered; forgiveness is given and both individuals are healed.

When I was a teenager, I stole a soda from a family that lived about a half of a mile down the road. They had never done anything wrong to me.
This family was highly respected in the community and they were really good neighbors. It is hard for me to believe that I would take something from my friends that didn't belong to me and use it for my own personal gain.

A short while later, I was walking towards home and I had to pass this family's home. I saw the mother on the front porch. She was ironing clothes.

As I got closer to her home, I was beginning to feel really bad. I wasn't sick, but I was having guilt feelings that hurt me on the inside. I could have just kept on walking, but a remorseful aching heart in my conscience would have followed me up the road.

I walked over to the house and I told the mother what I had done. I offered her ten cents, the price of the soda. She forgave me and let me keep the money. I walked home with joy in my heart.

When our hearts are heavy laden with the guilt of the many things we have done wrong and we are hurting on the inside. When it is time to make peace with God. Please don't keep walking. We need to tell Him that we have sinned and we are sorry for our sins. Now with joy in our hearts, we can walk on.

No Looking Back
February 16

We will have grace for the journey and peace along the way. All instructions must be followed or there will be cancelations. We don't have time to go over the entire book and review all the pages. I forgot to mention our guidance will come from the Holy Bible.

Before we get started, the first thing we need to know is that we must be born again. This is when Jesus comes into our lives and forgives our sins. He is then our Lord and Savior.

If we have a new life in Christ, we can begin our heavenly journey. It is very important for us to follow Him all through life. There will be no detours or return exits back into a life of sin.

I don't believe any of us would like for our trip to heaven canceled for our disobedience. I have to mention some people started out in the grace of God and yet somewhere along the way, they went back into the world of living sinful lives and they never followed Jesus again. I have to believe that they will not enter into the holy city of God.

Well, let's see what the Bible says: "Not everyone that saith unto me, Lord, Lord, shall enter into the kingdom of God." (Matthew7: 21). Deny Christ; He will deny us. We don't want any more cancelations. Let's continue, no looking back.

Run with the Son
February 17

Beware the shadow, no need to worry; this one is friendly. It lies silently on the ground, hid in the darkness as it patiently waits for the owner. When the sun comes out the shadow will appear. It never makes a sound when stepped on, a little bit shy on a cloudy day and will disappear quickly in the early hours of night.

All of us have shadows and they are faithful followers. Wherever we go, they will follow. Sometimes they will go ahead of us and lead the way.

It is very hard to catch up with a shadow, especially if the sun is its teammate. Occasionally I have been able to out run my shadow. Most of the time it has been one step ahead of me.

Shadows almost always cross the finish line first. That does not bother me for we are a good team. We always work together; one can't finish without the other.

I have noticed that the shadow runs better when the sun is shining. Shadows will follow or lead in a race, it all depends on the position of the sun.

We could think about this in our race for life. Running down the track with a short distance to go. If we run with the Son in the right position of our hearts, we will be guaranteed to win and claim the glory crown. Without Him we will be left behind. Run with the Son and win.

Talents Used, Souls Forgiven
February 18

God's blessings are abundant in our lives when we use our talents for His glory. He does not want us to hide them when there are so many people who need a little inspiration to revive and restore their faith in Him.

Let the singers sing the songs of love, grace and mercy for the entire world to hear. Worship Him with the songs of praise. Preachers and Sunday school teachers bring forth the precious words that you place in our hearts to help us live holy, righteous lives.

Many talents given, they are not all the same. Each one has been specially crafted and engraved with each of our names. Whatever the talent use it to lift up and magnify the name of Jesus.

If the high calling is to write a book, then let us write with love prevailing for our words will be in the homes and God will bless those who do not attend church.

God is deeply concerned about each of us. He is not willing for any to perish. Wherever there is a place, whether in a home, church or school, it does not matter if a soul is saved by grace.

"Use us Lord, in your own special way to be a blessing and to help those in need." We don't always see the results of used talents, but the people blessed will know they are forgiven.

I Can't Do It
February 19

There are some things in life that are really hard to do. Speaking engagements can cause butterflies in the stomach. A TV interview is even more of a problem. Thousand of people watch the program and they listen to every word.

I rt I was going to give a book review on a local television station. I have to admit there was fear in the thought of being in front of a TV audience. I never had to confront those fears; a book review was never scheduled.

I know that I am not the only one that has been nervous about doing certain things. We all have times in our lives when we need more confidence and stronger faith to achieve our goals and be victorious in life.

I want to pass on to you a few words of encouragement for future endeavors. These words also apply to me. I saw these words on the Internet: " I cannot do it, but God can do it through me."

We are weak and unable to take a stand by ourselves. It is very hard to accomplish our goals when we are alone. The things that are impossible with us are possible with God.

If I ever have to give an interview on live TV or there is something in your life that more faith and confidence is needed. We are never alone when we are alone with God. "We can't do it, but God can do it through us."

Deep Desire
February 20

We want a burning desire to thirst after the goodness and mercy of God. A drink of cold water is refreshing to the body. Let us all go on a little journey; fill up the canteens for we will be gone two or three days.

I cannot emphasize enough the importance of having a good water supply. Each person is responsible for his or her food. Let's just say for the sake of this story, no one is allowed to share any of their life saving components like food or water.

I know this sounds terrible and it is. Please bear with me as I explain. After being in the hot sun for several hours, the water supply begins to vanish. There are no ponds or lakes and remember no sharing.

After a short while some of the canteens are empty, throats are dry and parched. There is a longing for a good drink of water. The travelers beg for a drink from their companions, but none is given. This is a life or death situation.

So it is in our lives as we thirst after God. We come with an empty canteen and beg for mercy. He will not turn us away and leave us to die in our sins. A drink of water will satisfy our thirst and a touch from heaven will give us life forevermore.

A Light on a Dark Path
February 21

A wanderer in the night is stumbling in the darkness. A storm is coming. Dark clouds hover above. There are no houses or lights to be seen. Vision is very poor.

If only a flashlight had been retrieved from the disabled vehicle, there would be a slim chance of survival. It is too late now, the sun has gone down and the car is too far away for this young woman to return.

This is in the cold winter months when the wind blows and snow covers the ground. Snowflakes drift silently towards the bare earth.

After a short while the ground is lightly covered with snow. Visibility is a little better as the pure white flakes highlight the trees and even the rocks are easier to see.

It must be a miracle from heaven as the storm fades away and stars in the sky glimmer with a bit of hope. The moon shines bright and an old logging road is seen.

This could be her last chance to make it to a safe shelter. She begins walking down the trail and to her surprise there is a light in a cabin just a short distance away. She is rescued and safe at last.

When we are lost in the darkness of sin, don't give up! Just repent and a light from heaven will shine on our path to glory. Jesus is that light.

When Jesus Comes Again
February 22

The first time Jesus came to earth, angels sang: "Glory to God in the Highest." He was born in a stable and laid in a manger. There was no room for Him in the inn. Shepherds came and worshiped Him.

Mary and Joseph were very proud of their newborn baby. In the early stages of Jesus' life, the king wanted Him dead.

When He was a boy, certain groups of people listened to Him for He spoke as one with knowledge and great wisdom about God.

He became a young man with a heart full of compassion. The blind received their sight and the sick were healed. Those who had leprosy were cleansed. His life touched the multitudes with kindness, goodness, and unwavering love.

The first time Jesus came, the people gave honor to Him as He rode a small donkey through the crowd. They waved palm branches and gave Him the praise, glory, and honor.

Later in life when Jesus was on trial, an angry mob cried aloud: "Crucify Him, crucify Him!" He came as a humble servant obedient to the will of God the Father. He was crucified on a cross and died a horrible death.

The next time He comes, " Glory to God in the highest." It will not be as the meek and lowly one riding on a donkey, but as the King of kings and Lord of lords. Every knee will bow to Jesus Christ.

The Trumpet Sound
February 23

Many years ago when battles were fought with foot soldiers and riders on horses, trumpets were used to signal an attack or retreat. The trumpeter was probably one of the most guarded men in the military.

Let's visit an imaginary battlefield. We will just watch from a distance fully excluded from any action. I would say the man who sounded the brass instrument was always close to the officer in charge.

He didn't blow the trumpet anytime he wanted too. If he did the soldiers would be so confused that they would not know whether they should fight or run. The uncertainty of a signal could leave the men lying on a battlefield in blood.

The commander gives the order to charge, immediately the vibrating sound of the trumpet is heard and the fighting men run with their bayonets drawn ready for war. These brave men would also retreat at the trumpet sound if they were being defeated in battle. Now that the fighting is over, the two sides merge as one.

Travel with me back in time to the future and Jesus our commander in chief has special orders for us from the Bible. Watch and pray for He will descend from heaven with a shout and the voice of the archangel. I believe the trumpet will sound at the order of God almighty. From earth to glory the faithful followers of Christ will ascend.

Our Home in Glory
February 24

We were called away to service in a faraway land. Family and friends were left behind to attend the farms and take care of the children. Help them to grow up and be responsible citizens with love for our great country.

Faith would be one of the lessons of life. The family that prays together stays together, even if a loved one is sent overseas to fight for our freedom. Many miles separate the families and yet they are bound together with cords of love that cannot be broken.

Soldiers are far away and there is not a day that goes by without thoughts of going home and being with them and holding the children in their arms. The kids can hardly wait to see mom and dad.

Parents and other family members are also emotionally bound with a strong desire to see their son or daughter, brother or sister come back home.

The days and months pass into years and then finally it is time to go home. Arrangements have been made for the flight and soon everyone is together again. Each member is held close with a strong, loving embrace.

Home is the place where we go to be with our families and live in peace. We want to go home to our Father's house. He is waiting with a strong embrace of love to hold us tight and never let us go. We will forever be with Him in our home in glory.

Great Expectations
February 25

Great expectations come with high hopes and big dreams. Todays adventure will find the climbing gear and us in a valley with our tents erected at the foot of a mountain.

We had dreamed about this day with hopes of climbing this rugged terrain and being the first ones to place our flag on top of this huge land mass.

Now I'm not talking about experienced mountain climbers. We are all beginners except the guide. He is well trained in this profession. If we follow him and do exactly as he tells us, we will have a safe climb and eventually stand on the highest ridge.

The guide thought it would be best if we started out early in the morning. All of the packing supplies, food and water have been loaded into the backpacks. Everyone is ready to go.

There will be times when we will be in extreme danger with the possibility of falling to our deaths. After hours of climbing and following the guide's instructions, the summit is reached and all of us amateurs rejoice with our flag on display.

When Jesus comes into our lives, we have high hopes and great expectations of making heaven our home. If we will follow Him and obey His commands, the glory flag of our hearts will wave high as we rejoice in the victory.

A City in the Sky
February 26

In the very near future a big event will take place; we are going to a city. Some of us are ready and have made the final preparations for our heavenly flight. There is still a little time for those who are lagging behind.

We will not be using earthly transportation vehicles. A slow moving train has to stay on the rails. That is not a good choice for we will be airborne.

Forget about high-flying airplanes for we are going higher than we have ever been. What about a huge jet that can fly from one place to another with extremely fast speeds and can even break the sound barrier?

It is my understanding that when we go to this city in the sky; we will be there even before a rocket can enter orbit. I know we are not used to such high velocity traveling.

I hope I didn't discourage anyone with the travel arrangements. Our flight to glory will really be quite pleasant.

Please give me a few minutes to explain. Jesus is coming back to earth with power and great glory. He will be coming for those who have accepted Him in their hearts.

We don't know when He is coming, but when He does, we will be changed in a moment in the twinkling of an eye and we will be heaven bound. We don't want to wait too long and miss this flight.

A Prodigal Son Returns
February 27

Let us follow the life of a prodigal son. He is one that will carelessly spend his money and is very reckless with his life. The Bible tells us about a young man who lived in his father's house and it seemed as though he had the best of everything.

However, he was not satisfied with the good life and was determined to leave home and spend his inheritance on riotous living.

Far away in a corrupt city with a lot of pretend friends that only showed kindness when they could see the money. This lasted for a while and there came a time when this young man was hungry and he had no cash for food or clothes.

He could certainly use a friend, but there were none to be found. They were probably in other parts of the town seeking other prodigals with plenty of money to waste. They would hang around for a while until the victim was poor and lying in a gutter, clinging to life and then they would leave.

This young man was in the same position trying to survive. He even ate the food that was given to the swine.

He thought about his father's house, the love that was shown to him and the good life with real friends. He returned and his father saw him a great ways off and ran to him and welcomed him home.

Perhaps there is a prodigal son or daughter in our families that has gone astray and it has been years since we saw them. Keep praying and someday, we may notice they are in a big hurry, please don't worry! I believe they are coming home. Receive them with a loving embrace.

Walk by Faith, not by Sight
February 28

The daily routine of life will find us walking with Jesus. Our day will begin with Him as we kneel before the throne room of grace, talking with God in prayer.

Some of us will be going to work, school, or maybe just a walk at the park with our Savior. No matter where we meet Him the hand of mercy will be upon us and God's grace will abound in our hearts all through life.

I have found that walking with Jesus there is peace all along the way. The Son always radiates love that touches lives around the world. We are blessed in so many wonderful ways to have the Prince of Peace in our lives.

There are times in nature when dark stormy clouds hide the sun. The torrents of rain come with a vengeance with lightning flashing across the sky.

There is no need to worry for Jesus abides in our hearts and lives. He can calm the angry storms or our troubled souls. Hear the words of the Master: "Peace be still."

When our trials are heavy to bear and we are in need of a friend. We have a blessed assurance that Jesus always cares and He is a friend who is closer than a brother. Now that the storm has subsided, let's continue our daily routine and walk with Him all the days of our lives: walk by faith, not by sight.

Treasure in Heaven
February 29

Worthless items found in an earthly treasure chest. Many years ago these things were of great value and today they are still in demand. The purchase price is extremely high and their life span will be many years into the future.

A precious metal is extracted from the chest, which is used in the framework of buildings, bridges, and many other things. This is a valuable material sought after by many construction workers.

We see the devastating effect of corrosion as these materials are too weak to support any weight and bridges are condemned for safety reasons. Buildings are torn down and rebuilt with this steel product.

Another thing found in the chest is wood. Most of our homes are built with this natural born tree substance. Even a mansion on a hill will collapse into ruin when the deterioration process is complete.

Truly there must be something of value in the earthly container. After a thorough search, nothing is found.

I think we should move on to heaven's treasure chest and look for the things that are pleasing in the sight of God. We need to lay up for ourselves treasures in heaven that will last for eternity. Faith, hope, and charity will keep us unto life eternal.

Asleep at the Midnight Hour
March 1

The midnight hour was approaching. This was an ordinary night just like all the rest. Everyone had gone to bed and they were sleeping peacefully with high hopes of rising with the morning sun.

All of a sudden at the stroke of midnight, a sound was heard that awoke the family. If it were the sound of a trumpet, some of the members would have rejoiced for they would have been caught up in the clouds to be with the Lord.

It would really be a time of sadness for those who were not ready to go. They would probably not even know that the trumpet had sounded, but they would know that their family members were gone.

The TV and radio programs would have special alerts. Pilots disappeared in flight, no one at the controls, airplanes going down. Ships lost at sea. The captain and some of the crew are missing. Unmanned cars deserted on the highways.

Graveyards robbed, only the unbelievers, the unfaithful, and all those who have rejected Christ are still in their graves.

I do have some good news, the trumpet has not yet sounded. There may still be a little time to make things right with God. Sleep another day or decide tonight for Christ.

Restore to Life Eternal
March 2

Today we are going to ride a 55 Chevy down the imagination highway. My vision of hope and dreams goes back many years to reveal this beautiful car on display in the year of 1955. The color was a bright blue with a black interior.

It would be an honor to own such a vehicle. Just imagine me as the owner. The car would be waxed and cleaned on a regular basis to prevent rust and corrosion.

Well many years has gone by and to my dismay the car of my delight has lost its shine. Bad weather and salt covered roads has corroded the metal.

There is still hope for this classic car of the past. It is going to take a lot of hard work that includes sanding, replacing fenders, and repainting this old vehicle. When the work is finally done, My 55 Chevy will be restored to show room condition.

There are times in life when we have to go through a restoring process to renew our lives. We started out with Christ with a strong desire to make heaven our home. We committed our hearts and souls to follow Him all the days of our lives. The years have passed and we are not quite as close to Him as in the beginning.

It's not too late for a divine makeover. Go with me back to the cross. His precious blood will restore us unto life eternal.

A Safe Passageway
March 3

On a dark stormy night the ship is in danger of colliding with the huge rocks. It looks like the crew will perish at sea. The mighty vessel with the men on board moves closer to their impending doom.

The ship sways back and forth in the turbulent waters. It seems as though there is no escape for these weary sailors. They have fought the storm for days and now there is very little hope of making it safely to land.

After hitting a jagged rock, a huge hole was ripped in the side of the ship. More water rushes into the large boat and the men who are already tired and wore out from the storm continue to bail the water.

These brave men draw on their last bit of energy to keep the vessel a float and to save their lives. The ship is gradually sinking and a watery grave will claim the crew.

When all seems to be lost, a glimmer of light begins to shine. It is weak at first and then in a matter of seconds a high beam shines far out to sea.

The captain and men change the course of the ship and follow the light towards the lighthouse. A safe passageway was provided to keep the journeymen unharmed through the treacherous rocky sea. Finally on shore, they discovered there were problems with the electrical wiring in the lighthouse. No one lost his or her life.

In our journey of life, we are lost and without God. We will perish in our sins unless we repent and change course. Follow the light of life and Jesus will make sure we make it safely to our new home.

Open the Gates
March 4

The gate was securely locked to keep out any intruders, robbers, and anyone that did not have permission to enter the premises. There have been reports in the neighborhood of unlawful break-ins with people injured and even killed.

This particular resident made sure his family would be kept safe by adding extra security to his property. A special identification system was also built into the gate. The only way a person could enter this guarded place was to have a code number, fingerprint, and eye recognition.

There was one other way and this was completely controlled by the home dwellers. If a visitor appeared at the gate and wanted to talk with someone in the family, a profile of the person would be transferred to a monitor inside the mansion. If the person was accepted, the gate automatically unlocks and entrance would be granted for the waiting individual.

Suppose there is a time when we stand before heaven's gate. Everyone will not be allowed to enter this sacred place. There will be special requirements:

no ID's will be checked for Jesus already knows each of us by name. Without holiness no one shall see the Lord.

If the blood of Christ is detected in our lives, the gates of heaven will swing wide for a grand entrance. "Enter into the glories of the Lord."

Passing Through
March 5

Our next stop is a small town in a rural area with fine stores and good campsites. This is a wonderful place to visit. We will walk at the park and take pictures of the beautiful scenery and share them with our family and friends back home.

Everyone is reminded to enjoy their stay and enjoy the activities of the town. This is just a temporary place in our travel expedition. We will be leaving soon for we are just passing through.

This trip comes to an end and another one will begin. All of the travelers are encouraged to pack their belongings and be ready to leave in the morning. I know that none of the fine artifacts would be left behind. These beautiful gifts would be the talk of our hometown for many days to come.

Let's get moving to our new destination. There is so much to do and see; we can hardly wait to get to our next location. No one knew this would be our last day of worldly travels.

There comes a time in our lives when our journey will end. Death or the Rapture will take place and no one knows the day or hour of our departure. Whenever the time, be ready to meet thy God. We are just passing through.

Higher Ground
March 6

The floodwaters continue to rise as the rain falls from the sky. No one knows when this terrible weather will end. Cars are completely emerged and homes are washed away.

There seems to be no escape for the people in the valley. Going to higher ground saved many of them. The mighty river moves swiftly across the land, destroying everything in its path.

A huge tree uprooted by the storm is carried swiftly down stream to stop suddenly in the rough waters. Two small children are seen holding onto the branches to keep from drowning in the strong current of water. They are clinging for their lives.

Rescue is on the way. I hope they will be in time. These little ones cannot hold on much longer. Some men in a rescue boat risked their lives to save the children. Everyone rejoiced on shore as the parents held the kids in their arms with thankfulness in their hearts.

There are times when we were caught in the strong currents of sin, drifting aimlessly down the river of life. We would have perished had it not been for one man who gave His life to save us. Now is a good time to reach up to the nail-scarred hand and hold on to it. He gave His life so we could have life. " Thank you, Jesus."

Memories of the Past
March 7

Traveling down an old country road with thoughts of family and friends. There are special memories of the old home place. The house has changed a lot over the years. No one lives there now and the home is in really poor condition.

We knew it wouldn't be the same as when we left it. We stopped for a short while just to think about the old days and revive the memories of our youth.

I would say there are special times in our lives when we like to travel the roads of the past. Today is one of those days and we will be visiting our favorite places.

The sun is shining. Let's go for a walk at the park. Remember all the good times we had there. This is where we had some of our best picnics. We walked down the trail by the river and watched the colorful leaves fall to the ground.

It is getting late. There is still a little time to go fishing at our favorite spot. We won't stay long as there are other places of interest. This activity was really enjoyable or should I say it was peaceful at the lake. There will not be any fish to clean for supper.

While we are still visiting the precious memories of the past, our memory lane trip will not be complete unless we visit the church. Let's all go together with a little imagination.

The preacher delivers a wonderful sermon and the Holy Spirit touches us. The altar call is given and the minister has a countdown for Christ. My memory of the past is happening today as I knelt again at the altar and His same love lifted me up.

Calendar of Regret
March 8

Wait another day there is still plenty of time. We cannot choose the day of our salvation. It is not like an appointment when a certain date is scheduled and everyone is in agreement. We can mark off the days on a calendar. The last one is our final opportunity to meet at a certain place and fulfill all of our obligations.

I believe we need to take an imagination shortcut into the future. A group of people was confronted about their souls salvation. The Holy Spirit had brought conviction upon all of them. The altar call was given and some of the individuals accepted Christ into their lives.

One young man decided he was too young and thought it would be better if he waited many years to make things right with God. Time passed and he enjoyed the sinful pleasures of the world.

But now the day that was chosen is finally here. He dressed up in a nice suit and tie. This was going to be his salvation day. This elderly man could hardly wait to get to church and invite Jesus into his heart and life.

This was the big day for him to repent. As the man drove into the parking lot at church, He noticed there were no other cars. There was a sign on the door. "It's too late! The Rapture took place." This is the calendar of regret.

Patiently Wait
March 9

There are special times in our lives when we patiently wait for a certain event. All of us have experienced something in our lives where we had to wait days, months, or even years before it would occur.

When we graduated from high school or college, applications were filled out in an employment office and mailed to the employers for certain jobs.

We also visited manufacturing companies and other places of interest. The only thing we can do now is wait. The days slowly pass and no contacts are made with any of the personal.

All of a sudden the phone rings and our anticipation rises as we hear the employers name in the conversation. This call is from the personal office and they have a report of our job status.

Our hearts seem to beat a little faster, especially when we realize we have been selected for a special position and they would like for us to report to work on a certain day.

We are overjoyed at the thought of finding a job. I have heard that good things come to those who wait. It certainly seems to be true. As we go through life our highest expectations will be met when we patiently wait.

It is very important for us to know that Jesus is coming back to earth. None of us know when that special day will take place. We are warned to watch and pray.

If our patience grows thin and we get tired of waiting, it's only a matter of time before the corruptible things of this world will steal our salvation and we will be totally unprepared when Jesus comes in the clouds of glory. Patiently wait! Application has already been accepted.

Run to Win
March 10

The race is about to begin. There will be contestants from all walks of life. There is no age limit, but the children to the adults will run in their on class.

The winners will be chosen according to their endurance, steadfastness, and faithfulness. This will not be a race for the weak in heart or for those who rely only on speed. The unholy will have a huge disadvantage unless they have a change of heart somewhere along the way.

Awards will be given at different stages when the participants have completed all the requirements of the race. A crown will be given to those with good sportsmanship, kindness, and good deeds shown along the way.

It looks like it would be really hard to win this race unless the runners make things right with God. That is true.

Holy, righteous, and faithful contestants will receive a crown of life that fades not away. Why would anyone else want to enter this race? It seems as though the winners have already been chosen.

The duration of this race is not a one-day event, but it covers many years of each of our lives. God wants us to repent so we can go to heaven. He told us how to win; whether we repent or not, the decision belongs to us. He is the one that gives the crown.

A Place in Glory
March 11

Today is a good time to visit our imaginary place in the woods where our dream home will be built. The land has been cleared of the brush and trees. This is a beautiful site with a river close to the property.

The logs for the cabin will be cut from the forest. This home will require a lot of hard work, as all the bark on the trees will have to be removed.

We know that winter is coming soon and we don't have any time to waste. In this part of the country, winters can be quite severe. There is no way anyone could survive without a good shelter.

Early the next morning, the sound of trees was heard falling to the ground. Mules were used to transport them to the area of construction.

The father and his two sons worked extremely hard to cut and shape the wood beams. The mother was also busy preparing meals, caring water from the river for her family.

The work continued for a couple of months. The activities around the home had increased for the weather was getting colder and a few snowflakes were seen in the air. Finally the roof was finished and the family could move into their new log home, where they all lived peacefully all the days of their lives.

There is another building project going on. Jesus is preparing us a place in glory. "Let not your heart be troubled: ye believe in God, believe also in me. In my Father's house are many mansions: if it were not so, I would have told you. I go to prepare a place for you. (John 14: 1,2). We will be at home with Jesus in just a little while.

Christ our Best Friend
March 12

I would like to borrow a little bit of your time. Just a few minutes will be sufficient. The other day I saw my best friend in a supermarket. It has been several years since I saw him. We talked for a few minutes and then we shook hands and parted company.

All through life we make friends and they stay with us for a while and then they are gone. That does not mean the end of a friendship. The reality of life is that we will be separated for various reasons.

We all have our own ambitions that take us to many parts of the world. Some of the people we meet along the way will be our friends for life, even if they live in a far away country.

A good friend helps us along the pathway of life with encouraging words, kindness, and loyalty to give us strength when we are weak.

When we are cast down and forsaken, a friend will always give us a helping hand and will lift us up in times of sorrow. In the healing process of life, our friends sometimes have to leave and we are left alone.

I want to speak just a moment about a friend who is closer than a brother. Jesus will never leave or forsake us. There is nothing that will cause Him to depart. He is faithful to the end. Christ is our best friend.

This Same Jesus
March 13

Our story began when Jesus came to earth as the Son of God. His compassion touched many lives. He performed miracles with the sick being healed.

Parents brought to Him their children and He touched them. Even people that were too far away for Jesus to lay His holy hand on; they were cured when He spoke the Word.

Remember when He turned the water into wine, fed five thousand people with a few pieces of fish. Multitudes of people have been touched by His unwavering love.

His love is an everlasting love and it continues down through the ages, touching lives all alone the way. Had it not been for His love, where would we be today?

I think we already know the answer to that question. Let's be sure, no fellowship with God, still living in our sins and no hope of going to heaven.

Our faith would be in vain if Jesus did not rise from the dead. He arose from the grave. We have the same hope as those who watched Jesus ascend into heaven.

We know that this same Jesus shall come again and receive us unto Himself. He is the one who fed the multitudes, who gives us the bread of life, walked on water, and lifts us from the troublesome trials of life.

He calmed the storms by commanding them: "Peace be Still!" There are a countless number of times when the storms were raging in our lives and after Jesus gave the command, we have peace like a river in our souls.

This same Jesus who loved and gave Himself for us is coming again. Even so, come, Lord Jesus.

Stranded on a Highway
March 14

Stranded on the highway in a snowstorm, icy conditions prevented the travelers from going home. I had heard that twenty-four people had lost their lives because of the severe weather.

Tractor-trailers had jacked knifed and some of them had turned over, blocking the road and causing more accidents. The roads were not safe to drive on.

Walking on the slippery ice was also very dangerous. It was reported that someone backing up with snow moving equipment killed a pregnant woman in a parking lot. The baby survived and was in the hospital for critical treatment.

Kids were left at school and had to stay overnight. Hundreds of people were stranded on the highway with no food or warm blankets.

Some of the travelers walked to gas stations, pharmacies, grocery stores, and other places for shelter and to sleep for the night. This was a really terrible time in their lives. No way to get home. Finally the roads were cleared and the people returned to their dwellings.

As travelers on a journey to our home in heaven, the roads are sometimes blocked by unbelief and self-reliance. We cannot get through unless we depend on God. He will make a way when there is active faith to clear the road.

Keep the Faith Alive
March 15

There is one important thing that we would like to know before you leave this world. The hour of death is near as the family is called to his bedside.

We would like to know how to keep our faith alive. Is there something we can hold on to that will inspire us to live for Christ? Please tell us before you leave.

We know that you learned many years ago to love God with heart, soul, and mind. The dying man drew us closer and began to tell us a love story about a man who left his home in glory and came down to this vile sinful world.

He came to give His life and die on a cross for our sins. We already knew that Jesus died for us. Surely there must be something else our beloved family member could tell us. We questioned him more intently. There were no interruptions this time.

He referred to Jesus on the cross again, and he told us that our love, faithfulness, hopes and dreams were all a lie. We certainly did not want to hear those comments.

How could he say such things when his entire life was based upon them? We didn't know it at the time, but our family member was telling us how to keep our faith alive.

If Jesus is still in the grave, our love, faith, and hopes of life eternal are buried with Him. Right at the point of death, the dying man told us. "Jesus Christ arose!"

Ready or Not
March 16

The daily routine of life will find us getting ready for the various events of the day. Special clothes are selected that will be appropriate for the occasion.

Work clothes will be required for certain outdoors activities. A good winter coat will keep us warm. It is very important to wear boots, especially in the deep snow.

Before we go outside, we have to go through the preparation process. I don't believe there is anyone in this group that would volunteer to go outside without good boots and shovel the snow from the driveway.

When Sunday morning comes and it is time to get ready for church, our choice of clothes is different. A suit and tie will be a good selection or just casual clothing will be fine.

I am sure God would be pleased that we are going to church. Our daily routine will always find us getting ready to go somewhere and be there at a specific time.

Sometimes things happen whether we are ready or not. A plane will leave if we are unprepared for the scheduled trip. There is no turning back for late passengers once the airplane has left the ground.

Our main concern in life should not be our outward appearance, but the inner feelings of our hearts and souls. Jesus will be returning for those whose lives have been cleansed by the blood, pure and holy. Ready or not, He is coming.

Names Called in Glory
March 17

A woman holds a pen in her quivering hand at the signing of a contract. This agreement is final and both parties will be subject to the rules and regulations of the document.

Once her name is placed on the dotted line, whether it is for good or bad, joy or sadness, it will be too late to void the contract.

If there is a dispute about certain obligations, police officers or lawyers may be contacted to settle the problems. Some contracts can be annulled if they have not been fully implemented.

Let's say a car was sold and a signature sealed the deal. There were a few mechanical things that were not mentioned in the conversation or in the paper work. The buyer can be released from ownership of the vehicle if he or she has proof of the defects.

Now if she drove the car home and kept it for several weeks and then noticed various things wrong with it, she would be bound by the contract and would have to take full responsibility of the vehicle.

The book of life is one place where our names will appear and we do not want to change anything. We will not void or make any corrections by going back into sin. When our names are called in glory, our response will be: "Here, Lord!"

A Refreshing Rain
March 18

The outpouring of His love comes down like a gentle rain. Grass has faded from the intense summer heat and ponds could use a refilling.

Nature is a lifeless place without a fresh shower from above. Look around at the trees, dying leaves are thirsty for a touch from heaven, even a sprinkle would do. Everything in the forest is brittle and highly flammable.

Tomatoes in the garden hang low on the vine. The deterioration has spread to the corn, beans, and all the vegetables are in decline. None of them has the strength to rise another day.

The livestock will die, unless the rain comes. They are lying in the fields barely clinging to life. All of nature is affected by this drought. Families will perish without a good water supply.

Small clouds form in the distance. There is no response from the inhabitants of earth, as they are all too weak to get up. Dark clouds fill the sky. It rained for days and life came back to all the occupants of a dry parched earth.

There are times in our lives when we need a spiritual rain from above. A fresh shower will supply our deep thirst for God. The desires of our hearts will be revived with a touch from heaven. From death to life, we will live again. His love is coming down like a gentle rain.

A Stranger in the Camp
March 19

A good location for the campsite was found in the mountains. It is always good to get away for a few days and enjoy the pleasures of life. This vacation trip was planned many days in advance.

Fishing equipment was unloaded from the van and the tents were anchored to the ground. The campfire was built and we gathered around the fire. The fishermen were laughing and joking with one another. Everyone was having a really good time.

We began to talk about the future and the things that we wanted to do in life. There was a pleasant atmosphere as we spoke of the places we wanted to visit.

This conversation became more serious as we talked about life and death. The thought of living for many years brought joy to our hearts. Each of us held onto the expectations of a long life.

When death was mentioned, an odd feeling came over us. It appeared as though a stranger had entered our camp. The campfire went out, and we went to bed for the night.

Early the next morning, one of our friends had died in his sleep. All of our hopes and dreams of having a long life was cut short by death. By having faith in Christ, we will live again and go to a better place.

Thanks Again, Jesus
March 20

The gratitude of my heart was expressed at a restaurant the other day. I was sitting at a table enjoying my meal when all of a sudden, an accident occurred. I am thankful that no one was hurt.

Please don't worry! I exaggerated a little bit about the seriousness of this event. My imagination was trying to control the situation and I couldn't resist the power of thought.

Return with me to the restaurant so we can revisit the real story. An accident did occur but it was only a minor inconvenience. I was enjoying my meal when I accidently spilled a cup of water onto the table and surrounding area.

If I had stayed with the imaginary thoughts, a car would have run into the building and a kid who gave us the warning saved our lives.

It looks like I have a real problem; I didn't know my unrealistic thoughts would try to steal the story. Please bear with me as I promise not to be interrupted any more.

There was a kid in the restaurant and when I spilled the water, he came over with some napkins and helped me clean up the area. I thanked him and he went back to his seat. When I was walking towards the door, I thanked him again and he said: "You are welcome."

It is a blessed day in our lives when we are grateful and give thanks to Christ for all He has done for us. "Thanks again, Jesus!"

No Grapes on the Vines
March 21

This looks like it is going to be a bad year for the harvest of grapes in the slumber fields. At first the laborers were very productive in planting the seeds, tilling the ground, and just taking good care of the vineyard.

Time went by and these hard workers could not be seen laboring in the fields. A closer inspection would show a more comfortable environment of sleeping beneath shade trees.

They didn't bother to work the fields. Grapevines were unattended, but now it is time for the harvest; the slumber workers will be paid according to the pounds of grapes harvested. It sure is a lot of workers disappointed in this group. No grapes on the vines equal zero profits on the scale and very little money in each one's pocket.

Workers in another field were quite different, diligent in the harvest fields. They took a lot of pride in their job and they continued working in the fields. They began in the morning and worked all day until late in the evening.

Time went by, but these faithful laborers continued steadfastly, tilling the ground, and tending to the work of maintaining the orchard. There were times when they were found beneath the shade trees, but only long enough to take their required breaks.

No one in this group could be associated with the slumber team. The crop yielded an abundance of grapes and the rewards were many as the harvest ended.

The harvest is ripe and the laborers are few. What is done for Christ will last and souls will be saved too.

High Calling of God
March 22

Battles have been fought down through the ages. Men and women called to war. Volunteers and draftees answered the call to serve our country.

I remember the days of the draft when I was selected to serve in the armed forces of the United States. My notice came in the mail for me to report to a certain place for active duty. After training I was sent to Vietnam where I would finish my obligation to the Army.

Every one of us has been called out for a purpose, whether to fight in a war or stay at home and raise the family. Whatever the task, we should be faithful in our commitment to serve with loyalty and obedience.

Our summons for service comes in many different ways. Sometimes the call comes from the government by a letter, as it was with me. The Internet has been a good source of communication. It is really hard to beat this worldwide connection. People down through the ages have used the telephone to talk with one another.

Our best response is to be available for service. There is another type of call that I did not mention.

This is the most important one of them all. When this call comes, please don't neglect it, hang up, or run and hide.

This is a call from the throne room of grace. He wants us to serve Him with a full commitment of unwavering love. This is the high calling of God.

Gold in the Hills
March 23

Gold is discovered in the hills. I cannot tell you the place for fear of a stampede. The people's response is like animals that have been spooked by a lightning storm. The cattle all run together to escape the danger and sometimes die in the process.

These settlers have left their homes and families. They unhooked the plow horses and rode off in a gallop. No time to tell the wives goodbye or to hold the children in their arms and tell them how much they are loved.

Gold shiny nuggets discovered in an isolated part of the country. All land rights are open to the public and only a few people have staked claims. The gold is free for those who have signed the deed.

Some of the prospectors have already lost their lives in the stampede for riches. They will not be going home anymore. Life ended in a gold rush.

The hopes and dreams of a prosperous life will come to an end when the gold is gone and the pockets are empty. What does it profit a person who is in search of gold or earthly riches to lose his life and family in the end?

Earthly treasures are temporary; they were not meant to last. It is always good to prosper for a better life, but if it cost us our souls, what have we gained?

Break Up the Fallow Ground
March 24

It is hard to believe that spring is already here. It seems as though we were shoveling snow last week. Today we are getting out the plow and the horses have already been harnessed.

Plowing a garden is not an easy task. Rocks in the field have to be removed. It is very important to select a good gardening spot; one without rocks would be an excellent choice. I'm sorry, but we just have one field, so we had better get busy. The plow cuts deep into the earth for the turning of the topsoil.

Next week we will break up the fallow ground by tilling the garden and then we will plant the seed. A couple of weeks have gone by since the cultivated land has been planted.

The new garden still needs a lot of work in order to produce a good crop. Finally the days of harvest have arrived and we will reap the benefits of our hard work.

We cannot quit yet. There is a greater need for us in the fields of life. We are instructed by the Holy Bible to break up the fallow ground so the seed can be sown.

The time is now for us to share the Word of God. We are not yet finished with our work in the harvest field. Sow today and reap tomorrow.

Carry the Torch
March 25

A flaming fire is ignited in a cauldron to mark the beginning of the Olympics. The runner selected for this position was usually a celebrity or another famous person. One year for this spectacular event, Muhammad Ali, a famous boxer received this honor.

The torch would be lit and the person carrying it would run to the designated place where this flaming fire of the Olympics was handed to another runner. The torchbearer continued down the course until the last man entered the main area and lit the cauldron.

There were people from all nationalities competing for specific metals. A gold metal was given to the individual who won the event. I hate to end the Olympics without knowing the final results.

But we need some volunteers who are willing to carry the cross. Running by faith is required. All applicants who love Jesus Christ will be accepted. God needs runners who are committed to helping others win the crown of life.

These individuals will be the cross-bearers and their mission is to hold the cross high for His glory. Their responsibility will be to share God's love with others along the way. Carry the cross for the entire world to believe.

Build a Bigger Barn
March 26

The unseen danger of a small, growing farm has a drastic effect on the owner. Many years has gone by since this structure was built. The years have been prosperous with the gardens more productive than ever. An increase in the sale of livestock has added money to the bank account.

With all of these growing pains, it is quite evident a new barn needed to be built. Immediately the work began as the old barn was torn down.

Well the new barn was finally built, but the loss of corn was tremendous. The cattle sales also dropped, his workers quit for lack of funds. It would certainly be hard to recuperate from this tradeoff, an old barn for a new one.

This rich man was very greedy and thought only of himself. Sinful living had separated him from his family and loved ones. He was alone with no one to care for him. His possession was a great big, empty barn of despair.

This man who was once wealthy and had plenty of money is now hungry and living in a poor condition. One day he went to church and he told Jesus that he was sorry for his sins. He received God's grace that day and arose from the altar a new man.

That was a really good tradeoff, an old sinful life for a new life in Christ. The wealth of the soul is the love of the heart.

Never Thirst Again
March 27

This has been a year of extreme drought. The water supply is scare. Wells have gone dry. Farmers in the community have had to sell their livestock because the feed is too expensive.

Rivers and lakes are at an all time low. I heard the weather report the other day and the forecast was favorable, at least for a little while. Snow was predicted, but this would not be enough to replenish the dry earth.

Many of the families that live in the country depend on creeks, wells, and other resources for their survival. The drought is so bad that some of the inhabitants may have to sell their homes, land, and move away.

I have not heard of any range wars of fences being cut or anyone hurt because of the water shortage. I know it could happen with some owners who have property and water rights to their land.

On one side of the fence the livestock have enough water to stay alive. The other side is quite different, no water and the animals are dying. It will take a lot of rain to keep the peace in the valley.

So it is in life, we all need water for our survival. Our souls will perish if our spiritual thirst is not satisfied. If we are on the wrong side of the fence, Jesus will open the gate and give us the water of life. We will never thirst again.

Change the Tracks
March 28

We have already been on several trips and visited a lot of places. I don't believe we have ever been down the imagination railway. There is nothing like a little bit of adventure to keep us on the rails.

Let's get started. This will not be the normal safe trip without any problems. Now would be a good time to say a little prayer. It's all right to prepare for the danger ahead.

Please be warned this is a life or death ride. It is too late to get off the train for we are all ready in motion. Time goes by fast as we approach the intersection where the train will have to switch tracks.

A trackman is ahead of us and he seems to be having a problem with the switch. The lever is frozen and the man is unable to reposition the rails. It looks like there is going to be a head-on collision with another train.

Finally the switchman breaks the ice from the manual lever and the tracks are changed. There is a lot of rejoicing on these two trains as they pass safely in the night.

There is another danger that I forgot to mention. We are going down the rails of life and unless we change tracks, we will perish. Sinful lives are changed by faith in Christ and we are kept safely on the rails.

Saved by Grace
March 29

We all know the story of how Jesus came to earth. Angels announced his birth. He came to do the will of His Father. The purpose of His coming was for us to have fellowship, peace, and freedom from our sins by divine grace

This was no small task, seeing how corrupt the world had become and how far away we were from God. Just knowing how deep we were in sin would discourage anyone, except the Son of God.

Think about someone being stuck in the miry clay, unable to escape, and sinking deeper every day. This was our condition in life. We try to rescue them while standing in the same clay. It appears to me that we are going down just as fast.

We as sinners cannot save ourselves. The unholy, unrighteous, and ungodly will perish together, unless we are saved by a higher power.

Christ came to save us from our sins. He is the only one that is qualified and endowed by God the Father to accomplish such a tremendous task.

There is no need to worry about Jesus sinking in the clay. He is holy, righteous, and God's Son. Let us now take hold of His hand and be saved by grace.

The Calmness of Nature
March 30

A gentle rain will calm a troubled spirit. Rain from heaven is refreshing to our souls. If we are feeling mighty low, a shower from above will help us to grow. We don't need a storm for buds of faith to form.

Take a walk at the park and enjoy the scenery. Birds are singing sweet melodies for each of our hearts.

The gentleness of nature touches us with the good things of life.

Look at the flowers and see how they bloom. Behold the beauty and smell the fragrance. It looks like God planted these for our convenience.

The trees have their own stories to tell. The things they have heard in the shadows are kept secret from the public. We all need privacy, no matter where we go. It's nice to know the forest is silent and will not whisper anything heard.

I have noticed the sun is shining. The rays of light shine upon us. It fills our lives with radiance that always creates a smile.

In springtime the lifeless surroundings are revived with a little sunshine from above and everything is brought back to life. In our gloomy days, it just takes a gentle light from glory to dispel all the sadness and keep our hearts aglow.

Nature has a way of restoring peaceful qualities of life. God gives us eternal peace in Christ.

Shadow of Death
March 31

Our journey today will take us through the valley of the shadow of death. Please be aware, the only survivors will be those who are still living when Jesus comes, it is too late to retreat. We have an obligation to fulfill this appointment and die and after that it will be the judgment.

It seems as though there are a lot of fearful hearts. This would be a good time to pray and make things right with God.

Some of us will die before Jesus comes back to earth, "The dead in Christ shall rise first: then we which are alive... shall be caught up together... to meet the Lord in the air." (I Thess. 4:16,17)

We had better get started. I cannot give a time when this expedition will end or how long life will last. No one knows when the shadow will cross our paths and claim another life.

This is our destiny in life; we all have to pass through the valley. There are no exceptions. The tombstones are yet to be marked with each of our names. Some of us will leave at an early age, while others will be called later in life.

After a short while of walking, there seems to be a growing fear as more and more tombstones appear.

"Yea, though I walk through the valley of the shadow of death, I will fear no evil: for thou art with me." (Psa. 23:4) Looks like God answered our prayers.

He Is the Son of God
April 1

On a hill far away a man was crucified. God's only begotten Son hung on a cross. He was tortured beyond recognition.

His punishment started with a beating, a lashing with a whip. He was beaten thirty-nine times save one. If there were more than the law allowed, the one who did the beating would also be punished. Many of the victims died from the beating alone.

The crown placed on His head was made of vines with many thorns. I believe these sharp pieces of wood were about one or two inches in length and they were forced into His brow. The blood was streaming down the side of His face. His beard was plucked out.

Oh, this was a horrible sight to see Jesus in so much agony. What crime did He commit to deserve such a severe punishment? I believe because He referred to Himself as the Son of God and He could raise this temple in three days. He was talking about His own life of rising from the dead.

Jesus had to die on the cross, without the shedding of blood there would be no remission of our sins. We are the guilty ones with many sins in our lives. Guilty is our verdict. Jesus gave His life in our place to pardon us. Behold, He is the Son of God. " Glory, Hallelujah!"

Where will We Find Him
April 2

Our imaginary search will take us to many wonderful places. We will be looking for the Savior, the mighty God, the Prince of Peace, and we will rejoice when He is found. We will be traveling down the shepherds trail.

The first place we came to was a small stable where Jesus was born. We had arrived a few years later, after His birth and the manger was empty. Mary and Joseph took the family and moved to a different location.

We were still determined to find Him for He had something of great value and we couldn't live without it. Once again we set out on our journey, more years passed and we knew that Jesus would be older. Our greatest fear was to die without meeting Him.

A few days before we had arrived in a small village, it was reported a man was in the garden praying in great agony and His name was Jesus.

We hurried to the garden but to no avail. "Where is Jesus?" They told us about the hill where He was crucified. We were too late, but then we saw people rejoicing for Jesus had risen from the dead.

Unable to find Jesus before His death, please don't worry! "Blessed are they that have not seen, and yet have believed." (Jn. 20:29) He is alive and we have life in Him.

Walk on
April 3

Today we will just be going for a walk and gather a little inspiration along the way. Sometimes in life it is hard to take the next step, to gather enough strength to complete the course.

It is a lot easier when we know Jesus is right there walking with us. When we feel like quitting or we just don't think we can make it to the other side, He gives us a divine touch from heaven.

Our souls are inspired to keep walking. No looking back or returning to the ways of the world. I know there are times when we are weak and unable to stand. There is victory promised if we will take hold of His nail-scarred hands.

"Walk on" I heard those inspirational words one day and I was inspired to try a little harder, to put forth more effort. It's only two words, but for me, I was able to accomplish more when they were applied to my life.

There are things in life that will inspire us to have greater achievements. Sometimes when we are walking, we take our eyes off of Jesus and the glory crown is not in sight.

The best way to stay strong with unwavering faith is to keep pressing on; never turn loose of Jesus' hand. Two words for faith inspired living: "Walk on!"

No Time to Wait
April 4

A dramatic scene unfolds, as there is no time to wait for a response team. A woman was driving down the highway with a little baby in the car. All of a sudden this small infant stopped breathing and its face had turned blue.

This was a life or death situation. The aunt pulled the car to the side of the road and started screaming for help. She could not wait any longer, immediately she began the resuscitation process and the little child started breathing again.

While this emergency was happening, other knowledgeable people had gathered around the couple to provide the necessary help to save the baby's life.

They were there at the right time and place to offer assistance. The baby stopped breathing again and the rescue workers stayed with the baby and kept it alive. This precious child was taken to the hospital and was in stable condition at the last report.

In an emergency there is no time to spare. Every minute counts. A short delay would have devastating results. When there is no immediate danger, we are less responsive and will wait much longer before any action is taken.

There are certain things in life that we should treat as an emergency. We should be concerned about our soul's salvation before we stop breathing. Jesus is our only true source of life.

Crucify All Over Again
April 5

When we go back into sin we are crucifying Christ all over again. The spikes will not be driven into His hands and feet or the crown of thorns forced upon His brow. He already went through the suffering and pain. He died once and that was sufficient. How could He be crucified again?

Let's begin with our sins. At the time we came to Christ, we were unholy, unrighteous, and living ungodly lives. We believed on the Lord Jesus and He forgave us of our sins.

We took up our cross and began following Him. Our lives had been changed from the old sinful nature to one of holiness and righteousness.

Christ could never be crucified again. I believe we are all in agreement. If we go back down the sinner's path and allow sins to come back into our hearts, we are crucifying Him again by our actions.

No spikes or a crown, but our sins pierce his flesh as if it were the nails and our unrighteousness as though He was never crucified. If Jesus is crucified again, we had better check our own lives to see if we are the ones causing the pain.

Remember His love and how He died, crucified on a cross. When we return to sins, we are betraying His love. Please, Jesus have mercy on us. We have sinned.

Walk with Jesus
April 6

We plead the blood for direction in life. We all need divine guidance, whether we are going through the valley of sorrow or by the peaceful rivers of overflowing joy.

There is not a day that goes by without you walking beside us, and sharing God's great love. It is always a blessing to feel His holy hand, a loving embrace gives us the blessed assurance of unending grace.

Help us to walk the straight and narrow way. There are many paths to follow, but only one leads home. Our heart's desire is to be faithful and never turn to the broad road of sin. We will follow you, Jesus, wherever you lead. Our lives are in your hands and our souls too.

Onward is our journey to the gates of pearl. Give us strength every day to fight against evil, to overcome our enemies and be victorious in battle.

Love will always prevail and if we stay committed in loving you with heart, soul, and mind, we will never fail.

We are going to keep walking, talking with Jesus all along the way. We thank you, Lord for the promise of never leaving or forsaking us, but that you will go with us all the way.

A walk with Jesus with will find us walking the streets of glory and praising Him throughout eternity.

He Didn't Send an Angel
April 7

God has His special forces of angels. Each one has their own qualifications to perform certain things for God. We are all familiar with guardian angels. They are vigilant to watch over the inhabitants of earth and to give us divine protection wherever it is needed.

We go to the cross where Christ was hanging between heaven and earth. Jesus could have called for the angels to set Him free, but He didn't do it. He stayed on the cross even though His pain was unbearable. He was fulfilling God's plan of salvation, so we could be saved.

God has many supernatural angels, surely He could have used one of them to accomplish His will, and spare His Son. There have been many occasions in life where God sent an angel to perform certain duties, but not this time. None of them were qualified.

The salvation of mankind was so important that all of God's sacred angels with all their super natural powers could not accomplish His will, for us to be saved.

He did not send an angel to die in our place. He sent His only Son who was obedient even unto death. For a good man some would dare to die, but for us ungodly sinners, Christ died so we could live. There is no salvation in any other, not even an angel.

He Didn't Come Down
April 8

His love for us kept Him on the cross. He didn't come down when his tortured body was experiencing excruciating pain.

Think about Jesus dying. He was wounded for our transgressions and bruised for our iniquities. I know it is probably hard to imagine God's Son suffering.

When He lived here on earth and walked among us. He touched many lives and they were instantly healed. On a cross He suffered, bled, and died.

Remember Jesus was born as a little baby and grew up to become a man. Let's review His birth for just a minute so we can have a better understanding of who Jesus is: "Behold, a virgin shall be with child, and shall bring forth a son, and they shall call his name Emmanuel, which being interpreted is, God with us." (Mathew 1:23)

Let's go back to the cross where there seems to be some doubt about Jesus suffering. If He were a man, then He would have suffered and felt the pain. The Bible speaks of God with us and it also says: "Christ suffered for us in the flesh." (1Pe. 4: 1) Jesus was a man and God on earth.

He died as a man; He was resurrected as God. He didn't come down from the cross, if He did, we would still be in our sins.

Anyone Need a Ride Home
April 9

We are going on a travel adventure, perhaps the greatest one in our lives. We will not be going very far as this is a faith trip back in time.

There is no need to purchase an airplane ticket. We will make better time if we travel the waves of thought. Our return trip back home may be a different story.

We are going to a grave to see if Jesus is inside. If He is not, all faith trips will be canceled and any reservations to glory will be non-existent. Without faith we will be unable to return home.

We may have to take up a permanent residence in a far away country. When we leave for this destination, I am aware that some of us will have to catch a ride with the faith believers.

Once we arrive and find out the truth, each of us will be responsible for our own return trip. Hitchhikers will be allowed if more time is needed for them to believe.

Be prepared just in case the sepulcher is empty; our individual faith plane will have no power if unbelief is still in control or if Jesus is still in the grave.

We have waited long enough. It's time to go inside the sepulcher. Just as we thought, now we have the proof. The grave is empty. "He is not here; He has risen." Does anyone need to catch a ride home? There is no one in this group.

The Third Day
April 10

Jesus promised on the third day He would rise from the dead. They took Him down from the cross and laid Him in a sepulcher. He was not unconscious or in a coma as some people might suppose.

There should be no doubt in anyone's mind; He was dead. Jesus was buried in a borrowed grave. This deathbed was not going to be His permanent place with the deceased.   Soon He would be leaving; He had no intentions to stay.

Everyone knew that Jesus always spoke the truth and whatever He said, always came to pass.   One time He told the people, "I am the way, the truth, and the life: no man cometh unto the Father, but by me." (John 14:6)

Wherever Jesus went, lives were transformed by His truthful words. There is no reason to expect that Jesus had told a lie about rising from the dead. "On the third day, I will rise again." So many times we are impatient and cannot wait for the time to be fulfilled.

One day passed and then two, surely He is not going to come back to life. But on the third day, Jesus kept His promise and arose from the dead. He was alive, alive for evermore. Jesus did not lie. The grave could not hold Him.

No Flowers on the Grave
April 11

We are not going to visit the gravesite this year. It is always good to pay our respects to those who have died. Flowers have always been a wonderful way to express our gratitude and to show our love for a family member or a friend.

Please don't get me wrong. There are many places where our loved ones are buried and we will continue to reverence their lives.

We are associated with one person that deserves the honor, but His grave will be unattended and no flowers of gratitude or appreciation will be left at His burial site.

I know this is starting to get a little confusing. If He deserved the honor, why is He being neglected? We are not alone in our denial to go to this man's grave. There are many others who feel the same way.

It seems as r this man lived a life of disgrace and was so dishonorable that none of us would claim Him or associate ourselves with Him.

On the contrary, He was the greatest man that ever lived upon this earth. He is loved more than anyone else around the world. There are no flowers on His grave because Jesus is not dead. He is alive! We give honor and praise to Him as our Lord and Savior.

Faith Is Alive
April 12

Just imagine our faith controls everything in life. Disregard all mechanical and electrical applications for faith is now the main power source.

I don't believe anyone would benefit from having vain faith. We depend on our cars and trucks to take us to various locations. The key is inserted into the ignition and when it is turned on, the engine starts and the vehicle is ready to drive. If our faith has a flaw in it somewhere, no matter how hard we try, the car will not start.

We have to depend on someone else to take us to our destination. Our neighbors are always willing to give a helping hand. Let's give them a call and see if they will come over. Once again dead faith fails to respond and the phone hangs from the cord in a broken condition.

It looks like we are having a chain reaction. Car will not start; phone is dead, and other faith outlets are unresponsive. When faith is vain, nothing will work properly.

Let's go with the real facts about faith and go to the burial of Jesus. If He is still in the grave, our faith is vain, worthless, and we have no hope of going to heaven. Jesus is not in the grave. He arose and our faith is alive.

Faith Barriers Removed
April 13

When our way is obstructed with the boulders of life, faith is also hindered and we cannot get through. Let's think about a drive in the country. It's a beautiful day and a perfect time to enjoy the scenery.

We will be traveling on a road that is narrow and there are a lot of curves. I guess this is a good time for a warning. There have been rockslides on the steep mountain slopes and some of the travelers have lost their lives as rocks crossed the highway.

Now that we know the dangerous, life threatening conditions, let's begin. I forgot to mention the road we will be traveling is one way. This is not a two-lane highway. I thought we were going to enjoy the scenery. How is that possible when we are fearful of losing our lives?

There are a few trouble spots and once we get through the bad curves, and past the rockslide area, we will enjoy the most beautiful scenery ever created. Well we made it through the pass, only because state trucks had cleared the highway.

We are on a journey to a far away land; heaven is in sight. Jesus will remove all obstacles that hinder our faith on the highway of life.

No Excuse This Time
April 14

Todays story will take us way back into the mountains where the imagination will find an excuse for not going to church. An elderly man lived with his wife in a small cabin. He had worked hard all of his life and he had a wonderful family.

His sons and daughters were grown and they no longer lived at home. Occasionally they would come for a visit and stay a couple of days. The good wife would always cook for them.

It was always a sad time when they parted company. Now she really loved her husband and would do anything for him. She had prayed many times for him to be saved.

Every Sunday she would plead with him to go to church with her. He was really a kind man, who wanted to please his wife, but he always had an excuse for not going to Sunday school, so his wife went to church by herself.

She would go to the altar and pray and ask God to touch her husband and bring conviction in His heart. One day while she was praying at church; the front door opened, her husband walked down the aisle, knelt down beside her and received Jesus into his life.

Persistent faith and love will not fail. Excuses will never find God too busy to hear our heart's cries.

Jesus Saves
April 15

We have gone back in time and traveled many miles in search of salvation. Today our journey will take us to the past, present, and future. It all depends on where we first met Jesus and when He came into our hearts.

There are probably some people in this group that has not yet met Him. We would like to hear your testimony later.

I first met Jesus when I went to church and walked down the aisle to the altar. The Evangelist had just finished his sermon and was having a countdown for Christ.

Counting from sixty back to zero and then he said: "Heaven or hell, it's your choice." Praise God, I choose Jesus as my Lord and Savior. He lives in my heart and I thank Him for: "Amazing Grace."

I have heard other testimonies of Christ saving people at home, in jails, hospitals, and many other locations. One person told me he got saved when there was a severe storm.

I don't know the whole story, but I would think: the bolts of lightning were extremely close and the fear of death brought him to his knees.

By faith, meet Jesus at the cross, follow Him to the grave, and observe an empty tomb for Christ has risen. Jesus saves; now we can sing, "Amazing Grace."

"We are Va. Tech." Let's Go Hokies"
April 16

Today we are going to travel in time to the Virginia Tech campus. A terrible tragedy had taken place on April 16, 2007. Thirty-two people were killed, seventeen wounded, and six injured escaping through windows. The person responsible committed suicide.

This was a time of extreme sorrow and grief for the families and for the entire nation. Even though we did not know them personally, we still felt the pain. The dark shadow of death had crossed the path of these precious individuals.

We can still remember the words of inspiration that touched our lives in the memorial service. "We will Prevail!" These are thoughtful words that inspire us to keep going, no matter how deep the sorrow or how great the pain.

Keep holding on to the memories for in them are the lives of loved ones and our hopes and dreams are fulfilled in the love that never dies.

We all became a part of this tragedy and we were joined even closer together when the final words were given at this sacred assembly.

When the student body arose to offer their final farewells, perhaps there was other voices heard that day from the departed, and they led the group. "We are Va. Tech." "Let's Go Hokies."

Paid in Full
April 17

The risk of owing too much money can be hazardous to our lives. There are times we need to borrow for certain types of investments.

Arrangements are made at a bank for a loan and a certain amount of interest will be applied to the transaction.

This is the normal process of life. Money is needed and we go to a certain institution to set up an account. Normally we do not borrow if we think we cannot afford to repay the balance.

I can vaguely remember a story of many years ago; a man was in so much debt he could not pay it all back. I'm not sure; gambling may have caused his wasteful spending.

Anyway, one night this man had decided to take his own life because of his financial obligations. He wrote a long list of everything he owed. I believe he said at the end: "Who can pay so great a debt?"

He fell asleep with a pistol lying on the table with the note. A friend came by and saw the note and the weapon. The best I can remember, his friend wrote: "Paid in Full."

In our lives, the debt of our sins is so high; there is no way we can repay it. Jesus died on a cross in our place for our sins. "Paid in Full."

Pure Sweet Honey
April 18

The lure of sweet honey is in a log about half of a mile from a bear's den. The cold hard winter is over and the flowers have already bloomed. Bear cubs are seen playing and rolling around on the hillside. The mother of this small family is climbing over the rocky terrain in search of food.

The bees have been very active this year. Most of the time, hives are created in a safe place where there is no danger from wild animals. The bees had no way of knowing a bear and her cubs would take up residence a short distance away.

A big hungry bear begins to make her way through the forest on her way home to her new summer retreat. The smell of honey is hard to resist and it is not too far away.

She moved the huge log and the bees swarmed all around her. This lasted for several minutes before she left with a mouth full of honey. The mother bear was persistent and finally was rewarded with the entire honeycomb.

In life we need to have the same determination in our search for God. We should hunger and thirst after righteousness.

The sweet fellowship of God should draw us closer to Him and by our persistence we will be rewarded with the pure honey of heaven.

Meet Jesus at the Crossroads
April 19

It is really obvious that we all like to travel. Sometimes we go as tourist, explorers, or we just love a good adventure.

Today we are going to one of the most important places in life. It is all right to leave the GPS system at home. Our guidance will come from a higher power.

I have to agree this is the grandest place on earth. More lives have been changed for righteous living than any other place, since the creation of man.

Let's get started. We are going to the crossroads of life and we are going to meet the Savior of the world. This will be a journey that brings peace, love, and life to all believers.

It's been a while since there has been this much anticipation for one of our journeys. There is no need to bring a backpack or any of the other luxuries from home; they are just not necessary.

We want everyone to feel comfortable in this life changing experience. All of the sins that have been accumulated over the years, it is all right to bring them; as a matter of fact, we encourage it.

I know we didn't travel very far, but we are at the destination. Let us all pray together, "Lord Jesus, come into our hearts and forgive us our sins. We believe that you died and rose again. Thank you, Jesus, for salvation."

Life in Christ
April 20

Many years have elapsed since Jesus was crucified on a cross and was laid in a grave. He arose from the dead and ascended to heaven.

What does that mean for those of us who are living today? It means that Christ was brought back to life. He was revived from the dead and those of us who believe Christ is the Savior will have everlasting life.

Jesus' body was buried in a sepulcher. He stayed there until the third day and then He arose. The grave could not hold Him. He has power over death, the grave, and hell.

We too will have to die to sin. This will not be the death of our bodies. No funeral arrangements will be made. We will not be going to the cemetery to be buried in a casket.

There will be no kind words spoken for us in the sanctuary of the deceased and our names will not appear in the obituary column of the news paper. They are not going to bring out the grave clothes and sing any songs for the departed.

The Bible tells us that we must die daily to our sins. Our sins have been crucified with Christ and we are to live each day for His glory.

When we are saved, we do not die a physical death so we do not need a funeral. We die to our old sinful ways and we live with a new life in Christ.

Security Breach
April 21

A Notice has gone out to the public of a severe security breach. Computers were hacked and private information was stolen. High technology thieves affected thousands of people by stealing confidential information.

Debit cards connect us to many types of benefits. We can withdraw money from the bank or buy something on- line. If this information gets in the wrong hands, lives can be ruined and identities can be sold to the highest bidder.

I believe the security breach has been corrected and new cards have been reissued to the victims. Once identities have been stolen, it is very hard to clear one's name.

We all use security methods to protect our families and make sure they are kept safe. Our doors in each of our homes have locks on them to keep out intruders, those who would harm us.

No matter how hard we try, a thief can somehow break through all of our defenses, and even prisons with armed guards have had inmates escape back into society.

There is a security plan that will not fail. It is guaranteed to be thief proof. There is a special requirement to obtain this defense system. We need to believe in Christ and commit our souls to Him. He will keep our lives secure with divine protection.

It Is Finished
April 22

When our life long goals are complete and we have done our very best to accomplish the task, we rejoice in the finished work.

Just like athletes who have trained for many years to compete in the Olympics, they eventually come to the end of their life experience and hopefully they will be rewarded for their achievements.

We all have certain expectation of fulfilling an ambition in life. The dreams of going to college and becoming a doctor or nurse is finally realized when they have finished the college requirements and have received their diplomas.

Rewards will be given at the end of our journey. It all depends on how we finish the course. Life with faith, hope, and love will end for His glory.

There was one person who lived His life for the sake of others. His love and compassion is known throughout the world. By His obedience to God our lives have been changed forever. His mission in life was to bring us into a right relationship with God.

When Jesus was crucified, His last words on the cross were: "It Is Finished." He gave His life so we could have life. God's will, was accomplished.

Be Alert, Stay Alive
April 23

Deep thoughts of the imagination will take us to the wild country where our survival training will be used to save our lives.

We had better gather a little more firewood. It is going to be a long night. The forest ranger warned us of the wild animals in the area. Wolves have been known to attack livestock and sometimes people.

I didn't want to scare anyone off with the comments about vicious predators that search and kill for food. This is a warning that will help us to stay alive. Wild animals are hungry and they are on the prowl.

It is very important to keep the fire burning. I'm not talking about just a little fire. We will have a better chance of surviving if the flames are reaching high into the sky.

We are going to post a guard tonight and rotate every hour until morning. The campers awoke to the rising of the sun and everyone was ok.

In our spiritual journey with the Lord, We need to be constantly alert, vigilant, and always on guard again the wiles of the devil. "As a roaring lion, walketh about, seeking whom he may devour."(I Peter 5:8)

If we continue looking to Christ for our deliverance, we will rise with the Son of righteousness. Keep the fires of faith burning; we will rise with Him in the morning.

He Has the Key
April 24

This is really a sad time in our lives. When the shadow of death crosses the path of one of our family members, there is a tremendous amount of sorrow and grief that we have to bear.

Everyone gathers at church for the final farewells. Friends and neighbors come from miles around to pay their respects. Once the coffin is closed, teardrops fall to the ground, as this is the last visual meeting with a loved one.

Flowers are placed in the sanctuary to show love and appreciation for this departed soul. The pastor delivers a message that touches each one of our hearts.

There are other speakers also that inspire us with words of hope and comfort that this death is only a temporary thing. Songs are sung that lift our spirits with thoughts of life after death.

As the Holy Spirit walks among us, we feel a divine touch from heaven and we know all is well. We know that those who have died in the Lord have the blessed assurance of rising from the dead.

We know they shall live again because Jesus also died and He took back the keys of death, hell, and the grave. He lay in the grave, but He was resurrected by the mighty power of God.

A grave that held Him cannot hold us. He has the key and He gives life to all who believe.

Faith to See Christ
April 25

There are certain events that took place in the life of Christ. None of us were living when Jesus walked on the earth. We were not eyewitnesses of the healing miracles, walking on water, or when He fed five thousand people with a few pieces of fish.

We did not see any of those things. It is only natural to think if we had only been there our faith would be so much stronger. It's hard not to believe when all of heaven and earth were revealing Jesus as the Son of God.

It is really amazing to me, some of the people were standing beside Jesus when He touched the sick and healed them. Perhaps they were there when He restored the blind man's sight or when the lame man walked.

Yes, I am really stunned that these spectators were up close and personal and yet they did not believe. A faithless generation cannot see from hearts of unbelief.

It is really remarkable for millions of people around the world who never saw Jesus, any of His miracles, or at the cross to see His crucifixion. We were not there when He was buried and rose again and ascended into heaven.

Our lives exist not because of our sight, but according to the belief in our hearts. "Blessed are they that have not seen, and yet believe." (John 20:29)

Faith Never Quits
April 26

The fulfillment of life is our determination to keep going. No matter how tired or regardless of the pain, we cannot win the victory crown if we give up.

There are times when our burdens are so heavy that we just don't have enough strength to proceed. If each of us will keep holding to the nail scared hand of Jesus, we will make it.

The cross each of us has to bear will be heavier at times. Sometimes in life we are stricken with a life threatening illness, "Be strong and of a good courage and the Lord will strengthen thine heart" (Psalm 27:28). Keep holding on, for our God is able to deliver. We are almost home.

Let us take one step, one day at a time. Never give up or quit. If we get too tired to go on, it is all right to stop and rest to regain our strength, but no matter what, please don't yield to defeat!

Jesus never called it quits even when His cross was heavy to bear and the pain was unbearable. He stayed on the cross for us. If He gave up, there would be no way we could be triumphant in life.

One step, one day, it may be all it takes for us to win the victory crown.

He Died for an Enemy
April 27

Is there anyone here who would die for an enemy? Let's give this question a lot of thought. Military opponents are considered to be our enemies.

We have brave men and women in the armed forces, fighting for our freedom. These brave soldiers are at risk of losing their lives and some of them have given the ultimate sacrifice of life for their country.

The war continues overseas with soldiers on both sides inflicting severe wounds and death on the battlefield. I have heard of soldiers sacrificing themselves to save one of their own.

It really takes a courageous person to die for a friend or a perfect stranger. But if it is the enemy, is there anyone in this country who would die for them? Some of us would dare to die for a friend, who would die for an enemy?

Well I know of one man who was beaten and had to suffer with excruciating pain. He was nailed to a cross with a crown of thorns forced upon His brow and spikes driven into His hands and feet.

We didn't participate in the death of Jesus, but His life's blood was on our hands for our sins. Jesus prayed, "Father, forgive them; for they know not what they do" (Luke 23:34). He died for those who crucified Him and for us.

If in This Life Only
April 28

This is really a terrible day for our nation. It is the death spiral of Christian life. All churches are closed until further notice. No prayer meetings will be scheduled. There will be no services in homes or in private buildings. Bibles will remain closed. All Christians will volunteer to turn in their crosses and stop following Jesus.

Whoever thought that all of these things would occur without any resistance from anyone. Things of faith disappear right before our eyes. Those who claim Jesus as their Lord and Savior are living a lie.

All hopes of going to heaven are false illusions. I have to stop here. I cannot handle anymore, discouraging words that betray the truth.

We need a Holy Ghost anointed scripture to restore our faith, hope, and love. "If in this life only we have hope in Christ, we are of all men most miserable" (I Cor. 15:19). If there is no life after death, we are still in our sins.

All previous closings, false announcements, lies, and cancelations of faith are hereby reverted back to their normal truthful conditions. All believers still have the blessed hope of going to heaven. This story began in a death spiral, what happened to change it? Jesus arose!

He Gave His Life
April 29

Let's travel to a wide-open range where the horses are wild and free. A beautiful white stallion leads the herd. This is a magnificent animal and finally it was saddle broke and ready for the trail.

One day a person was injured really bad and they had to get a doctor or he would die. There was only one horse that had enough stamina to cross the mountain and could run like the wind.

A rider rode the horse for miles at a full gallop, but it was too much for the white stallion. He fell to the ground and never got back up. He gave all he could give in this rescue attempt. Other riders were nearby; a doctor was located and he saved the injured person's life.

Let's return to another life or death situation. There is only one person who was qualified to save our souls. No other person or even an angel could heal our deep wounds caused by our transgressions.

God's only begotten Son was crucified on a cross. He came to rescue us from our sins; Jesus gave all He could possibly give for our salvation.

He died so we could live. When we come to Jesus, He will bind up the wounds and cleanse our hearts of all unrighteousness.

Partners in Crime
April 30

The pathway of corruption keeps us buried alive in forbidden territory. There are places in life that we should avoid, but if an evil sinful desire is dominate in our hearts, it cannot be restrained. When sin runs rampant there is no controlling the devastating effects it will have on our lives and on the people around us.

There are many sins out there that would destroy us if we partake of them. We have already put a lot of blame on sins, but the real culprit is our minds. Certain thoughts and actions begin the whole process of sins unconfined and unrestricted.

I guess sins and our minds are actually joined together as a team. They are partners in crime and everything else that corrupts good living. One will not respond without the other.

We have already been on this pathway too long. We had better take the first exit to escape the consequences of sin. Guilt is a good quality that has an effect on the mind. Those of us who feel guilty for having done something wrong will try to make it right.

This is when Jesus comes on the scene and our minds are transformed by faith in Him. The sins we used to do are not appealing anymore. Sins died when the mind was revived in Christ.

Come From Behind
May 1

The race of champions will begin in just a few minutes. These three runners are the special qualities of life. We will call them by their real names, Faith, Good Deeds, and Love.

Before the race begins, let's take a quick look at the qualifications of each runner. Faith is able to move mountains. I am sure that would be a good choice. Good deeds have inspired people around the world with kindness to help one another. Love is the navigational point of God's mercy. Now I know why this is the race of champions.

There is something that is really confusing to me; these three entries have always run as a team. They are now separated and run for themselves.

All three of these runners are scheduled for the event; the third qualifier has arrived, but there seems to be some problems at the stadium.

I am not sure, but it seems like love has been temporally denied access to the racetrack. Amid all this confusion the two other runners have already lined up at the gate.

The gun is fired and they are off and running. It sure looks like faith or good deeds will win. Everyone in the crowd stands in amazement; love has entered the race and has already caught up with the others. It could easily win, but it looks like these three have merged into one team and they are all declared winners.

Dust on the Bible
May 2

Our journey today will take us back in time to an old home where a sacred book is found. We don't have to worry about dinosaurs or prehistoric creatures of the past, at least not on this trip. We are not going that far back. This is the computer age with advanced technology and books in print are gradually becoming extinct.

Everyone's attention is drawn to this holy book. It looks familiar, where have we seen this many printed pages in a single volume?

The dust was removed from the cover and to the explorers astonishment, the name of the book was revealed, "Holy Bible." I am glad this was just an imaginary trip, but in some ways it is true.

Bibles are still found in dwellings around the world. They are located in various places in the home. Some of them have so much dust that it is hard to read the title. The pages have not been turned in years.

This book was created for daily living and devotion to God. It was not created to be a relic of the past. God's inspired Word is a living book of life for all who will believe and read its sacred pages.

"Where have I seen this book?" If there is too much dust on the Bible, there is not enough time with God.

The Choice is mine
May 3

We have a very important adventure that requires us to go back in time. We will be traveling with the pioneers to our new homes out west. The Federal Government is looking for some brave individuals to deliver the mail by pony express. Presently the Indians are at war with the settlers.

Please be aware there will be risk and it is a possibility that some of us will not be returning to the homeland. I feel it is my responsibility to give these warnings because I took the liberty to sign the government contract for all of us to be pony express riders.

I hope there are no hard feelings. Just one more thing, the federal agency will prosecute anyone that fails to deliver the mail. It looks like I've got a bigger problem than being chased by Indians.

There seems to be a lot of angry friends who have circled around me for some unknown reason. I think I had better get out the peace pipe and send up a few smoke signals to cancel all imaginary thoughts of this trip.

That was too close for comfort. I am so glad that our commitment to God is a personal one. Each of us is responsible for our own decisions in life, including accepting Christ as Lord and Savior. Salvation is granted on an individual basis. All my friends agreed: "The choice is mine."

Class for Sins Dismissed
May 4

We have a very important assignment today. A pencil with a good eraser is required to make any corrections in our corruptible lives of sin. An ink pen will be used for writing prayers of faith with a more permanent closure.

I hope everyone has come prepared for these life-changing events. This process will not take very long. Even though it took a lifetime to create our sins, we will take a few shortcuts in the elimination process.

It would be impossible to list all of our sins, I doubt if anyone here has brought enough paper for such a difficult task. The most harmful sins have been listed and erasers are already removing them from the page.

It looks like no one will finish any time today. The problem with pencils erasing a page is that the sins are still in our lives.

This would be a good place to take a shortcut. Ink pens will be used to write a more permanent way to dissolve our sins. Hand written prayers start to appear on the page. Words written in ink cannot be erased. Let's take one more shortcut and this will be the last one.

"Lord Jesus, We believe that you died and rose from the dead. We are sorry for all of our sins, please forgive us and come into our hearts." "Thank you, Jesus." Class for sins dismissed.

A Pen in God's Mighty Hand
May 5

The expressions of my heart will be found in a short story. Words of faith, hope, and love abound in the pages. When I share my thoughts of inspiration, I want others to know Jesus Christ as Lord and Savior and I pray that God will use me in His own special way.

Writers use many types of instruments to reveal their thoughts. Many years ago authors would use feathers to write their documents. A small container would hold the ink and the end of the feather would be inserted into the liquid solution.

There was not much room for errors. Ink pens were invented and they have been used by a wide variety of people. Some of them are made with a metal sleeve that holds a plastic ink cartridge.

These two types of pens could not write by themselves. Someone had to hold it in his or her hand. I like to think God is using me as a pen in His hand. The words that I write are not mine alone, but they come from the throne room above. He helps me with every short story to convey His message of love.

It is such an honor for me to think God trusts me enough to write the things that will touch many lives through my book. A pen in the mighty hand of God, I could not ask for a greater blessing. Words inspired are heaven sent.

The Cross and Beyond
May 6

Our journey today will take us to the cross and from there we will return to our present homes. It will be best if we travel by the imagination route.

Now that we have arrived at the time of the crucifixion, Jesus is hanging on the cross and a crown of thorns had been forced upon His brow. He is bleeding from the wounds in His hands and feet.

Many of the people are crying as they see Jesus suffering and in great pain. He was taken down from the cross and buried in a sepulcher. On the third day He arose from the dead.

Our imaginary journey actually begins hundreds of years after the resurrection. We have returned to the place of His death. The cross no longer stands and people are no longer put to death in such a horrible way.

As we travel along the back roads, we notice there are churches in the community and the residents are praising and worshiping God. All along the way, we meet people whose lives have been changed by the sacrificial death of Jesus.

The grave is empty and the cross no longer stands, but the one who lives in our hearts is alive forever more. The world today wants to see a living Savior. Live for Jesus and they will see Him.

A Sharp Axe
May 7

It's not too early to cut some firewood for the cold winter months. I have notice one man out in his tool shed, sharpening his axe. His plan is to begin early in the morning and stay all day. He has probably learned from experience that a dull axe will create more work and less wood.

After working for a few hours in his shed, he picked up the sharpened tool and started towards the forest. A friend of his was also going to gather the winter fuel supply, but this man did not bother to sharpen his axe. He just grabbed the old dull instrument and joined his friend in the woods.

Well the chips began to fly and the sound of trees was heard falling to the ground. After a while the man with the sharp axe had a good supply of wood, probably enough for the harsh winter ahead.

Now the other man, he was really tired. Swinging that dull axe completely wore him out and only a few trees lay on the ground. He would definitely have to return to the forest and cut more wood. The next morning he was sharpening his axe.

If we want to be an effective witness for Christ, shouldn't we study the Word and pray before we go into the harvest field? Our labor of love will not be in vain if we have prepared ahead of time. Anyone need a sharp axe?

Flames of Faith
May 8

We had better not wait any longer; this fire is going out. We don't want anyone to be caught out in this freezing, cold weather. The wind chill factor is below zero. If the fire dies, we will not be able to survive.

There are a few cinders still burning. If we hurry, the fire can be restored and we will live another day. There are some small twigs that will help in the burning process. One stick is laid on at a time; too many small branches would smother the fire.

At last a small flame is seen flickering on the small pieces of wood. The anticipation of life for this survival team grows stronger with each passing minute. More wood has been gathered and the larger sticks are also burning.

The warmth of this brush fire has restored their hopes of survival. Now that the fire is going, it will be everyone's responsibility to gather more wood and make sure the flames do not go out. This team stayed awake all night and the next morning they were rescued from the cold artic air.

We are a lot like the survival team that depended on the fire to stay alive. If our faith flames have just about gone out, we had better hurry and add another log to the fire. It takes just one spark to ignite the flames and to keep the fire burning; we had better get some more wood.

Detour Turn Right
May 9

There is a sign at the end of the road with a warning that we should all obey. There have been accidents in which people have lost their lives.

I am trying to give the warning now, just in case there is more negligence on the highway. There is only one word on the sign, but it has a very important message. The word is: "Detour."

That sign does not stir up any strong emotions in our lives. It's no wonder the people just keep on driving as if the sign never existed. I wonder if there would be more interest if the sign had a stronger warning, "Detour, enter at your own risk."

Well we are not allowed to change words on any of the signs. Let's proceed with caution and obey all instructions to turn at the designated place.

Later while we were driving down the road, listening to the radio. A news alert came over the airwaves that told of a bad accident just past the detour sign. There were casualties as the drivers failed to heed the warning.

This is where the imagination story ends and where a real life situation begins. This is a warning from God above. Please pay very close attention. It's only one word, but it can change our lives forever. Is everyone listening? The word is: "Repent." Make a right turn and go straight.

No Talents Left
May 10

Lives are truly blessed when they use their entire God given abilities to serve Him. Those who have dedicated themselves to love God with all of their hearts, souls, and minds will rest in peace at the end of their journey.

The fulfillment of our lives is to be used of God and all the talents given by Him will be completely used up. It would truly be a wonderful blessing to come to the end of our journey and find there is nothing left to give. We gave it all for His glory.

God has many wonderful gifts of grace that He has given to each one of us. Special talents are handcrafted for our own individual needs. He has designed them for each of us personally.

His handiwork always comes with the anointing that will bless us and will be an inspiration to His people around the world. Our lives are blessed when a song is sung, a sermon is preached, a book is written, and the lists goes on for His Glory. These gifts are given so we will love, praise, and worship Him.

God's creative talents are designed for us and anointed by Him so everyone will be blessed. The fulfillment of our lives is to come to the end of our journey and know there is nothing left to give, we gave it all. No talents left.

Mother's Day
May 11

This is a very special day for us to honor and remember a wonderful person who has inspired us all along life's way. Sometimes a card is sent to relay sincere thoughts to our mothers. If we still have the opportunity to express our heart felt thanks, let's pay a personal visit and tell them how much they are loved.

Think for just a few minutes on the qualities of her life. She is always caring and concerned about her children. A mother's love will lift us up when the problems of life are dragging us down. Her love binds the family together with an unbreakable cord.

There is no one on earth who is so close and dear as a mother. Her children bless her for the goodness of being a caring affectionate person.

She is known by her faithfulness and unwavering love that has kept her in the arms of God. She has taught us the true meaning of life. Love God first and foremost, commit our souls to Him, and we will not go astray.

Her love for us is made stronger every day by her faith in Jesus Christ. She imparts that same miracle of grace to her children. We would like to give a special thanks and a loving embrace of gratitude to each of our mothers. We love you mom!

A Flickering Flame
May 12

The life of a flickering flame will go out when the fuel supply is empty. Beware death lurks in the shadows. If we walk in darkness, we will stumble and fall.

Tonight we will be walking the desolate paths of darkness; each one of us will have a lantern to guide us safely through the corridors of sin.

This instrument of light will keep us alive if we keep it trimmed and burning. We need to keep the wick at a certain level, raise it every once in a while to keep a strong burning flame.

I want everyone to be aware; we will not be traveling as a group. The oil we have in our lamps will not be shared with any of the participants of this life saving endeavor.

The oil supply that is in each lantern cannot be refilled, as there is only enough fuel for each of us to finish the course. If we share then our life's journey will end when the flame goes out.

There are many paths to choose, but there is only one that will lead us home. We had better get started; every minute counts.

The quicker we find the correct path will increase our chances of survival. We have traveled many miles and years. Some of the lanterns have gone out and others are burning as they cross the finish line. Straight and narrow is the path that leads to life; blessed are they who find it.

Train Wreck
May 13

The old train moves slowly down the track, no one is aware of the danger ahead. Loved ones at the country store wave goodbye to their friends and family members.

A couple of kids are real anxious about seeing their new parents and going home with them. The orphanage took very good care of the children and now a mediator is escorting them to the city for a new life.

In just a very short while the passengers may be involved in a train wreck of disastrous proportions. No one knows that the bridge has been damaged by the floodwaters.

A young girl who always walked along the railroad tracks to school, noticed the collapsed trestle and she knew it was just about time for the passenger train to come around the bend.

She was on the opposite end of the bridge. All the travelers on the train would die unless she could warm them. She crossed some of the loose crossties and made it to the other side just in time. She risked her own life to save the passengers on the train.

I know of a man who gave His life to rescue the perishing. If it had not been for Jesus, we would have died in our sins.

Fear no Evil
May 14

My adventuresome, friends, we have a special cleaning job that will be very dangerous. We have been hired to perform maintenance on the buildings across America.

There are thousands of windows that need to be cleaned. We would like for everyone to volunteer for this unusual task. I know this seems like a boring job. Does anyone really like cleaning windows?

We can make this endeavor more interesting, but there is the danger of losing one's life. Let me explain, we will be working on high-rise buildings and each of us will be hanging from a rope that is anchored to the structure.

I hope I didn't discourage anyone; we will just be thousands of feet in the air with each of our cleaning supplies attached to our harnesses. I said this is just a volunteer operation, now would be a good time to accept or reject the challenge.

I forgot to mention that I have never done this type of work before; normally I am afraid of heights. I guess that is why my knees are shaking and I am trembling all over. "Hey, wait for me; don't run away so fast!"

There are things in our lives that we cannot accomplish because of fear. When Jesus walks beside us, there is no reason to be afraid of any evil. "Greater is He that is in you, than he that is in the world" (I John 4:4).

Gather in the Grain
May 15

The fields have been planted. It's time to gather in the grain. We want everyone to get a good night's rest. We will begin early in the morning and work all day. This will be our normal schedule until all the grain is in the silos and other storage areas.

Our payment for working in the fields will not be money for today's employment. I hope I didn't say the wrong thing as some of the laborers have already started to walk away. I had better explain before the field is completely void of workers.

Everyone will be working today for his or her own food and to supplement the lives of the needy. The grain that is gathered will equal one month's supply of bread, cereal, and other food sources for each person's survival.

If our labor in the field is minimal, the food rations will also be small. Each of us will be required to gather a certain amount of grain for our own personal monthly allowance of food. I hope everyone understands these new rules.

The sun is beginning to set and it is time to go home. Everyone gave a good day's work and the measurement of the grain was sufficient for all life sustaining reasons.

In our daily living for Christ, He wants us to go into the harvest fields and be productive workers. The harvest is white and ready for harvest. Gather a little more grain to feed the hungry and help those who are in need of a Savior.

Work in the Harvest Field
May 16

Yesterday was a good day to work in the harvest field. No money was earned, but the hungry were fed and many needs were met in Christ.

The rest of our week will be entirely different as Christian's will be the laborers in the field. God has called them for service to bring forth the message of salvation. The harvest is ripe and it is time to help someone come to know Jesus as Lord and Savior.

All faith volunteers will be accepted into the labor force. This includes the young converts and those who are established in the faith. By the way we would like to welcome all faith believers to join with us in this endeavor.

Let's get started, as there is a lot of work and not much time to accomplish this task. The harvest field is the world and our entrance will be from any personal location.

It is always good to pray first and seek guidance from God. He is the coordinator of this labor force and He will perform all spiritual transformations. He has commissioned us to go in Jesus' name into the villages, towns, and wherever lost souls can be found.

We need to tell the people that Jesus is coming in the clouds of glory. He will be coming for those who have accepted Him into their lives. The harvest is ripe and the laborers are few. God will reward our labors of love.

Strawberry Pie
May 17

This year there is an abundant supply of berries. I thought it would be nice to have a delicious pie. There were harmful toxins in the surrounding area, but I was unaware of poison ivy vines on the ground.

The plants with the three shiny leaves were easy to be seen as they covered the strawberries in the forest. I was probably so intent on picking this fruit of the vine that it never occurred to me that I was right in the middle of a venomous strawberry patch.

Please don't worry, as this danger has been slightly exaggerated by an over active imagination. I picked strawberries most of the day and finally it was time to go home. Soon a big pie would be baked and I would enjoy it with my dinner.

This was supposed to be a very enjoyable afternoon. Well to my dismay, there was an itching between my fingers and toes; I could not resist scratching the infected area.

There is danger in our lives if we go to the toxic fields of sin and partake of the poison. A dose of repentance may be required for the antidote.

A Fresh Refilling of Faith
May 18

It started out to be a normal vacation in the mountains. The mother, father, and two small children had packed the camping gear into the van. This trip had been planned for months in advance.

This small family had traveled for many miles without seeing anyone. There were no stores, houses, or even gas stations. The father was beginning to get worried as he noticed the van was running really low on fuel. They would have to stop somewhere and soon.

He thought they would have been at their destination by now. Is it possible that along the way, they missed the turn off and failed to get on the right road?

His wife got out the map and began retracing the route. She found that they were not lost, but were within miles of their camping resort.

The problem was still a fuel tank that was nearly empty and they were in a remote part of the country. Finally they saw a gas station and the van sputtered to a stop right next to the fuel pumps.

Our journey to heaven may seem like we took a wrong turn somewhere along the way. Sometimes we just need a little more patience and a fresh refilling of faith to see the lights of home.

Weeds in the Garden
May 19

The garden is slowly dying, unable to breathe. I know there are other things we could be doing, but this is an emergency.

We could really use the help to recuperate these stricken plants. If we have a lot of workers, then we will be able to accomplish this task at a faster rate. There is no danger involved, not even poisonous plants as we have encountered in the past.

Our problem this year is an overgrowth of weeds. I don't know who is responsible for this negligence and I hate to call on my friends to pull these killer weeds. Please be calm; this is still a harmless operation. The garden products are the only ones that are in danger.

If the weeds are not removed from the garden, we will not have any food for our survival and then I will have to upgrade the status to extremely hazardous living conditions.

I am glad to see everyone has been positively persuaded for the enhancement of life. I had no idea weeds could be pulled so fast.

In our spiritual gardens there are many sins that are like the killer weeds. If we do not get them under control, they will destroy our relationship with God.

A Porch of an Idle Life
May 20

An elderly man sits on the porch, watching the people drive down the road on their way to church. He always greets them with a friendly wave and the travelers return the same gesture.

Since he retired, a lot of things have changed in his life. We need to go back to the time when he was going to church. It would be hard to find a more faithful member.

If anyone needed a helping hand or was sick, he would not hesitate to offer assistance. His loving kindness was known throughout the community. Somewhere along the way he walked away from God. He left the church and laid down his cross.

This retreat did not happen over night, but gradually church services were missed and there was less time for prayer. His daily walk with the Lord declined and after awhile he stopped singing "Amazing Grace."

It is really hard to tell this imaginary story. I hate to think of anyone backsliding on God. This life related instance deserves a better ending.

The travelers who wave on Sundays want to know what happened to the man on the porch. "Did he die?" "No, he went to church with Jesus." Listen, "Amazing Grace."

Silver and Gold
May 21

Silver and gold will buy the necessities of life. These precious metals are recovered from mines and they are melted into molds.

There are many items that are produced this way. We have watches, bracelets, and many of our computers have a certain amount of silver in them. Does anyone here have a silver dollar or a gold coin?

There are some things that cannot be bought, even if there is an abundance of this type of currency. We can buy groceries, pay hospital bills, and many other things.

One person many years ago found out about the things money couldn't buy. He was in need of food and other physical things for his livelihood. Peter and John were walking by this man who needed healing; He was unable to walk. This poor man was begging for money to keep from starving.

Christ disciple (Peter) told him, "Silver and gold have I none; but such as I have give I thee: In the name of Jesus Christ of Nazareth rise up and walk" (Acts 3:6). Immediately the man was healed and walked.

One touch of the Master's hand is of more value than all the gold and silver in the world. Arise to a new life in Christ.

Allegiance to God
May 22

We the believers in Christ do hereby make an allegiance to God to surrender our lives completely to Him. Our promise is to faithfully yield to His service in complete obedience to His (will) plan.

It is our solemn resolution to commit our hearts, minds, and souls, to love Him all the days of our lives without any restrictions or constraints.

We truthfully and without reserve will proclaim to the world that Jesus is the Christ; the Savior of the world and all who believe in Him will be saved.

Our faith pledge is one of belief that Jesus arose from the dead and ascended into heaven. We confirm that our lives as Christians exist in the fact that Jesus is no longer in the grave, but He is alive forevermore.

We will respectively honor His name with the truth that He is the Messiah, Mighty God, Prince of Peace, and Everlasting Father. We will reveal without any compromise that there is no other name given under heaven whereby we must be saved.

Our oath is given on this day to faithfully obey, serve God with loyalty, and devotion. We commit ourselves to living holy, righteous lives, and in complete reverence to God the Father, God the Son, and God the Holy Spirit.

The Battle is not ours
May 23

This is a special recruiting assignment for all eligible participants. I remember several years ago when I was drafted into the Army, we had to take a mental test. The results of it would determine our occupation in the military.

There were people selected for the infantry and artillery units. These combat positions were very important for the survival of the armed forces. These soldiers were the ones who were sent to the battlefield to fight the enemy.

We have a different type of enlistment for all the brave men and women who are up to the challenge. There are certain qualifications that we must meet before any of us can enter the combat zone.

Only volunteers of faith will be accepted by God to fight for peace and the stability of life. Those who do not believe in Christ will be rejected from this warfare. It is time for all cross bearers to advance to the front lines. "Onward Christian soldiers," is the battle theme.

This is the Lords fighting forces against all evil. We must be strong and of a good courage and He will strengthen our hearts and give us the victory in the end.

One very important thing for us to remember, this battle is not ours, but the Lords. He will fight for us and together we will win the war.

Rich in Spirit
May 24

Our adventure today will take us into gold mining country. If we have an opportunity, we will talk with the prospectors about finding gold and the benefits of happiness, joy, and peace in their hearts.

I hope everyone has camping equipment for this hiking trip. Think about this journey as a learning experience that will give us a better understanding of the true riches in life.

There is no need to worry for we are just going to stay a little while, just long enough to learn that the richest vein in the world will not bring peace to our souls. One prospector was rich, but he was poor in spirit. He had no time for God.

The second prospector we met did not have any gold. He worked his entire life to find it. This valuable ore was not found. Perhaps he tried to find happiness in all the wrong places.

Before we left this poor wretched soul, we told him about Jesus who loved us enough to die in our place on a cross. This miner broke down in tears and asked Jesus to come into his heart.

All of this man's life, he searched for an earthly treasure, but on his knees in prayer he found the greatest of all riches, peace with God. He is now rich in spirit.

His Search Is Endless
May 25

A search and rescue operation continues for the lost souls of this generation. Jesus came down from heaven to walk the dark hills in search of those who need a Savior.

We will find Him in the valleys of despair or in the dark alleys where the homeless live. He is there in the gutters with the outcasts, holding out His nail-scarred hand to rescue fallen man from the clutches of death.

There is no greater love and concern for our soul's salvation than what Jesus has for us. The love of Jesus was manifest at Calvary and extended to every day of our lives, as we are witnesses that His love never dies.

It is not an uncommon thing to find Him in churches around the world where Pastors convey to their congregations the love of God in Christ Jesus. His love never ends, as it always abounds in our hearts and lives.

There have been many hospitals visited by many caring Christians. They came to visit the unhealthy and Jesus was always there before them, laying His holy hand upon the sick and ministering to their needs.

Don't be surprised if Jesus is in prison, visiting a person on death row, He is there to give him life. It seems as though Jesus is everywhere; that is true and He is right here in our midst with a special touch for all receptive hearts.

Memorial Day
May 26

This is a time in our lives when we remember the sacrifices of our brave men and women, those who fought and died for our freedom.

Memorial Day is a federal holiday that began at the end of the Civil war. Later it was recognized as a tribute to honor all service personal that died while serving our country.

These soldiers told their loved ones goodbye as they went to war. None of them knew if they would be returning to their homes, if they would ever see their families again.

They didn't know if this were the last time that little child would be held in his or her arms, or ever see their marriage partners again.

There have been wars all down through the ages. War has left its mark upon our brave men and women of the armed forces. Some were wounded in battle and received serious injuries.

We would like to give special recognition to all military personal for their service to the United States of America. We remember and show our appreciation to those who gave their lives as an ultimate sacrifice.

Freedom is not free. A salute is given in their honor. They are no longer with us, but they will live on, in our hearts forever.

The Potter and the Clay
May 27

The enthusiasm runs high as the potter thinks about a new creation. It is already formed in his mind. He knows exactly what the object will look like, even before the work is started.

This creative project will take many hours to complete. That is ok, because the potter is a very patient man. No matter how long the job takes, he will stay with it until it is exactly the way he wants it.

Before the work begins, the potter has invited all of us to his studio to watch the process and learn some important facts about shaping and molding pottery.

The craftsman tells us about the object he wants to create. Our vision of the same item seems to be a little blurred. All we can see is an ugly lump of clay.

The potter begins his work and gradually the modeling material begins to take shape and after awhile a vase is formed. The potter draws us in closer to see an imperfection in the model. He returns the clay to the table and recreates a beautiful vase.

The molding and reshaping of our lives is to create the image that God has visualized. If sins have entered into our lives and corrupted our souls, then we need to return to the cross and be touched by the Master's hand.

Get Out Now
May 28

The weather forecasters have just announced a monster storm is coming. Severe winds and thunderstorms are predicted to come with a vengeance. This is a high alert warning for the entire eastern region of the United States.

Everyone is under strict orders to evaluate at once. There will be no responders left behind to help rescue the stranded or to save anyone's life.

In just a short while the devastation of the storm will occur. There is not much time to spare. If there are family members and friends living nearby, go quickly and warn them. "Get out now! A monster storm is coming."

The evacuees scramble to find their kids and loved ones. As some of the children have been playing at their neighbor's homes. Once the family is gathered together, they proceed down the highway.

Dark storm clouds are already forming overhead. There was enough time to escape, but the roads were so crowded that no one could get through. Well the storm finally passed and there were many casualties.

Just past the imagination horizon the sun is shining in the real world. We have a warning that will come to pass. "Jesus is coming with power and great glory." If we are still living in our sins, the message of salvation is to repent. "Get out now, by faith in Christ."

Endure to the End
May 29

Many years ago a group of people were having a family reunion on a small island. They had not seen one another for many years. This was a real exciting time for them.

There was always a strong bondage of love between each family member. This was the first opportunity for them to meet together and fellowship with one another. Jobs and other activities had kept them separated over the years.

Well it is time to go home and get back to the regular routine of life. Now this family had rented a yacht for this special occasion. The captain and a few crewmembers transported them to the island.

No one knew the return trip home could be fatal to every person on this large recreational watercraft. Dark storm clouds were beginning to form and flashes of lightning were seen a short distance away. This vessel was already too far away from the island to return.

Their only hope was to keep going and pray that God would somehow intervene and rescue them from this life-threatening storm. After a while the violent winds ceased and the rough waters were calm.

In our heavenly journey with the Lord, there will be times that we have to endure the storms. Our only hope is to keep going, we have gone too far to turn back now. All faithful believers who endure to the end shall be saved.

Astray from the Fold
May 30

The sheep are in the watchful care of a shepherd. They come to him when he calls and he will use his staff if necessary to protect them.

When the sun begins to set, all of the sheep are gathered into a fold. They will remain there until morning and then the shepherd will lead them to the green pastures.

Some of the landowners came by to warn him that wolves have been sighted in the area and that some of the lambs were killed.

Now this shepherd is very careful to protect his sheep, but one day a small lamb had left her mother's side and was feeding by itself in a brush covered area.

The shepherd had called for his sheep and when he counted them, one was missing. He left his helpers in charge of the fold.

In the distance he could hear wolves howling and he was more afraid for the defenseless little animal. He risked his life to save the lamb. Time went by and he found it alive in a bramble bush and brought it safely back to the fold.

If there are times in our lives, we go astray, wander too far from the fold, and get tangled up in the brambles of sin, the Good Shepherd will set us free and take us safely home.

Red Flag Warning
May 31

The weather forecaster has issued a red flag warning for some of the counties in Virginia. Please be advised that today the conditions are extremely hazardous with a possibility of strong winds.

No fires are allowed at any time of the day until it is considered safe by the officials. The weather will be monitored on a daily basis for any improvements to these dry conditions.

Now would be a good time to warn the neighbors and those who will be going on camping trips, burning brush, or any other activity to avoid all fires. The law will be strictly enforced with penalties, including jail time.

It just takes one little spark to land on the roof of someone's house and after a while the home is destroyed. Hopefully no one will lose his or her life because of the flames.

There have been too many incidents where a family member or a friend has lost their lives in a fire. While these fire conditions persist, the only sensible thing for us to do is wait for rain.

Maybe there should be a red flag warning of hell; the conditions are persistent in our lives because of sins. Try waving the flag of truce to a forgiving God and see how fast we avoid the flames.

Lost and Found
June 1

An ad has been placed in the lost and found section of the newspaper. A reward will be given when the item is found. Usually there is a description of the object.

Let's just say it is a gold watch that has been in the family for many years. The value of this timepiece is very sentimental, as the deceased father owned it. The watch was engraved with his name on the back.

Now this family has authorized us to advertise in the paper and other places to try and relocate this beautiful watch.

One person called and said he found the watch and if we would send a certain amount of money, the watch would be returned to us. When we asked him about the name, he failed to respond and hung the phone up.

The search continued and finally one day after the small family had moved away, the new owners were cleaning out the garage and a small shiny object was seen in the corner of the building. It was the watch and he returned it to the family. They rejoiced together, lost but now found.

Perhaps there was a time in our lives when we were close to God as His prized possession. He loved us and we still walked away. But one day, glory, hallelujah, Jesus found us and brought us back to the Father's house.

In the Miry Clay
June 2

We have a very important message to deliver and it must arrive on time in order for millions of souls to be saved. This is an emergency! Sound all alarms.

There is no time to waste. It has been reported that individuals are sinking in the miry clay. God is calling all Christians to active duty.

Their response is urgently needed to rescue the perishing. No ropes are needed for this life saving process, but souls will be saved if we deliver the message.

Our first requirement is to go before the throne room of mercy and seek divine intervention from Jehovah. He will deliver those who are sinking in the miry clay of sin. God wants to use us in this rescue attempt.

There is no hesitation as the believers go into the communities, towns, and in every neighborhood with the gospel message.

"Believe on the Lord Jesus Christ, and thou shalt be saved" (Acts 16:31). The message for them is the same one for us. "If we confess our sins, he is faithful and just to forgive us our sins, and to cleanse us from all unrighteousness" (I John 1:9).

"Jesus, I am sorry for my sins," at that moment, Jesus reached down and saved all who confessed.

Follow the Son
June 3

Our journey in life will find us in a small isolated town. We had to travel the imagination route through dark streets of despair and corruption.

It was evening and the sun began to fade away. As long as there was light, we could follow the signs and read the road map. We had traveled for many miles and enjoyed looking at the scenery.

Our new home was being built in the country and we were real anxious to see it for the first time. The contractors informed us that the house was ready and we could move into it anytime.

We had never been to this part of the country before. This was a good time for us to relocate and enter into the next phase of our lives.

Somewhere along the way when the sun had nearly disappeared from sight, we took a wrong turn and found ourselves in this sinful place.

There was a church meeting a short distance away and we entered the building. They gave us shelter and guidance for a safe trip to our new home.

This is what happens in our lives when we stop following the Son. We end up in the corruptible places of sin and unless we get back on the right road, we will not see our new home in glory.

He Paid the Price
June 4

Let's go back in time to when we first met the Lord. This is when we received the salvation of our souls. At that time some of us did not have very much money. Those who had gold and silver still could not pay the price.

Whether we were rich or poor, it did not matter. The price of our freedom would cost a whole lot more than what we could afford.

It looks like we would be prisoners for all of our lives. It is a terrible thing to be bound by sins, unable to escape, no matter how hard we try, our consciences would always remind us of our unrighteous ways.

If we offered money for our freedom, it would be denied. All the gold and silver in the world could not set us free. It certainly seems like sin is a permanent quality in our lives that will stay with us as long as we live.

I am sure everyone is curious of how some of us were set free. The chains of sin were broken. I said that there was no price we could afford for our freedom.

That is true, there was only one man who could pay the price and that was Jesus. It cost His life on an old rugged cross.

"Ye are bought with a price: therefore glorify God in your body, and in your spirit, which are God's (I Corinthian 6:20). Sins are not permanent; they can be washed away in the blood.

Asleep on our Watch
June 5

It was late one night; everyone had gone to bed. Now this was really a peaceful community. The neighbors were friendly and there was no reason to expect any danger.

The doors were always locked, just in case a burglar would try to break in and steal from the family. There was always someone from the citizen's patrol, walking the streets to make sure the homes were safe.

A policeman would come by and check the businesses to make sure they were locked and secure for the night. His job was to guard the community and be alert for any prowlers with evil intentions.

This neighborhood was so peaceful that the security personal became relaxed in their obligations. They used to come by on a regular basis, but not anymore. Nothing is going to happen; everything will be all right.

Instead of performing their security watches, the person elected for citizen's patrol might look out the window of his house.

The patrol officer was so sure that no thieves were in the area that he would take a nap in his car until morning. Everyone was asleep when the burglar came, and he killed one person.

Jesus is coming for those who are looking for Him. Will He find us asleep on our watch and thinking He is not coming? Be alert and stay alive.

Not Guilty
June 6

There seems to be a lot of evidence against the offenders. We had better get the best lawyers in the country if we want to win this case. I am not sure that will help. All the circumstances and witnesses prove that we are guilty.

After looking over the multitude of offences for all of our sinful ways, we had better upgrade to the most intelligent lawyer team in the world to represent us.

This whole legal establishment of lawyers, judges, and even the jury were false representatives of justice. There was as much corruption in their lives as it was in ours.

It does look like we have a chance of being declared innocent. If they have to judge themselves as well as us, everyone will be set free.

We started feeling pretty good about the outcome of this trial. The lawyers presented their final arguments and then we waited patiently for the jury to return.

The verdict was announced, "Not Guilty!" Let's just see what happened. We were guilty as sin; no one was excluded. If we were found guilty, all of us would be punished for our sins.

There is coming a day when we will stand before a holy, righteous God. His judgment will be of truth, righteousness, and according to repentance, guilty or not?

He Is a Friend
June 7

When there is someone we look up to and respect. It is really an honor to be called his or her friend. Jesus cares for us and His love never wavers, but always grows stronger with each passing day.

He is a friend who will visit us in the hospitals and stay all day and night. Jesus is our friend; He stands at our bedside making intercession to God on our behalf.

He is faithful all through life as a friend and a Savior to abide with us all the days of our lives. We are never alone as Jesus is always with us.

I am sure there must be a little bit of curiosity here. Where do we find such a friend? Some of us would say in church, at home, in a hospital room, or any place our hearts are tender for mercy.

We would all agree that He is a friend that is closer than a brother. Jesus said that He would never leave or forsake us, but He would go with us all the way. This is not a halfway promise.

Some of our friends are considered temporary; they go part of the way and then disappear. Jesus found us first when we were unlovable, living ungodly lives, and He had mercy on our souls. He still calls us, my friends.

Be of Good Cheer, It Is I
June 8

We are going to be visited today by a few friends from the Bible. According to my imagination they will be traveling thousands of years to be with us. They will be here in just a short while to visit the hospitals. Please make them welcome.

It looks like Abraham is the first one to arrive. Remember how he was going to offer his own son for a sacrifice and God provided a lamb. He is a very important man and he is coming to visit the sick.

Moses just now entered the premises. Truly this was a man of God. He led the people out of Egypt and they crossed the red sea. God used him to bring us the Ten Commandments.

There is another group of people that just now entered the hospital. They are the Disciples of Christ. We all remember how they followed Jesus and witnessed His miracles. It is a wonderful thought to think that all of these people came for a visit.

Those were just imaginary thoughts; they didn't really come. Please don't be discouraged for Jesus Himself came from glory.

This is what He really said, "Be of good cheer, it is I" (Matthew 14:27). He came in person; His visit will be on a daily basis. Behold, the Son of God.

One Day with Jesus
June 9

Early in the morning at the beginning of the day, we are going to take a walk down by the riverside. There are no dark clouds with bolts of lightning, flashing across the sky.

Any emergency gear or survival kits can be left at home. We will not need them this time. We are just going for a walk with a friend.

I know how much this group likes adventure, but occasionally a peaceful walk at the park will inspire us for the more challenging events in life.

This will be a day with the Lord. I am sure that everyone would agree, if it had not been for Jesus, we would not have made it this far.

We have a few more miles to go before this journey is complete and we walk the streets of glory. Now there have been some individuals who decided they would travel alone.

It really brings great sorrow to my heart to know that they perished in the miry clay. When Jesus was trying to reach them, they would not take hold of His hand. I hope there is no one here who thanks he or she can make it without Him.

Well maybe after this walk with Jesus, we will be more convinced than ever to follow Him all the way. One day with the Savior removes all doubt and we all confessed; "He is the Christ, the Son of God."

The World or Jesus
June 10

Yesterday was a good day to walk with the Lord. Since everyone enjoyed it so much, we thought another day with Him would be just as rewarding.

Remember He is always on call; Jesus will make a personal visit to help anyone who has a need. All through the night, Jesus was busy visiting the sick, comforting families who lost loved ones, and rescuing lost souls.

He never sleeps and responds quickly to all prayer request for His help. When we gathered for our morning walk, some of the people were in doubt if Jesus was going to show up. They had heard that He made many personal visits last night.

We assured everyone that He would be walking with us this morning. This group was very energetic and just couldn't seem to wait. All along the way they talked about worldly things and was curious why Jesus didn't show up.

At the end of the day everyone gathered together in Jesus' name. Their conversation changed from the world to the love of God.

All of a sudden Jesus was walking among them and touching their lives. Why did He come now? I guess because grace begins in each of our hearts when Jesus is allowed to walk with us. Walk with the world and we walk alone.

Faith Is Believing
June 11

The trials of life are like the wind blown sands of time. We never know how long they will last or how often they will occur.

Sometimes our vision is blurred from the difficult times in our lives and it is hard to see the path when the wind and sand covers the tracks. We stumble and fall as we try to get back up. Our strength is nearly gone and we are just too weak to go on.

With Christ as our Savior and guide there is no giving up or calling it quits. If we cannot see through the storm and we have fallen from the heavy weight of our circumstances. We can escape this tragedy if we will only allow faith to see and our hearts to believe.

Sometimes just a couple of well-placed words will inspire us to: "Get up!" Inspirational thoughts will give us strength and courage to rise from our stormy trials. Take one step and then another; keep going, it will not be very long now until we claim the victory crown.

Faith is a survival technique that when used properly, it will save lives. It is far better than any emergency equipment. For a quick rescue take hold of the unseen hand of the Savior. The eyes of faith will see when we believe in our hearts.

Greater Is He
June 12

We are in the training process of defeating an enemy. As we travel through life our combat skills must improve on a daily basis. Every day is a battle, so we must always go forth in Jesus' name.

This warfare is so threatening that I will not even use my imagination to obtain the victory. There is only one way to fight and that is with the Word of God. It is quick and powerful and sharper than any two edged sword.

This is not an ordinary battle. Our enemy has been around for ages. The Bible tells us: "We wrestle not against flesh and blood, but.... powers, against the rulers of the darkness of this world, against spiritual wickedness in high places" (Ephesians 6:12).

The enemy (Satan) will try with all of his might to defeat us. He will use any resources that are available. How can we win against such a mighty foe?

Let's see what the Bible says," For unto us a child is born, unto us a son is given... and his name shall be called Wonderful, Counselor, The mighty God, The everlasting Father, The prince of Peace." (Isaiah 9:6).

The war was fought at Calvary and Satan thought he won when Jesus was nailed to the cross. Three days later, Jesus rose from the dead. He was triumphant over death, the grave, and hell.

We are promised the victory in Jesus because He lives in us and greater is He than he (Satan) that is in the world.

The Right Path
June 13

Our adventure today will lead us down a path to the cemetery. When our time on earth has expired; a graveyard awaits our arrival. No one will be denied.

Each of us will have a tombstone with each of our names engraved on it.

This was just a short visit to the graveyard. I am glad that all of us were able to walk away. We will not always have this same opportunity.

Let's get back to our adventure that is supposed to be an exciting experience. I believe we were walking down a path. It is more interesting when we are walking with Jesus and having fellowship with Him.

There are many paths in life to choose, but only one that will take us to our home in glory. This would be the straight and narrow way of following Christ.

It truly is a wonderful time to know of God's great love and have Jesus in our lives. Jesus said, "I am the way, the truth, and the life: no man cometh unto the Father, but by me" (John14: 6).

There are two paths to follow, one leads to heaven and the other to hell. There is the path of those who accept Christ and the one where He is rejected.

We all have to die, but we do not have to die in our sins. "If we confess our sins, He is faithful to forgive us"

Spiritual Rain
June 14

The ground is parched and dry from a lack of rain. Crops have been planted and they will not survive unless they receive a fresh water supply.

Irrigation systems are working overtime to save the vegetation and the livestock. The weather forecaster announced rain for this week. The anticipation was running high as we gathered our drinking vessels and barrels to catch this life restoring liquid.

Well the rains came and drenched the earth. All living things came back to life. Some states have probably experienced these conditions; we did not.

Water is the essence of life, just like a spiritual rain is needed to revive our failing spirits. Without that touch from heaven, we would not have enough strength to go on, and eventually the lack of fellowship would end our relationships with God.

Rain is controlled by nature. But the Holy Spirit revives us. Our lives are restored by a gentle touch of the Savior's hand, and by the grace of God that always abounds in our lives.

Call upon Him now for a gentle shower from above. "Jesus!" The spiritual rain descends from heaven to revive our souls and give each of us life.

Fathers' Day
June 15

It is a very special day in our lives when we can honor our fathers. Their love is expressed in so many ways. If they are still living, let's give them a special visit and tell them how much they are loved.

This can be a time to remember the special characteristics they give to the family. Their tender caring ways are unrestricted for each of their children.

A father's love will help his offspring to live holy, righteous lives. I recall a short illustration of a boy, walking in the snow. He was following in his father's footsteps.

This is a time for us to honor our fathers for the directions and guidance we receive from them. There are so many times we would have gone astray if it had not been for our loving, caring fathers.

Sometimes we are separated for various reasons. Our visits by miles, jobs, schools, and many other things keep us apart.

If the days and years have been broken without any fellowship for many years, it's never too late to say, "I love you," from the father and the children.

We express our gratitude and love for our fathers and ask God to keep them in his loving care all the days of their lives.

Neglect our Salvation
June 16

It seemed to be a peaceful night as the security guard checked the jail cells to make sure his prisoners could not get out.

All of the locks were examined for safety reasons. I am sure this guard was a little more nervous than usual. He had special orders that if these two men escaped, he would be put to death.

Let's just say for imagination reasons, there are two other criminals convicted of many sins. Well everyone is secure in the cells and the jail keeper is taking a nap.

Suddenly he awoke from his sleep and found all the doors were open. He was going to take his own life because he thought the prisoners had escaped. They were still in jail. Paul and Silas, told the jailer to believe on the Lord Jesus Christ and he would be saved.

The other prisoners did not escape either. The door was open, but they would not walk away as free men. They had the opportunity, but they did not take it. The criminals neglected their freedom. They were still prisoners and they would be punished for their crimes.

How shall we escape from our sins if we neglect our salvation? If we refuse the pardon that Jesus is offering us, it appears to me that we are still sinners and will be punished. If the door is open, invite Jesus to come in.

My Good Friends
June 17

There are times in our lives when we go for walks and enjoy the scenery. We have already had many enjoyable days at the park. Somewhere along the way, Jesus always meets with us and we have fellowship with Him.

Since we have become really good friends, we have been drawn closer to God. I cannot count the times that Jesus touched our lives because of our friendship.

It is true that we have never met in person, but there is a strong bond of love between us. Jesus binds us together in spirit.

The meditations of our hearts are pure and without reserve for the lost of this world. We have a deep concern for those in our families, friends, and even enemies.

The love of God will never let us rest as long as there is someone in need of salvation. My good friends, the lost are crying, they are in need of a Savior. He will wipe away the tears of a sin stained life, just as He did for you and me.

Please join with me in the search; a poor thirsty soul is dying without any hope. Just a drink of water will satisfy the thirst.

"Our Father, if you need someone to carry a fresh water supply to help those in need. Remember my good friends and me."

His Visitation Hours
June 18

Every once in a while Jesus will make an unannounced appearance. His visitation hours are unknown to us, unlike a hospital where visitors are allowed to see the patients at a certain time of day.

There are times we have to schedule an appointment to see a doctor, dentist, or another health care provider. They usually stay with us for a short while and then send us on our way.

We do not know that Jesus is going to meet us at a certain place or time, unless there is an emergency or special need. He will then touch our hearts and draw us by the Holy Spirit.

Several years ago while walking at the park, I had the good pleasure of talking with a friend. If my memory is true, we spoke of our fathers who had passed away.

We shared comments of how wonderful it would be to walk the streets of glory and praise our Savior forever. As we continued to walk by the river, we talked about God's love, mercy, and Jesus giving His life for us. Before we parted company, we had a special visitor from heaven.

Jesus made an unannounced appearance. This is a time of rejoicing to be visited by the Son of God and know everything is well with our souls. "Jesus, you are always welcome to walk with us on the pathway of life."

A Personal Visit
June 19

I have a very important meeting today. It is with a very good friend of mine. If there are some of my adventure seekers that would like to meet Him, please feel free to come along.

The main purpose of His visit is to get some volunteers for life changing assignments. Each person who is accepted will have to meet certain qualifications.

This is a personal visit to talk over some eternal concerns. Some of us have already accepted His plan of transformation for our lives. He will keep all conversations private.

As He speaks with each of us individually, please don't be surprised if He mentions sins. If He does, there is no need to be alarmed for the life changing process cannot begin until they have been forgiven.

I will assure every person here that this is not a painful process, at least not for us. But it was for Jesus when He hung on an old rugged cross and died so we could be forgiven of our sins.

His precious blood was spilled to wash away all of our transgressions. Everyone who accepts Christ will receive a new life in Him. I am glad Jesus came by today. Nearly all those who met Him, walked away saying, "Thank you, Jesus."

Grace Always Abounds
June 20

Our expedition today will take us on a very dangerous mission. It is best we rely on our imaginations if we want to get out alive.

Some of our friends are held captive in the dungeons of sin. We want everyone to come prepared for the worst. The conditions of sinful living can be seen anywhere the peoples hearts are not right with God.

This is a place where all of us in this group were held captives because of our sinful lives. One man (Jesus) made a way of escape for us and we have been following Him ever since. The one who saved us is in our hearts and lives. He will be with us in this rescue attempt.

Our biggest danger is being lured back into the trap of corruption from whence we came. If we stay too long and partake of the poison, the enemy will bind us with stronger sins.

I am confidant that everyone here will remain faithful and that none of us will be taken as prisoners. "For where sin abounds, grace does much more abound."

We told our friends and loved ones about Jesus. Immediately, when they believed in their hearts, the shackles of sin were broken. Jesus sets the captive free and gives us liberty. Grace always abounds. "Thank you, Jesus."

Led by the Holy Spirit
June 21

The workers have been assembled into the field to gather the corn. Now this has been a very good year for the farmers. Their hard work and good weather conditions have really helped to produce the best crop of the year.

We cannot forget the mules that were used for plowing and pulling the wagons of corn. They hauled the corn to the silos and other storage areas. Now that the work is done, the mules are placed into the barn.

Everyone settles in for the night, unaware of a burning lantern that had fallen into some loose hay where all the horses and mules were kept. Smoke from the fire escapes through the door and the roof.

The barn is now ablaze, but the farmers aroused from sleep by the terrified animals rushed to the scene to save their livestock.

The only way to save the mules and horses is to cover their eyes so they cannot see the fire and then lead them out of the barn. These brave men risked their lives to save these animals and all of them were led to safety.

This happened in the imagination world, but what about in our lives today. How can we escape the flames of a burning hell? The Holy Spirit must lead us to Christ who is able to save to the uttermost.

Come and Dine
June 22

I just want all of my good friends to know we are invited to a fish fry. We are not going fishing; the food supply is already being prepared for our consumption.

The chef is already well known as the best wine maker in the country. We don't have to worry if there is enough food. He has proved that little is much when He blesses it.

I am sure everyone here remembers how He fed five thousand with a few pieces of fish. Now that we know the identity of the chef, are there any objections to Jesus serving us?

I guess everyone here already knows that I have a mischievous imagination. It has been known to merge with my story. Sometimes it invites people to a fish fry that was intended for the disciples after Jesus was resurrected.

Well now that everyone is already here. I will not turn my good friends away. This is a private meal, but I believe it is for everyone who will accept the invitation, "Come and Dine."

Jesus was not only speaking to the disciples but to all of us. As a matter of fact, I think He would be really disappointed if we kept this invitation to ourselves and refused to invite people into His presence. "Anyone care for another piece of fish?" "Thanks for coming."

Life Saving Responders
June 23

We have a very important assignment today, as there are responders needed for various life situations. There is no special training required for we will be responding to the high calling of God.

When the opportunity arises for us to offer assistance to help anyone in need, we will not hesitate to help him or her. As always this is a volunteer operation.

We appreciate those who endeavor to show kindness, love, and complete dedication to God. Before we begin, let's review some of our local responders to better understand their life saving qualities.

Our local communities are well prepared for any type of emergency. If we have a building or someone's home is on fire. Then we have responders who will put out the flames. Sometimes they will go into a burning structure to save lives.

There are times when everything seems to be quite and peaceful. A siren is heard in the distance, a rescue unit has just been called to an accident on the highway. If they respond quickly to the wreck, lives can be saved.

I think we are beginning to understand our positions as responders. Each of our life saving techniques is different than the others. We are more concerned about each person's soul and what we can say or do to help them find Christ. If we respond in time and they accept Jesus, their souls will be saved.

Storm Chasers
June 24

We are going on an adventure to an extremely dangerous territory. The equipment we need for this experience is a camera and video equipment. Good pictures and live action will alert the people of the hazardous living conditions.

It does not seem like a terrifying mission, but there is the possibility of life or death. We need some qualified individuals to be storm chasers.

This job will be up close and personal. All those interested, please follow me to hurricane alley. There is always a lot of action is this area.

I must remind everyone this is not a thrill seeking opportunity of fun and excitement. We have a very important job of warning the people. All precautions will be taken to ensure everyone's safety.

Well now that we have arrived at the scene. Let's go to work. A hurricane has been sighted just a few miles ahead. The winds are well over a hundred miles per hour.

This is a monster storm. The cameras are clicking and live video is in action as vehicles are tossed about like toys. The storm chasers report the news and lives are saved because of their heroic efforts.

The challenge for us in our daily lives is to warn the people to repent. Get out of the storms path and seek shelter immediately in the Son of God.

Safe and Secure
June 25

We have been authorized by a higher power to commit our most prized possessions to His protective care. I assure all of my good friends of the stability we have in Him. There is no better way to protect our investment than in the care of almighty God.

Banks have been used around the world to secure our earthly treasures. However, thieves have robbed some of them. Surely Fort Knox would be an excellent place. This is where the gold is stored and I don't believe anyone has ever broken into this armed facility.

These security places are really good, but they are just not sufficient to keep our valuable assets. There is another unit of protection that I had not yet mentioned. We will probably have to get the President and the congress to allow this intervention.

Call out the National Guard and all military personal to provide security against all evil forces. I hate to discourage anyone, but they just do not have the capabilities to maintain a secure environment for our needs.

The suspense has gone on too long. Each one of us has a soul and that is our most prized possession. "I know whom I have believed, and am persuaded that he is able to keep that which I have committed unto him against that day" (Timothy 1: 12). A committed soul is secure in God's care.

Under the Radar
June 26

I hope we have some radar specialist, traveling with us on this journey. We could certainly use the technology in our rescue efforts.

Those qualified to operate this tracking system are encouraged to join the navigation team. Radar is a very sophisticated system that follows airplanes and keeps them from crashing into other aircraft.

It has been announced that an airplane is flying under the radar and it may have crashed into the sea. The search continues for the passengers and crew.

Bad weather is hampering the rescue operation. We all hope that everyone has survived this terrible ordeal. After several days of searching, we have decided to abort this mission.

We would like for all those who volunteered to search for the crew and passengers stay with us as we turn off the radar and focus on a different rescue.

We will be concentrating on the surveillance of a loving God. His watchfulness over our lives is a continual process. There is not a day that goes by without Him knowing everything about us.

He even knows when we try to go under the celestial radar and descend back into the world. No matter how deep we sink into sin, God will never abort the mission to rescue us.

Sins will find us
June 27

There are several suspects who have committed a variety of crimes. It is very important that we find these desperados, as they are extremely dangerous.

The security patrol is seeking help from various agencies. If anyone has a good team of bloodhounds, we could use them in tracking the fugitives. We want everyone to spread out, and let the dogs follow the trail. These canines are well trained, but even the best dogs cannot follow a water trail.

It is not advisable for our good friends to help search for these criminals; this mission is just too treacherous. We want everyone to be alert and notify the law enforcement of any unusual activity or visual contact.

The prisoners escaped late last night from a high security installation. They have been on the run for about three hours. It has been reported that they are armed.

Escaped convicts will take advantage of all natural resources, creeks, and even a rocky terrain. Their main objective is to escape for their lives. After several hours of searching, the men were captured and returned to prison.

Let's just say we are the runners from our own personal sins. We can run and hide, but our sins will find us. If we repent, God will have mercy.

Jesus, the Only Way
June 28

Our adventure today will be for those who like to climb high mountains. The terrain is very rough and strong winds are predicted later this week. We have already noticed a huge drop in the temperature.

Our survival depends on very strict instructions from the guide. He told us to obey his commands, stay close to him, and by no means separate from the group.

The leader of this group has been on many expeditions. He knows how dangerous it is for anyone to venture out alone. He gave the warning again to make sure we all understood. If there was any disobedience in the ranks, the consequences could be fatal.

There were some places on the mountain where we could rest and even sleep for the night. Everything was going well until the morning. We all awoke to the startling fact that some of our friends had decided to take a short cut to the top of the mountain. A short while later, it was discovered they had fallen from a ledge to their death.

Jesus wants us to follow Him. Obedience to His commands will ensure we have a safe journey to heaven. If we try to go it alone, climb up some other way, we will not make it. There is no other way but by Jesus.

Come unto me
June 29

This would be a good time to remember when we started following Jesus. The Master calls at certain times with personal invitations. "Come unto me," this is one of them.

All of us in this group can think about that special time when we met the Savior and surrendered to Him. Our lives have not been the same since Jesus came into our hearts.

His love grows stronger by the day; we hold onto the promise that He will never leave or forsake, but He will go with all the way. Jesus is still calling people today, "Come unto me!"

Sometimes the call is for us to repent of our sins and confess Him as Lord and Savior. This is the beginning of a new life for each one of us when we answer the call. Please don't turn Him away and reject His love and mercy.

There are times in our lives when the burdens are hard to bear and the troubles of life weigh us down. Jesus wants us to cast all of our cares upon Him. The call is still the same, "Come unto me!"

When there is a longing in each of our hearts for peace. There is no reason to be dismayed, just reach up and take hold of His nailed scarred-hand.

He gives us peace the world cannot take away. He is calling now "Come unto me!" What He has done for others, He will do for us.

Bind Us Together
June 30

One day at church a man was speaking to the congregation about unity in our lives. He had a very good illustration that I would like to share with my friends. This image of a bundle of wood would be a good example for the members of a church congregation to unite together as one.

Eleven sticks were tightly bound together and one stick was by itself. He tried to break the eleven pieces of wood and he could not do it. Finally an attempt was made on the single piece and it was easily broken.

I am sure we all remember the story in the Bible about the betrayal of Judas. He betrayed Jesus for thirty pieces of silver. Afterwards his conscience bothered him so much that he hung himself.

There was a time in this man's life when he was a lot stronger, but he separated himself from the disciples and just like the single piece of wood was easy to break.

The eleven disciples stayed together because of their strong bonds of love for Christ, they held fast, secure, and they were unbreakable.

As individuals each of us receives our strength from the Lord. He gives us more than enough grace to be victorious in life. Judas separated himself from the disciples and from Jesus. We are stronger together, and weaker when the main one (Christ) is rejected.

Debt is paid
July 1

Today we will get a look at the high price of our sins. This cannot be measured on a grocery scale or in monthly payments. The cost is way too high to even consider a large amount of money.

Our payment is not for us to have more sins, but that our debt would be paid for the sins we have already committed. If we pay for something then we are supposed to get a return on our investment.

I believe the transaction would be like money for a car. We pay and then we receive. The debt of our sins is similar to the market place, except we do not make our payments.

Jesus paid the price when He gave His life on an old rugged cross to die for our sins. Our transgressions cost Him the loss of blood, a severe beating, unbearable pain, and a crown of thorns upon His brow. He gave His life to pay a debt He did not owe.

They did not use the blood of bulls, calves, or even lambs. None of those things would be sufficient to cover the price of our sins.

Nothing but the blood of Jesus for sins He did not commit. He paid with His life and now we receive forgiveness, salvation of our souls, and a home in glory.

What He gave and what we received should cause every person to fall on their knees and say, "Thank you, Jesus." Debt is paid in full.

Final Review
July 2

God is on the throne and He knows everything about us. Let's just suppose He is examining the final pages of our lives. We can make it more personal by each one of us being the one that is reviewed.

This book is open and there are special characteristics that God wants to see in each of our lives. Each page is filled with kind deeds of helping neighbors and friends.

More pages are turned to reveal some important things that happened along the way. This book is really interesting and it shows the good qualities of life.

Each page is filled with kindness, love, and mercy. God notices a forgiving attitude has been a consistent process in this book. It looks like each of us really lived a good life.

But the final review brought tears to our Father's eyes. There was no mention of His Son in the book by certain individuals.

A good life is commendable, but without Christ, a life is void of real peace and forgiveness that comes from above.

The gates of heaven will not open unless we have Jesus in our hearts. It's late, but it is not too late. Confess Him now, and God will open a new chapter of life in glory.

Only by Permission
July 3

It is really a nice day to enjoy the comforts of home. This is the place where we like to meet with our friends and family members.

We have a mat in front of the door that says "Welcome." When the doors are locked and no one can get in, is it possible that the display sign is telling a lie?

I guess our visitors could answer this question. They are the ones that have to stand outside and wait for the door to be unlocked.

One thing is for sure; no one will be allowed to come in without permission. If the door remains locked, they will graciously leave. Let's visit your house where a good friend of mine will be visiting.

He waits patiently outside the door for permission to come inside. After waiting for a short while, he decides to leave. There is a possibility of a return visit tomorrow.

Well to everyone's dismay, at the midnight hour, death came to claim one of your family members. Jesus is the one who was standing at the door yesterday. No one invited Him inside, so He graciously departed.

Today may be our last opportunity to unlock the door of our hearts to let Jesus come in. He will only come in by permission. Our greeting should be: "Jesus you are welcome, please come into my heart."

God Bless America
July 4

We go back in time to the signing of the Declaration of Independence. According to history, we were officially separated from Great Britain in the year of 1776. This national holiday is known as Independence Day.

We celebrate July 4th to commemorate our freedom and to raise a new flag that will wave in every continent. We are one nation under God with life, liberty, and the pursuit of happiness for all.

This is our country and we are proud to stand with her for life or death. Our loyalty has been proven down through the ages with battles and wars fought here and abroad.

Men and women who were called for service paid the high cost of keeping our freedom. Some of them gave the ultimate sacrifice by dying for the country we all love, "America."

It has been said that freedom is not free. The blood flows deep on the battlefields and there are many graves with each of these brave men and women's names engraved in stone.

America continues to fight for our freedom overseas. It seems to be a never-ending war. We are the United States, the home of the brave, and the land of the free, and one nation under God.

"America!" We stand beside her, and we will die to protect her. "God Bless America."

The Master of the Clay
July 5

We will visit today a place where clay is shaped into a certain object. This will be an interesting adventure for us to watch the transformation of this modeling material.

I am sure everyone will be impressed when we meet the Master of the clay. There is no one like Him for He labors continuously in His shop.

All of us can think of times when we needed a special touch to mold and reshape our lives. He does not hesitate to make a personal visit, no matter if it is day or night. He is always on call and will respond in a moments notice, even if we come in for emergency repairs.

Sometimes the imperfections of sin will corrupt our lives and we definitely need a touch of the Master's hand for Him to cleanse the impurities of our hearts.

The door of His shop is always open and He welcomes all visitors. No one is turned away. He is never too busy to hear our heart's cries.

I don't believe we have been properly introduced to the Master of the clay. "Our Father which art in heaven, touch us now and mold and make us into living vessels of honor."

Behold, the Man, Jesus
July 6

The discovery of a man's true identity is shown in the characteristics of His life. We are going to visualize the life of Christ so we will have a better understanding of His love for us.

There are many interesting things about Jesus and we would like to know, "Who is this man?" Those of us who know Him would say, "He is the good Shepherd."

There is no need to fear any evil because we know He is always beside us. As a shepherd watches over his sheep, so does Christ keep us in His loving care.

He is a man who can calm the storms that prevail in nature. We would all agree, when the trials of life are hard to bear, Jesus never leaves us. He speaks to the storms of our souls. "Peace be Still."

I see there are some folks here that are not quite satisfied about the identity of Jesus. Please go with me to the cross. We will witness through the eyes of faith, the crucifixion of Jesus on the cross.

He is dying for our sins; the suffering is unbearable. They took Him down from the cross. He was buried and rose again the third day. "Behold, the man, Jesus!" All of us who know Him say, "He is the Christ, the Son of God."

Life or Death
July 7

It looks like it will be a good time to take a vacation. We are going to get away for a while and spend some time in the mountains.

This is a yearly event that has been planned several months in advance. Perhaps there are some fishermen in this group that would like to go along with us.

This is not going to be a luxury vacation. All of the modern conveniences of life will be left at our homes. There will be no electricity to give us light in the evening. Forget about running water, unless there is a creek nearby.

I guess I should warn everyone of the possible danger of hungry bears in the area. Please be advised that no firearms are allowed on this trip, but knives are acceptable.

This will be a time for us to live off the land. Our food will be fish, berries, and other natural resources.

The purpose of this vacation is survival training, to stay alive.

We just now received some bad news. One of our family members passed away this morning. We will have to reschedule our trip to a later time. This is an unexpected tragedy of the loss of our loved one.

Our adventure was to spend one week in the wild country. We had made the plans and were well prepared to stay alive. No one knows the day or hour when death will cross our paths. We can be prepared for life in Christ.

Shelter in the Rock
July 8

I don't know if there is anyone here that has worked in a forest. We could certainly use the help. We will be cutting trees for lumber.

There are several positions open at the sawmill. This is where the trees will be debarked and sawed into boards. This is the last process before the lumber is hauled to factories.

We welcome all lumberjacks to work with us in cutting the trees. There are many more job opportunities. This company will be hiring all week.

Please come by and sign the application form. Now that the crew has been hired. The work will begin first thing in the morning. All week we heard the sound of chainsaws and trees falling to the ground.

Everyone was hard at work and no one noticed a young boy had entered the danger zone. This area was strictly prohibited, no one was allowed below the tree line.

The lad didn't notice the warning signs as he was trying to catch his pony. All of a sudden, shouts from above alerted the boy to the danger; maybe it was too late.

A huge tree was falling right towards him. He crawled in under a rock ledge and was saved. We can go to the rock of ages and we will find shelter in Jesus and we will be safe all through life.

The Fire Escape
July 9

The residents in the hotel are being evaluated. A fire is raging through the facility. People are running for their lives to escape the flames. There are men, women, and even children trapped inside the burning structure.

The fire department is responding to the emergency. Hundreds of firefighters and residents of the community have joined in the efforts to save lives. Dark smoke fills the rooms and the flames reach higher.

The only hope for each person is to make it to the fire escape. Everyone is instructed to move quickly towards the emergency exit. Each person climbs down the escape unit and it appears that everyone has made it safely outside.

But a father does not realize his daughter is also safe. He goes back into the burning building to save her. My imagination cannot let this man die in the flames. He is also saved.

It will not be this easy to save people from a burning hell. The reality of life is not controlled by ones imagination, but by faith in the Son of God.

Believe on the Lord Jesus Christ and thou shalt be saved. It is not very hard to say, "Jesus, I am sorry for my sins."

Pardon Me
July 10

Let's say we are walking at the park and someone accidently bumps into one of us. The words most commonly used are: "Excuse me, or pardon me."
Most of the time, the reaction is good and both parties continue on their way. If there seems to be some contention, it may be best to walk away.

Today we will be approaching the throne room of grace. There are many offenses, sins, and transgressions that we have done wrong. We know there is not enough time to express our grief for a lifetime of corruptible things.

The few words that we choose must be strong and sincere. They must come from the depth of our hearts. A really long speech is not needed to make things right with God. However, He loves having company and He will stay with us, as long as we desire.

He is our heavenly Father and He definitely wants to spend time with His children. Before we are adopted into His family, we need to return to the apology for our sins.

Whether we use a lot of words or a few, be sincere. "Jesus come into my heart, I am sorry for my sins, please pardon me." He will never walk away from a repentant heart.

Stagnant Life
July 11

After several miles of traveling, we finally reached our destination. This is a popular camping site that is visited by many tourists. We were really looking forward to hiking through the woods to our favorite fishing spot.

We set up camp and enjoyed some of the recreational activities. This seemed to be the perfect time of year for meals prepared over a fire or on a grill. The next morning we had breakfast of bacon and eggs.

The time had finally come for us to begin our hiking trip through the mountains. We were surprised at the amount of brush that was cluttering the trail.

It looked as though no one had walked this path for years. In times past, the trail was always easy to follow. Our journey through the woods was taking a lot longer than we had planned.

After battling the elements of trash and debris, untangling fishing rods caught in the shrubbery, we finally make it to our destination.

Our hearts sank with grief when we saw the stagnant water and more garbage on the pond. Our favorite fishing spot was polluted and this part of our imaginary vacation was ruined.

The impurities of a sinful life will not only hinder, but they will stop the flow of grace unless Jesus is allowed to clear the way. The pathway of life is not cluttered with sin. Jesus' precious blood cleanses our sinful hearts and makes us holy, pure within.

Light in Darkness
July 12

We were living in sins dark valley until a light from heaven shined upon our lives. Let's travel back in time; we don't have to go very far to reveal a life changing experience. There for a long time we all lived in darkness and would stumble and fall. The night represents our sinful conditions.

Our daily routine consisted of unrighteous, ungodly living, and in the participation of sins. We definitely did not have good directions, no one can see in the dark.

Our adventure today will take all of us from the valley to a mountain where we will be walking along a ledge of a dangerous ravine. I feel it is my obligation to warn everyone; there is a strong possibility of death. Some of us will not be going home.

There is no guide and it is in the middle of the night, pitch-black darkness. One misstep and a grave on a hill awaits our arrival. How could anyone survive in these terrible conditions?

There is only one way and that is through and by the Lord Jesus Christ. We commit our souls to Him and He will lead us safely home. Some of us in this group want to know how we can survive the dark ledges in life.

Jesus is the light of the world. Those who follow Him will not walk in darkness, but will have the light of life.

Keep Holding on
July 13

A massive fire was spreading through a large living facility. A contractor was seen on the outside of the building, standing on the window ledge. The fire was becoming more intense and the walls were ready to collapse.

There was not much time to save the man, a few minutes at the most. He maneuvered himself in position to hold on to the window ledge and then he swung himself to a lower unit.

The fire department had extended the ladder to the individual, but was it too late? The   contractor was within an arms reach of the equipment and the flames from the burning structure were reaching for him.

He climbed onto the ladder and the fire department had width-drawn it about three feet when a section of the burning building fell to the ground.

The construction worker was saved just in time. The rescue operation was a success and we are thankful the man's life was spared. This was a true story.

One other part of this rescue caught my attention. The contractor was holding on to the window ledge and then he let go when the fire was blazing all around him.

Is it possible that we are holding on to the wrong things in life? If we are holding on to our sins, the flames are getting higher. Let go, and take hold of the Savior's hand and keep holding on.

The Stain of Sin
July 14

I suppose everyone was wondering why no one had seen me in the past two weeks. It seems as though I had completely disappeared. Some of my friends probably thought I was being held hostage by my imagination. If I was a prisoner, then I managed to escape just in time to imagine this story.

We need some help in the woodworking shop. All those interested in staining a nice piece of furniture, please come to the craftsman shop at the end of town.

There is no need to bring any tools. The desk has already been completed; it just needs a good coat of stain. After working about four hours, we were finally done.

We were admiring the beautiful finish when we noticed a dark spot right in the middle of the desk. It seemed as though all of our hard work was in vain.

A customer had already paid for this piece of furniture and he was going to pick it up in four days. The wood top would have to be completely sanded and refinished all over again. A beautiful desk was now ready for the customer.

Sins of our lives penetrate deep into our souls. They are the stains that corrupt and defile us. Jesus' precious blood is the only thing that can purify our sinful hearts. Then God will accept us into the family.

The Worth of a Soul
July 15

It appears to me that today would be good time for an excavating project. Some very rare vases have been discovered in the earth. These artifacts are very old and can be easily broken. None have been found in perfect condition.

We are sending out this information so all collectors and antique specialist will be ready to inspect these priceless objects. Digging in the earth is a very tedious operation. It can be a little boring, but we appreciate all the help we can get.

Several glass containers have been dug up and taken away. They need to go through a cleaning process. It is really hard to tell if the glassware is of any value while it is covered in mud.

Well it has been several hours now of carefully removing the dirt so as not to break any vases. Finally some ornamental pieces are found. The value of them exceeds all expectations.

 Suppose we go through a divine excavating project. The search will be more intense as it will be in the depths of our hearts.

It appears to me that at one time we were all broken vessels, polluted by sin, until Jesus found us and made us whole.

The value of our souls is according to the price He paid, and if we repented of our sins. How much are we worth?

Blind Spots of Faith
July 16

While I was traveling down the road one day, a car pulled right out in front of me. She had stopped at a stop sign to see if there was anything coming down the road.

I was turning left at the intersection where this woman was located. But all of a sudden, without warning, she cut me off. I just barely had enough time to slam on the brakes. An accident was avoided. There have been times in my life when I have done the same thing.

I'm sure most of us have been in the same situation. We look and know that the roads are clear, but they are not. Sometimes we cannot see because of blind spots in our mirrors and other places in the car.

One day when I was coming home from work unaware of the danger ahead. There were some college kids at a crosswalk. They were laughing, and texting, not really paying much attention to the traffic.

Blind spots are very dangerous and so is texting while walking across a highway. I didn't see them coming and they didn't see me either. Well, there was not an accident to report. We all made it to our destinations.

As we travel down the path of life, we need to keep our eyes on Jesus. Sometimes we cannot see Him because of the blind spots, worldly cares, and sinful pleasures. This is when we are in the greatest danger. Will He see us in the Rapture?

Race for Life
July 17

The media has broadcast a special event that will take place on a certain day. All competition sports are announced with a month, day, and year. We want everyone to be aware that these calendar dates does not apply to our daily lives.

This will be a race for a crown and a new home. All active runners will have a chance to win the prize. There will definitely be many winners. All those who cross the finish line will receive a lifetime benefit of eternal bliss.

Just to make this race more interesting. We have included a position of permanent residence in the celestial city. All of these rewards will be presented when each of us finish the course. Whether we start to run as a little child or later in life as senior citizens, our chances of finishing the race are the same.

I have noticed that some of the runners are totally unprepared to run in this competition match. All of their lives they have been carrying packsacks.

These are loaded down with heavy sinful weights. We all know that we cannot finish a race with the burdens of sin, dragging us down.

Just so everyone has the same opportunity to win, Jesus will take all corruptible things from our lives if we ask Him. We will win with Christ as Lord and Savior.

Transformed Lives
July 18

When we receive Jesus Christ into our hearts, there is a transformation that takes place. Immediately our sins are forgiven. This is the result of repentance   when we tell Jesus we are sorry for our sins and we ask Him to forgive us.

It does not look like we have been changed. All of our physical features are the same. We need to go deeper into the depths of each heart and soul and hear the confessions of the born again believers.

Each of us could talk about the many sins that we had committed and how we were delivered from them. By God's amazing grace, He set us free. The blood of the lamb cleansed the contamination of our sins and made us whole.

The transformation may not be noticed at first in our lives. We used to walk by those places that held us captive and we always yielded to sins evil temptations.

Since Jesus came into our hearts, the world gestures have lost their appeal. Now we are attending church and praising God for His great love.

Ones we were sinners, living in the gutters of life until Jesus walked by and lifted us out. Our lives are different now, the world can plainly see.

A Decision for Life
July 19

As we travel through life, we will have to make many decisions. Let's say there are two paths in life to follow. One of them is with Jesus; the other is the sinner's path.

I would like to invite all of my friends to meet me at pathway corner. We are going to take a walk down memory lane. We are going to revisit the past, and then we will proceed to the present and future.

Let's briefly go back in time, before we met Jesus. Most of us don't like to go back that far, including me. Just for a brief length of time to help someone find the right path. Is that all right with everyone?

We were away from God, no fellowship with Him, and living good normal lives, just like everyone else. Most of us probably started thinking about our sins when the Holy Spirit brought conviction upon us.

We realized that we were sinners and our lives were not pleasing in the sight of God. We were on the wrong path, until Jesus forgave us of our sins.

Now that we know of God's great love and the sacrifice Jesus gave at Calvary, we are now walking a new path. This one leads to glory and a home in heaven.

There is a decision that each one of us needs to make. The path of the unrighteous will keep us on the sinner's path, or the path of life where sins are forgiven and Jesus is Lord. He is calling, "Follow me." Stay on the right path and the gates of heaven will open.

Too Faraway to Focus
July 20

It's been a while since we walked at the park and enjoyed God's wonderful creation. This would be a good time for all of my photographer friends to take some snapshots of the imagination landscape.

I am not very familiar with cameras. Perhaps there is someone here who could show me the best way to take pictures. Someone made a comment that the evening hours would be good for cool colorful scenes. So all of us decided to go in the late hours of the day.

This was really good information for us to know when the landscape scenes are best for photography. I still didn't know how to use the camera.

After a while the photo images were shared among us and we commented about each one. They were all good, except mine. This was an embarrassing time for me, as my pictures were out of focus and I was ashamed for anyone to see them.

My good friends understood my hurt feelings. They showed me the adjustment to control the distance of objects. We all went home with beautiful pictures.

Our Father has created us in His likeness. Sometimes we get out of focus; maybe it is because we are too far away from God. Our personal image will always improve when each of us gets closer to Him. Please don't be discouraged; God's creative image in us is still being developed.

Bread for a Beggar
July 21

There was a poor beggar, standing on a street corner. He would beg for some money to buy food. His little child was taken care of by her grandparents. This poor man was unable to work and he relied totally upon the generosity of strangers.

Sometimes he stayed out all day in the bitter cold weather. Always begging for food, money, and hoping that someday he could take care of his daughter whom he loved so much.

At the end of the day he would stop by the pantry. The owner would always greet him at the door. This place of business sold bread and other types of groceries. The clerk of the store would always bring a fresh loaf of bread and give it to the poor beggar. There was never a charge for this food.

As he sat at table in his little shack on the hill, he always prayed, thanking God for his daily bread. Well it was discovered that the beggar had a wonderful speaking voice. Soon a broadcasting company hired him. Just imagine them now, living in a mansion on a hill, happily ever after.

In our lives we are all like the poor beggar, except we are hungry and need food for our souls. There is a deep longing in our hearts for Jesus. When we go to Him, we receive the bread of life. It is always free if we ask Him.

All Have Sinned
July 22

Many years ago a woman was about to be stoned for her sins. This was really a cruel punishment. We know that she didn't murder anyone. What did she do that was so bad that the men were going to stone her to death?

It appears to me that the law of justice was nowhere to be found. She did not have a trial and no lawyers to represent her. Immediately these men had gathered big rocks for her slaying.

Before we continue with this story, we want to make sure that she has a fair trial. This is a special mandatory meeting for all of us to gather around and witness the final results.

No one can stay at home this time so please come with me to the rock quarry. The final verdict is one we can live with. There is one man who will defend her. Whatever is decided on her behalf will also be our judgment.

This woman was taken in adultery, in the very act. According to Moses law she should be stoned. They tempted Jesus by asking Him, what do you say?

He stooped down and wrote on the ground. He said unto them, "He that is without sin among you, let him first cast a stone at her" (John 8:7). Remember, the truth is already evident by not throwing a rock. One stone that is thrown will be the lie that convicts us all. Is there anyone here that will throw the first one? Let's go home, we have all sinned.

Garden of Sin
July 23

The garden of sin is the place where sinners will grow to maturity. This is no particular area that has been tilled for seeds to be planted. Each one of us has our own personal spot of sinful activities. We will refer to our corrupt ways as the things that are placed in the garden.

When we sow the seeds of unrighteousness then our sins grow as the weeds. After a while there are so many transgressions that we cannot see the real image of life. The quality of our lives is damaged.

As with the garden there is a time for harvest of bringing in the vegetation. After it goes through the preparation process then it is ready for the market.

It is really a terrible thing to go through life surrounded by the weeds of sin. Our personal lives will be like withered tomatoes on the vine. The one's that never made it to the market.

Our best resource for a productive life is to first get rid of the weeds of sin and that requires the blood of Christ. Immediately our lives are restored to a sinless condition.

Please don't go back into sins garden and end up on a fruitless vine. The harvest is ripe and the Lord is coming for the blood washed sinners. Be ready!

One Lost Lamb
July 24

Soon it will be dark in the hill country. The shepherd is busy bringing his sheep into a more secure area for the night. Everything seems to be peaceful and quite. The shepherd knows all of his sheep by name and He calls for each of them. One small lamb does not respond. It is nowhere to be found.

The search began immediately for the stray. Ninety-nine sheep were left in the care of dependable servants. This shepherd will search the dark hills and stay as long as it takes to find the little one.

There are wolves, bears, and other wild animals that are a threat to small defenseless creatures. Sheep have no way of protecting themselves. They depend entirely on the shepherd to watch over and keep them safe.

After a while of searching, the shepherd heard the squalling of a lamb, not very far away. He moved quickly through the underbrush and briar patches to the place of rescue. The small animal had fallen onto a ledge of a cliff. The shepherd reached down and saved the lamb.

There are times in life when we go astray. We have wandered too far from the fold. Sometimes we are just barely on the edge of total disaster.

Jesus is the Good Shepherd and His love for us is never ending. He will not be satisfied until we are safe and secure in our Father's arms.

No Doubt in Faith
July 25

There are special appointments that we make in life. We visit many places that will help us to improve our health. Today is an excellent time to have an eye exam. According to my schedule it is in the afternoon.

We will learn some important things about faith while we are there. Saying that we believe leaves a whole lot of room for doubt. While sitting in the chair and looking at the chart on the wall, some of the letters are blurred.

The Optometrists begins to rotate the alphabet scale. And he will ask which row of letters can we see the best. After we tell him, then he wants us to choose the frame of the best focus.

We come now to our faith test. I would say most of the people in this group didn't even know there was such a thing in the exam room. The Optometrists will ask us to read the smallest line we can see.

The letters are spoken and sometimes we are not sure of the letters and we might say, "I believe it is an o, r, k, and we are just not sure." It could be something else.

I am glad our real faith is not based on an image on the wall, but in the Lord Jesus Christ." I know whom I have believed, and am persuaded that he is able to keep that which I have committed unto Him" (2Timothy 2:12). Our faith is a full belief without any doubt. We believe and know Jesus is Lord.

Runaway Train
July 26

We have waited a really long time for this vacation at one of the national parks. All of us were really anxious about this trip. This is the first time any of us has traveled by train.

Steam engines used to be a regular sight on the railroad. This would be our main transportation to and from our vacation resort. We were skeptical of riding this old train. After all it had been in a museum for half of a century.

We thought it would be safe so we all got on board. None of us knew we were in for a life threatening experience. There was a young engineer who was driving the train for the first time.

We were riding along when suddenly the train came to a screeching halt. A man was standing on the tracks, waving his hands frantically.

But the real danger was just ahead on a blind curve, a rockslide was covering the railway. It would have been certain death if we had continued down the track.

If we continue on the track of sin unrestricted and full steam ahead, we will not make it to our home in heaven. Jesus stood between heaven and earth on a cross to stop our runaway lives.

Each of us is the engineer of our own destiny. What will it be, stop (repent) or keep going?

God's Housekeepers
July 27

There is one King and He stands at the Father's right hand. We receive guidance from Him and He walks with us all through life. Our journey with Him is having God's blessings in our lives all the way to eternity.

We are His servants, the housekeepers of our lives. He reveals the unclean, corruptible things in our hearts and He never makes us do the household chores.

We just receive reminders from the Holy Spirit that without holiness no one will see God. This is enough inspiration for us to sweep the floors of the internal dirt and grime. A clean, pure heart will be one of the first things He sees when He comes for a visit. "Blessed are the pure in heart: for they shall see God" (Matthew 5: 8).

The floor is really looking good. But to really make it shine, we need to yield whole heartily to the One who is divine. There are some impurities that are deep in our souls.

A normal household cleaning will not remove these stains. Only God's love and mercy, the sacrificial blood of His Son will be sufficient to clean and restore our sinful lives to grace.

When Jesus comes for a visit, will He find filthy rags of unrighteousness cluttered in the closets of neglect?

There is still a little time to start the washing machine for a deep spiritual cleaning. Accept Him for a fresh, soul cleansing life.

A Personal Delivery
July 28

Our journey today will take us to the apple orchards. It is very important to have good drivers. This apple shipment must go to the market place on time or the owner will lose his home and the orchard.

The banker would be glad to sign the foreclosure papers. He would probably do anything to keep this shipment from getting to the market. We heard that he had a plan to stop a train right on the intersection, so the apple shipment would be delayed.

We can interrupt this disaster if my good friends will volunteer as truck drivers. We want the very best, and I am sure we have them. If anyone can get through, it is my faithful friends.

It is already known that the train will arrive in town at a certain time. This is also when the apples are expected to arrive.

There is only one-way to be successful in this delivery, and it is for the vehicles to cross the tracks first. The trucks barely crossed the railroad in front of the train. The poor man paid his bills in time.

As we travel through life, there are many obstacles that will hinder us from our destination. The Lord wants us to make a personal delivery. It will be a commitment from each of us to serve and love Him with heart, soul, and mind.

Is there anyone here up to the challenge? We are not going down, under, or around, we are going through.

A Blind Beggar
July 29

Let's go back in time to when a blind man was begging for alms. This man sat by the wayside. I suppose this was a place where a lot of people walked down a path to the market place. He sat on a section of land that was close to the road.

There was a lot of commotion that day and the blind man wanted to know what was going on. The travelers told him that "Jesus of Nazareth passeth by." He would be here any moment.

This blind man stopped begging, "And he cried, saying, Jesus, thou son of David, have mercy on me." The people "rebuked him, that he should hold his peace: but he cried so much the more, Thou son of David, have mercy on me" (Luke 18:38,39).

When Jesus found out the man's request, immediately the blind man received his sight. It is a glorious time in our lives when Jesus is passing by. We are blessed beyond measure when He stops to greet us personally.

Our lives are similar to the blind man; physically he could not see. We cannot see spiritually until Jesus opens our eyes. He is walking by, each of us should call out to Him, "Jesus, thou son of David, have mercy on me."

Lies of Deceit
July 30

We are going into a very dangerous territory today. The best way to avoid these treacherous villains is to speak the truth. "Let the words of my mouth, and the meditation of my heart, be acceptable in thy sight, O Lord, my strength, and my redeemer" (Psalm 19:14).

These villains are the lies that steal from the truth. If they are unattended, the end results will be disastrous. These corruptible words seek out victims of all ages.

No one is safe from lies of their perilous pursuit. Children and adults please be aware of the contamination process. One lie leads to many more.

There are many fatal consequences by speaking and believing the untruthful words. False words will ruin lives and they will follow us all the way to the grave.

All of us are not held captive to the villains of sin. The chains of our corruptible lives have been broken by the truth. Jesus is the way, the truth, and the life, no man cometh unto the Father but by Him.

When we speak the truth, the villains will perish by our own words. Be careful what we hear and more reverent to what we speak. Lies will deceive, but the truth in Jesus will set us free.

A Decision for Christ
July 31

There are many decisions that we have to make in life. When we travel down the highway, there are signs to direct us. If we follow the right one, then we will make it to our destination.

Maps used to be the only source of guidance. Travelers would study them so they would know exactly which way to go. Sometimes this presented a problem for a person traveling alone.

It is not very safe to maneuver a vehicle while looking at a map. The best course of action would be to pull over to the side of the road. Then review the best route to take and proceed with caution.

If a person decides to read the map while driving, it is highly possible that he or she will be in at a traffic accident down the road.

A GPS system will give us guidance to our destination. But it is not entirely reliable either. There is also the danger of another accident on the highway. We can decide which method we think is the best, a map or GPS.

Since we are already deciding on the best route to take in life, why not accept Jesus? He will not lead us astray. We will never be alone, as He will go with us all the way.

There is no danger of being lost. We just need to make a right turn and go straight. Sure looks like a good choice to me. Jesus is giving the call, "Follow me."

Left Town, No Regrets
August 1

While driving down the road, we were thinking about the old town that held us captive because of our sins. This is where we grew up and lived all of our lives.

I am sure there are others in this group who have lived in bondage, bound by the shackles of sin. Perhaps the old town was just an image of the sins in our personal lives.

Our thoughts will take us back in time, just long enough to help others escape the daily routine of unrighteousness and ungodly living.

The old town in each of our lives has a luring appeal with pleasures of sin. Some of us probably didn't even know that it was our sins that were leading us down the dark alleys of corruption.

Life in the old town was just a normal routine. We would go to our jobs, schools, and various other places. There were no shackles or chains holding us down.

Why would we want to be set free from a captivity that doesn't seem to exist? Once we realize that we are all sinners then we need to leave our personal sins behind.

When the Holy Spirit convicts us of sin, then it is time to leave and that is what we have done. We left town with Jesus and there are no regrets. Please join with us on our way to glory. Soon we will be at home in heaven.

One Word Assignment
August 2

We have a writing assignment today and we would like for everyone to participate. It will not take very long to complete, as we will just be working with one word and that is: "Jesus."

We would like for each person to write this name in a place that will leave a lasting impression in our lives. A good example would be in a book, but soon the pages and the name would fade away.

At the completion of this assignment, please turn in your suggestions. When everyone is finished writing the name, we will decide on the most permanent position for our personal benefit.

Someone wrote it could be placed on a TV or radio program. That sounds like a good place. Millions of people are attentive to these broadcast stations. After a short while the signals would fade just like pages in a book.

This looks like a good one; write it in the sky with an airplane. See how quickly it turns to a cloudy haze. What about on the sand? It does not take long for the waves of the sea to erase it.

There is one place for a lasting impression. Write the name of Jesus in the tables of our hearts. This will be a personal position that will last for eternity. We agree; Jesus will never depart.

Heaven is Real
August 3

We promised everyone that we would schedule a new camping trip. Since I don't have a boat, we had to make arrangements with the imagination department. They really give good customer service.

When I think about it, I don't believe I have ever been turned away.

Well I've been informed by the agency that there is an old boat in the community. It is not in very good condition, but it was the best they could find with such a short notice.

We looked it over and decided to buy it. Now this boat had not been in the water for a couple of years. It had just been painted and it was really beautiful.

Now that we have arrived at Claytor Lake, we would like for some of our good friends to go with us for a boat ride. We were really surprised when everyone ran away so fast.

We were in the middle of the lake and the boat began to sink. The game warden came by and rescued us. If we can't have confidence in our own imaginations, whom can we trust? There is only one and His name is Jesus. He is the way the truth and the life.

The reality of life is that He is the Savior of the world. Those who believe in Him have life eternal. Heaven is real and Jesus is coming. Does anyone want to go with Him?

Keep the Fire Burning
August 4

The forest ranger came around to all of the campsites. He came to warn us of a bear that had killed some livestock. The warning was for all the campers to be aware and keep the fires burning. After each meal, place all the leftovers in a secure trash container.

There was a young man and his wife, camping with their two small children. He was a policeman and he had brought along his guard dog, a German shepherd. Their campsite was by itself next to some thick brush.

Almost everyone had gone to sleep for the night. There were a few campers staying up late to make sure their fires did not go out.

The bear came into the area next to the tent, but the German shepherd saved everyone's life by running the bear away. It is good to have a protective imagination.

We need to keep the fires of faith burning in our daily lives. When the flames are low and we are not very close to God, we had better run back to Him.

Let the burning flames of faith grow higher and our devotion stronger. We need to draw closer than we have ever been before. Draw nigh to God and He will draw nigh to us. He will give us divine protection day or night. Our faith in Jesus will keep us safe in God's arms.

Almost Persuaded
August 5

There is going to be a big race today. We have made plans to go and enjoy this special event. As always our good friends are invited. Our invitation is to one and all.

Now some of us have never been to a race. It certainly sounds exciting. My racecar enthusiasts have encouraged me to go. It took quite a bit of persuading, but they finally convinced me.

I have noticed that some of my friends have declined to go with us. No matter how hard we tried to get them to come. They would not yield to our request.

They had just as many excuses as me, if not more. They held fast to their arguments and would not surrender. However some of them came very close to committing themselves to the event.

As we all know closeness does not count. We arrived at the racetrack and watched the cars cross the finish line. Everyone had a really good time and then we went home.

There are times in our lives when almost persuaded can keep us from the kingdom of God. Almost believing that Jesus rose from the dead will not open the gates of heaven. A partial belief will keep us in our sins.

We must be fully persuaded, no doubt in our hearts that Jesus is the Christ. An almost decision to accept Him will leave us behind. Heaven is waiting; does anyone here want to go with us?

Ten Commandments
August 6

We have a very important message that God gave us from heaven. When it was first delivered to the people, it was written on a stone tablet. God wrote on it with His finger and gave the tablet to Moses for us.

Now these words have gone down through the ages as His guidelines for our lives. They tell us how to live and they keep us from doing the wrong things. "Thou shalt not:" These words are familiar all through the text.

God did not ask us if we would please live by these words. He commanded us to obey the Ten Commandments. It was so important that God did not give us a choice, but a direct order.

We see today how unlawful and disrespectable some of the people have become in our generation. They do not want God's laws or anything to do with Christ. The laws of God have been removed from libraries, courthouses, and many other facilities.

This is the voice of a few and the response of a government that has forgotten God. "Take it down, get rid of it, and we don't want it." That is not true! "We thee people" stand in unity that there is one God and He is the Father of all. "In God we trust." He has created us and we are the people who will honor and always respect the Ten Commandments. We will obey God!

Sins Miry Clay
August 7

The dark hours of death will come without a warning or an announcement to the family members. There are times when we know that life is coming to an end. We don't know the exact day or hour of our departure.

Some of us may be sinking in the miry clay right now. We know that we have not made things right with God. The burden of our sins is a heavy weight that will go with us to the grave.

Sins have been tagging along all of our lives and controlling actions, corrupting hearts, distorting minds, and even ruining our relationships with God.

We know it is late in life and the shadows of death are already moving closer. Sin has been around way too long and would be glad to go the rest of the journey.

This miry clay keeps drawing us deeper into sin. It is up to each of us if want to have sin as our escort through the valley of the shadow of death or Jesus.

We do not have to go to the grave with our sins. They are not permanent fixtures to our bodies or leeches that will not let go. We will perish with our sins if we do not repent. It is getting dark and soon life will be no more.

Jesus is here and He is reaching down His nail-scarred hand. Pray with me, "Jesus, come into my heart and forgive all of my sins." We all rejoiced together as Christ pulled us from sins miry clay. "Thank you, Jesus."

The Verdict
August 8

We are scheduled to be in court to answer for our offences. A lawyer and a jury have been selected to defend us. These proceedings will take a while for we have many sins.

The judge asked us to arise and to affirm that we will tell the truth. We all agreed. He reminded us, we do not want any lies, no partial truths, or any false statements. The judge asked the first question? "How do we plead?"

"Your Honor, we will not mislead or dishonor the court with lies. There are many sins that we have committed and we confess to all of them. We are not denying any of the evidence that is brought against us. We have sinned, but our plea is not guilty!"

The judge was startled with our confession and could not believe we were claiming to be innocent. "Your Honor please let me finish."

Jesus died for our sins and we have been forgiven. He paid for our offences with His blood. We cannot be punished for sins that no longer exist.

The jury has now reached a verdict. "Your Honor, we find all the believers not guilty." No one here condemns us; we are free.

Temptation Trap
August 9

We had a very unfortunate accident the last time we went on a camping trip. After we got the sunken boat back on land, it was hauled into the shop for repairs.

The people in this imagination repair shop looked very familiar. I know we had seen them somewhere before, but where?

The boat was repaired and we were told that it is in excellent condition. According to the repair mechanic the old rotten boards were replaced with new ones. We picked up the boat and knew that something was not right.

It was almost like history was repeating itself. I suppose it was like buying an old boat from the same imagination team. We new something was wrong, but what?

We arrived at Claytor Lake, and asked our friends if they wanted to ride. They ran away just like the first time. While we were fishing for Bass, all of a sudden the boat sprung a leak and we had to be rescued. It was then that we remembered our last imagination encounter was with the same team.

It looks like some of us have a really hard time of staying away from sin. The same ones keep calling us back and immediately we fall into the same temptation trap.

Jesus delivers us from our sins and He does not want us to return to our old sinful ways. Remember where He brought us from and don't go back to sin.

Tomorrow
August 10

Since we have met, Jesus has helped us through many difficult situations. He never leaves or forsakes us. Our lives with Him are blessed daily by His presence.

There is one place in time that He may not greet us with the morning sun or a walk at the park. If we make it through the night, Jesus will be with us as always. There is a strong possibility that we will not make it through this time zone.

There are no guarantees of physical life in this adventure. We will not be starting in the morning for this will interfere with our personal lives. Everyone will be going on this mission; there will be no exceptions.

Before we begin our travels, it is best to make things right with God. It would be good if each person here would invite Jesus into his or her heart. The time zone we want to enter may not allow us the opportunity to make peace with God.

This really seems like a scary journey, but we have already traveled it many times before. Today is no different. I guess I have kept everyone in suspense long enough.

The place of the unknown is tomorrow. Yesterday is gone; today is the present time. Can anyone tell me for sure if tomorrow will ever come? Receive Jesus today and life will go on, everlasting life.

Bad Apples
August 11

Nice fresh apples in the marketplace will make a delicious treat. Take them home and make an apple pie. This will be a really fantastic desert, a good way to finish a meal.

We bought enough apples to last a while. They will be kept in the kitchen if anyone would like to have one at a later time. Throughout the week this food source gradually began to disappear.

We were enjoying this fruit when someone noticed a bad apple in the basket. Who would have ever thought corruption would exist in such a place. There seemed to be a certain amount of anxiety and fear that all the apples would be ruined.

It was decided by the hungry participants to get rid of the rotten apple. Throw it away or it will destroy the entire lot. This bad fruit was removed and thrown away.

Let's say there is a stain of sin that has developed in each of our hearts. If we leave it alone, the corruption will spread and will eventually ruin our lives.

Plead the blood of Christ for forgiveness. We must keep our lives holy, pure, and without spot, to present our bodies a living sacrifice unto God. Sins forgiven, life is restored.

The Reality of Life
August 12

Our adventure today will take us by ship to the ocean. A pirate vessel sunk in a certain area many years ago. We will be using special equipment to retrieve any artifacts.

If any of my aquatic friends would like to join with us in this imaginary exploration project, please be ready to go first thing in the morning.

Everyone should be aware that there are predatory fish and a great white shark leads them. He is about eighteen feet long and can easily sink a small craft.

A small fishing boat was seen a short distance away. The two young men did not realize they were in shark-infested waters.

To make matters worse a huge white was swimming right towards the men. Well we rescued them just in time and we all went home. It was just too dangerous even for a courageous imagination.

It is not likely that any of us will ever encounter this type of a life threatening experience. There will not be sharks, great whites, or sea monsters with violent intent.

Death may come in the peaceful hours of the night while we are sleeping. It will usually come without warning; when it is least expected. There is no need to fear death for Jesus is always near. Death is a reality; so is life by faith in Christ. Jesus saves when we believe.

One Image Equals Two
August 13

We have a very interesting project today that will require some artist skills. This will be a portrait, but it will have to reveal the old and the new changes in a person's life. It will show a sinner's life and then in the same picture a Christian will be the final image.

This really sounds like a difficult project. Let me see if I understand the instructions. We will create one portrait of one person that equals two lives.

If there are any professionals in this group, please come immediately to the studio. Your services are urgently needed. I am really disappointed that no one showed up. It looks like I will have to use my amateur talents to paint this portrait.

First I am going to create the image. A person has volunteered to pose as a model. This is a good Christian that had all the characteristics of a sinner.

The first profile has been completed and now I am moving to the second phase of the creation. Look at this picture. It is one image with the bad and good characteristics on the inside.

The outward appearance shows one person. God looks upon the heart. He knows exactly what is on the inside. A sinner saved by grace can look in a mirror and will see a Christian.

Enticed by Sin
August 14

We have a lot of dedicated fishermen in this group, or adventure lovers of the great outdoors. There is usually plenty of action when we go camping. The survival rate has been pretty good.

There is no need to worry about any boat rides. Today's journey will take us into the forest. We will be fishing the mountain streams for trout. Please bring the waders and any fishing accessories for this outdoor activity.

The place we are going has some really strong water currents. Please be advised that at certain times of the day, the streams are extremely dangerous with high water levels.

We want everyone to be very careful and have a good time. One elderly man decided he would go up stream and fish by himself.

Our safety procedure was to keep everyone in sight. It did not work this time; a better fishing spot enticed him to a more appealing place.

While he was there, a slick rock caused him to fall into the rising creek and he could not get up. We heard his cries for help and he was rescued.

There are times in our lives when we are enticed by the lure of sin. It is sort of like calling us back to our old sinful ways. Resist the devil and he will flee. Just to be sure he leaves, plead the blood of Jesus.

Restore to Life
August 15

Well it is that time again for a fresh coat of paint on the house. This past winter has been especially hard on the board siding. There are places where the paint has cracked and withered away.

The first thing we need to do is scrape the old scaly paint from the planks. We will be working from ladders and scaffolds. All of the old residue will have to be removed.

This is a time consuming job. If everything goes well, we should be finished in one week. Our time will begin early in the morning and we will finish in the late evening hours.

Now that the old finish has been removed, let's begin the painting process. We like to use the paint that already has the primer in it. This saves time and we will still have a good protective coat of paint on the home. We finished in one week. "Thanks for your hard work."

Sometimes we let our lives of faith degenerate to a poor condition. Our normal standard of living has been downgraded to unsatisfactory.

In order to restore our spiritual relationship with God, we need to reapply the blood of Christ to our hearts. It will not hurt to confess our sins all over again. Lives will be restored when we return to our first love, Jesus Christ.

Faith in a Storm
August 16

It was a very stormy day at the old homestead. There were lightning flashes across the sky. Roaring thunder could be heard for miles.

There seemed to be no end to the unrelenting rain. The creeks were swollen and the riverbanks overflowed with the gushing water. Strong winds were breaking tree branches.

This was the worst storm we have had in years. A father kept looking out the small, wire mesh window for his son who had not yet returned from a cross-country hike.

It was extremely dangerous for anyone to be in this type of weather. No one was traveling in automobiles. All roads were closed because of the high water.

Now this young boy was trying to escape the wrath of the storm. He saw a cave on the side of the mountain. If he could only make it to that shelter, then his life would be spared.

After crawling over broken limbs and rough rocks, he finally found shelter in the cave. Soon the storm was over and the father and son were together again.

There are times of severe heartaches when we go through the storms of life. Keep the faith, unyielding to the circumstances that separate one person from the other.

The storm will pass and bring into each person's heart a stronger love and a more sincere relationship.

Never Give Up
August 17

Let's go back a few years to a race. The goal of most of the runners was to finish the course. I am sure there were those in this group whose main objective was to win the race.

There one was young girl on this competition team that had a really strong determination to win. My imagination tells me that all through life she was recognized as a person with stamina and endurance.

She stood out among her classmates as a leader and as person who would accomplish all of her goals in life. Her fellow students looked up to her as their role model. They respected her because of her never give up attitude.

The race was in process and the runners were close to the end. This young lady was in the front position, but the miles and hills bore heavily on her physical condition.

She was utterly exhausted and only a few feet from the finish line. She fell to the ground and could not stand by herself. Rescue workers helped the girl up. Her legs were trembling as she struggled to cross the finish line.

She did not come in first place, but she won all of our hearts. Her attitude in life will be the same one that helps us to cross over onto the hallelujah side. "Never give up."

High Security
August 18

There are many important positions in life that require dedication and trustworthiness. Those who work in banks and other financial positions are responsible to the public. The money is kept in vaults for security reasons.

Some times guards are hired to protect our investments. They are well trained and will use force if necessary. There are many security devices that are located in businesses all across America.

It is good to take precautions to ensure our money is safe. All of this protective equipment is used for our benefit. We have peace when these security measures are in place.

If a thief enters into a facility, then cameras will help identify the perpetrators. Those who are found guilty will be punished for their crimes.

There are protectors of the peace and these law enforcement officials keep us safe from lawbreakers. Policemen protect our lives from those who would steal, harm, or even kill us.

Security is a very important thing in all of our lives. It is really a comforting thought to have someone on guard day and night.

Our best assurance is for God to hold us in His everlasting arms. There is no fear of Him dropping us. As a father loves a child so does He love us. We have peace with God.

Thorns and Nails
August 19

While I was looking out my window one day, a bird had landed in the top of a rosebush. After watching it for a couple of minutes, I saw a nest and it had baby birds in it.

This was an unusual birthplace with sharp thorns all around. I just couldn't see the little birds getting out of the nest without those thorns piercing their small bodies.

The days went by and the mother bird fed the little ones. After a while they were ready for the big test. It seemed like survival training to me, learning to fly from a patch of briars.

So I looked out the window another day and all of the birds were gone. None of them were entangled in the long stems of briars. This is one time that an empty nest was a welcome sight.

Has anyone here thought about our birthplace? We were born into a world of sin. Corruptible things are all around us. The sharp thorns of sin would keep us from living holy, righteous lives.

There is only one way for us to be delivered and that is by the blood of Jesus Christ. Jesus took the thorns that were meant for us. The nails pierced His hands instead of ours. He died so we could live.

The Wrestling Match
August 20

We will be wrestling today a very powerful foe. He has been around for a long time. Those who have fought with him would say that he is the cruelest of all fighters.

We have all met him somewhere along the pathway of life. His main objective is to dominate and rule with fear. This professional defender of evil will do anything to win, no matter how bad the opponents are hurt.

Our enemy is known worldwide by the name of "Satan." Each of us will be in our own personal conflict with him. There is no need to worry about our weak frail bodies against the powers of darkness, the forces of evil.

If Jesus is our Lord and Savior, we will not fight alone. Otherwise we are no match for the vengeful attacks of the enemy.

Christ has all power in heaven and earth. Those of us who follow Him know that Satan was defeated at Calvary. Not only was he beaten there, but in our lives daily as we plead the blood of Jesus.

When we stand with Jesus, the greatest defender of faith, the most loved person in the world, God's beloved Son, the devil trembles at His name.

How can we be victorious in life? Accept Jesus as Lord and Savior. Never go into battle alone. Walk in the light, as Christ is the light of the world. The darkness of evil will have no power over us. All faithful believers will receive the glory crown.

In the Line of Duty
August 21

Early this morning a terrible disaster took place. A policeman was walking at the park. He was probably enjoying the scenery and thinking about his family.

His job was to protect and ensure the safety of all citizens. I don't know how long he had worked on the force, but he was a kind-hearted man who cared deeply about the people he served.

Yesterday there had been a shooting at a hospital. A young man was in police custody when he took the guards gun and shot him. The criminal escaped and was on the run.

No one knew that this morning there would be a fatality at the park. What seemed to be a peaceful walk turned into a terrible tragedy. The policeman lost his life that day. Later this criminal was recaptured.

The family members at the patrol officer's funeral gave honor to him. There were probably words about his dedication and loyalty to the community. The family and all the people who knew him were deeply saddened by his death.

I like to think this policeman received a promotion in heaven. His badge of loyalty here on earth was traded in for a position in God's security force. A policeman fell in the line of duty. A new guardian angel took his place.

The Right Road
August 22

There are many roads in life that will take us to various locations. It is very important for us to choose the right one. Sometimes they will take us to a dead end street. When that happens, we can usually turn around and   drive back down the road until we are on the correct route.

Occasionally we will make a turn in which there is no way back. We can only go so far on the wrong highway and then we have to face the consequences of our choices.

Several years ago a bus was traveling down a major highway. There were a lot of people on this vehicle. The driver made a wrong turn and crashed, killing some of the passengers.

This was a very costly mistake by the bus driver. One wrong turn and families would never see their loved ones again. Those who lost their lives would not be going home.

As sinners we are automatically going the wrong way. It is not too late to turn around and get on the straight and narrow way, which is Jesus Christ.

If we stay on the wrong road, our sins will keep us from going to our heavenly home. Today is the day of salvation. Choose now which road to take. The right road with Christ is life forevermore.

Glory-Land Road
August 23

As we walk the glory land road, each day is an adventure. Our expectations of heaven grow stronger by the hour. We know it won't be long till we are at home with Jesus.

Our Father in heaven awaits our arrival. Keep pressing on. He is patiently waiting for his sons and daughters to come home. There will be rejoicing when we gather around the throne.

The time we have left here on earth will slowly pass into one eternal day. There will be no regrets or looking back to the days that are gone. We are going to keep walking the hallelujah way.

Our time on earth will end when our final sunset has disappeared on the horizon. The graves will not hold us as we are going to rise with the Son.

We are walking the glory land road with peace in our hearts and the hope of glory divine. When the midnight hour strikes, it will be time for our heavenly flight.

There is just a little time left to make sure our garments are pure and white. Our days on earth will soon be no more. Don't be surprised if Jesus comes in the morning, noon, or night.

There is no reason to be dismayed if we never go by the way of the grave, since the glory land is in sight.

Deceivers Among Us
August 24

There are certain times when our true identities will be revealed. This investigation will take us back through the years of our personal lives. There seems to be some identity problems. A lot of character traits have been disguised and we noticed that there are false deceivers among us.

I forgot to mention that Jesus will be the one who identifies each of us. He is the Security Chief and no one will be allowed into the kingdom of God unless He approves of him or her.

It has been reported that some of the people have tried to get into heaven by falsely representing the truth. There is no evidence of the blood of Christ in their lives.

We can go through life doing good deeds, attending church regular, but if we do not know Jesus as our Lord and Savior, then the gates of heaven will not open.

It is time for the truth to reveal the identity in each of our lives. Jesus will not ask us how do we plead. He already knows if the blood was applied to our hearts.

None of us want to hear these words, "I know you not, depart from me." It would be so much better to hear, "Enter into the glories of the Lord, thou good and faithful servant." Apply the blood of Christ and the gates will open.

River of God's Love
August 25

Our journey today will take us back into the mountains. We will be riding bicycles on some of the trails and enjoying the scenery.

A picnic has been planned at the lake. This will be a good time for us to get to know one another. Please come and bring a friend.

The bike riders had already started down the trail. They would be at the lake in a couple of hours. None of us were aware of the life threatening danger.

A young man had been working on his bike. The sprocket chain seemed to be too loose. He thought it would be okay, so he started down the hill with the other riders.

They were getting close to the picnic area when the chain broke and there were no brakes on his bicycle. This seemed to be a death ride. Guiding his bike into the river saved his life.

The river of God's love is constantly flowing. A little guidance from heaven will save our runaway lives. We can keep going down the sinner's trail, riding the death bike.

If we want to be saved, now is a good time to head for the river. God's love for us is revealed in His Son, Jesus Christ. So take the plunge of faith and receive life eternal.

A Crack in the Frame
August 26

It has been noticed by the building inspectors that small cracks have developed in the frame of the building. They do not appear to be very large, but engineers have been called in for a final analysis.

They decided the metal frame is too weak to support the structure. There would have to be some repairs or the building would be condemned.

If the cracks are not welded, the fracture lines would grow and eventually the infrastructure would collapse to the ground.

The welding crew began working immediately on the cracked seams. After several weeks of bonding the metal together, finally the frame was stable. The strength of the building was solid and as strong as ever.

Our lives will also vary in strength according to the small sins that have developed in the framework of our souls. They are just tiny cracks that are barely noticeable. There is no need to worry about them.

We should not take any chances to have our lives completely ruined. One small sin will multiply until our immune systems of faith are demoralized.

It is time to get out the welding rods and let God repair the cracked seams. It just takes some forgiveness from the throne room of grace to restore our moral values. The precious blood of Christ will bind us together with a love that will never fail.

Revisit Old Sins
August 27

We are going to venture into a very dangerous territory. There have been many travelers who have gone back into the dark valleys of despair. Unfortunately all of them did not return to the safe haven of peace and contentment.

This journey is way too hazardous to go by any normal human routes. We have decided the best way to go back in time is to get connected to the imagination travel agency.

Most of the time they have been successful in their retreat efforts. Sometimes they escaped with severe wounds and near death experiences.

What makes this adventure so dangerous is that we have to go back in time before we met Jesus. We will be walking the streets of the outcast and entering into the towns of corruption.

There will be times when the miry clay will try to drag us down to the depths of sorrow and dismay. This trip is a long journey for some of us.

Let's take a short cut and go through the fields of unrighteousness and visit our old sins along the way. The transgression towns will not turn us away.

We have gone far enough, let's all go home. Jesus is calling, "Follow me." Never go back down the corruptible paths of sin. There is no guarantee we will make it back to the safe haven.

God will make a Way
August 28

This would be a good time to go exploring in a new cave that has just been discovered. It is on a mountain slope surrounded by thick brush and rocks. This is a new cave and we do not know how safe it is for the public to enter.

A few explorers tied a line outside to a tree. This would be their guidance system to help them find the outdoor entrance.

Finally the men came back out as a rockslide had just started blocking the exit. Three of the men barely escaped, but one man did not make it. He was trapped on the inside with very little oxygen.

Immediately the first responders were called to save this young man's life. They were about to give up when this trapped explorer came walking down the mountain. He told them how he survived by following a glimmer of light. This led to another escape route.

There are times when we are surrounded by our problems. It seems as though there is no way to resolve them. The one and only solution is blocking the way. When there is no way, God will make a way. When He does, we will be walking down the mountain.

Keep the Stream Flowing
August 29

The valley is dry and the cattle will soon die if they do not receive fresh water from the mountain stream. It has been noticed that the water supply is gradually disappearing.

Farmers in the valley depend on the flow of the creek to keep their livestock and gardens alive. They also need water for their own personal lives.

There have been a few good rain showers and this has been a real blessing for those who live in the valley. The main water source is the mountain stream.

Most of the time when it rains, it is at the very top of the mountain. The streams are usually overflowing the banks and the water supply is in abundance. Valleys do have some rain but not near enough.

Farmers held a meeting; one man who lived on the side of the mountain said there is plenty of water where he lives. His home was right next to the stream.

After a careful investigation, a dam was discovered about halfway down the mountain. Beavers had blocked the stream. All of the tree branches were removed and the water began to flow again.

If the stream of God's love is weaker than before, perhaps somewhere along the line, a barricade was built with some favorite sins. These corruptible things will separate us from the main source of God's love and mercy.

In order to receive a fresh supply of grace, we need to open up the channels of our hearts by the blood of Christ.

One Day Shy of Eternity
August 30

This is a trip that has been planned well in advance. We are going to meet at the airport and we will be leaving first thing in the morning. It is very important to arrive early for security reasons.

Each of us will be scanned or have a body search for weapons or anything that would jeopardize this flight. The security personal will make sure we are properly identified.

If we are late coming to the airport and the plane is already airborne, we will not make it to our preferred location. Get up early, be at the airport on time, just one more thing, and please don't oversleep. We cannot afford to miss this flight.

The plane will be leaving in ten minutes. Some of the travelers have not yet arrived. Please tell the captain to wait for these late sleepers. The flight attendants told us they were sorry, but the plane would leave on time and it did without the slumber people.

We are traveling to our home in glory. Jesus told us to watch and pray. There is coming a time when the careless, unwatchful, sleepers of the faith will be left behind. The last day is wasted, one day shy of eternity. We almost made it.

Entangled in Sin
August 31

The fishermen started out early this morning. They wanted to spend the day at the river. It was reported that minnows were being used to catch Large Mouth Bass.

These men went to a remote spot where some trees had fallen into the water. Seaweed vines were hidden along the bottom of the riverbed.

After several hours of fishing, it was time to go home. None of the men were aware of the vines that had gradually wrapped around the motor.

The boat was held fast by the underbrush. One man cut the vines loose. The men all made it home safely with the catch of the day.

There are times in our lives when we will be entangled in the cares of this world. Our sins are like the seaweed that wraps around us. Jesus is the only one who can break the vines.

Once Christ has set us free, He does not want us to go back into the places where we will be entangled with sin. If for some reason we slipped back into our old sinful ways, plead the blood of Jesus.

"If we confess our sins, he is faithful and just to forgive us our sins, and to cleanse us from all unrighteousness"
(1 John 1:9). It is all right to go fishing, just not in the worldly places of sin.

Keys of Faith
September 1

An old flower vase had been purchased at a flea market. The woman who bought the flower container was real anxious to get home and show it to her family members.

This ceramic piece was not very expensive, as the price had already been marked down to fifty percent off. The flea market vendor was even thinking about throwing it away.

There were no visible dates or signatures on the outside of the vase to identify it as a collector's item. It just seemed like an ordinary glass ornament.

Soon this woman would find out the real value of this priceless treasure. One day she was cleaning the glassware, getting it ready for some flowers.

She removed the dirt that was packed inside the vase. To her amazement, there was a beautiful diamond ring in the clay compound. The value of this ring was about twenty thousand dollars according to my imagination.

The worth of our lives is not seen on the outside, but on the inside of our hearts. There will not be diamonds of material worth.

Our priceless treasure is of a far greater value. We hold in our hearts the keys of faith to the kingdom of God. One day soon our belief in Christ will give us access to the gates of heaven.

Salvation's Exit
September 2

Before we met Christ our travels would take us down the same road to our jobs and other important places. We would travel down the road of corruption, over the bridge of sin, and just past the exit of salvation.

That sounds a whole lot like the highway we used to travel everyday. That is true. These directions are to help us better understand how we missed the glory land road.

As sinners we continued to live day by day. Our routine was pretty much the same as driving down the road. We were consistent in our daily endeavors of sin. Our lives were corrupt with transgressions, but we kept going.

The bridges helped us to stay on our route. There were no interruptions in our sinful lives. We didn't even slow down for these structures. Our driving force of sin was not hindered by any bridge crossings.

There were many times we passed salvation's exit. I am so glad that God did not give up on us. Now that Jesus has come into our hearts, we are going down the glory land road of righteousness.

We are still going over bridges, but without any interruptions in God's grace and mercy. A salvation exit reveals the blood of Christ; we will take the exit by faith and live eternally.

House of Neglect
September 3

There was a small family that lived in a really nice home. The children had all grown up and moved away. The father retired from his place of employment.

He spent most of his time working on the farm. The house was starting to need a few repairs. He would always say, "There is plenty of time; I will paint the house next week."

Even when the roof started to leak and water was dripping in the living room, he promised to fix the roof in a few days. His wife put buckets on the floor to catch the water.

There was never enough time for a fresh coat of paint or shingles on the roof. Tomorrow seemed to be his favorite saying. It was always a false promise.

A house of neglect will soon be a place of ruin. Those who live inside will have to face the terrible consequences. This man could have made the repairs, if there was only enough time.

There is something much more important in our lives. If we neglect our souls salvation, keep putting it off until later in life, a day will come when there is no time left.   God will say, "This day thy soul is required of thee." A later day promise will not hold water.

Drifted Away
September 4

They were in a boat far out to sea, drifting away. Their eternal destiny fades with the evening sun. The bright hopes of heaven disappear into the night. Fellowship with God is a thing of the past.

This story is told for those who loved God with heart, soul, and mind. But somewhere along the way, they pulled up the anchor of His grace and slowly drifted away from Him.

Now they are lost at sea without a guiding light to show them the way. They are all alone in a perilous sea. Occasionally a death angel will fly by to check on the crew.

He does not stay long, as there is still a glimmer of hope that these men will be restored to life, fellowship with God. As long as they are breathing, there is life in their bodies.

God still loved them even though He was forsaken. He reached down to hold the crew in His arms; He gave them a strong, loving embrace.

It was more than the men could handle. They all broke down with tears in their eyes. How could God still love them after the way they treated Him?

His love is a never-ending love that will never fade away. These men drifted away in life, but they came back to God with repentant hearts and were saved again by grace. Drifted away, it is time to come back to Him.

An Old Fire Escape
September 5

Many years ago a fire escape was built on the side of a hotel. This framework was a strong type of metal and it was painted with a really durable paint.

The life expectancy of this unit was about ten years. If the maintenance were performed on a regular basis, then it would last a lot longer.

Over the years this strong fire escape began to diminish with weakness in the frame. The upkeep was poorly done and no one took the time to paint it. Rust and grime had weakened the support system.

An inspector came by to examine this structure. He found that it was too weak in certain parts of the frame. A notice was given to the hotel owner to build a new fire escape.

This one was just too dangerous to be used in an emergency. A person or group of people trying to escape would die in the process or be severely injured.

We need to inspect all of our spiritual equipment to make sure our personal lives are safe and secure from any fires that may occur.

The Chief Inspector is coming by; hopefully everything will be in good order. He will be looking for things of neglect.

If He finds that our lives have deteriorated, He may suggest a restoration of faith or a fresh blood cleansing experience. We all want to escape the fire.

Fiery Furnace
September 6

We are going to a place where a king had the authority over all of his servants. His commands were the law of the land. Those who disobeyed would be punished with death or another type of cruel torture.

All of the people were told to bow down at the sound of a flute or harp and worship a gold image. Anyone who refused would be put to death in a fiery furnace.

Three young men were completely devoted to God. He was the only one they would serve. He tells us in His Word that we are not to worship any graven image.

These brave men knew they would be put to death in a furnace. This was a horrible way to die, when they could have easily bowed to the ground and pretended to worship the idol.

Their dedication and loyalty was to one God, the creator of the world. They were not going to bow down and worship a statue made by man, even if they had to die. "O king, that we will not serve thy gods, nor worship the golden image" (Daniel 3:18).

They were thrown into the fiery furnace. It was heated seven times more, but God delivered them. "Our God whom we serve is able to deliver." The battles of life will be won when we stand for God in obedience to Him. Our faith in God is not pretending nor bowing to a false image.

Keep Running
September 7

Many years have gone by for some of us since we entered the race for life. Each and everyday we ran towards the goal, each of us holding up our cross all the way.

Through the lonely valleys, by the troubled waters, we continued on by God's grace. We endured the storms and trials of life without wavering from our faith in Christ.

There was no turning back to the old sinful ways. Our dedication to God was faithful and true. So we kept running with a determination to win the glory crown.

All of these thoughts really sound good, but the truth is missing from the reality of life. We cannot truthfully say that we have done all of those things.

There were times when the cross was too heavy to bear and we laid it down. Jesus came by to help us pick it back up and continue in life's race.

The lonely valleys of heartbreak and sorrow would keep us from going through, until Jesus stood beside us and healed our broken spirits.

Some storms were so powerful with unrelenting force; we could not go on, unless Jesus would calm our troubled souls. "Peace be still."

We are still running, but it is because of grace. When we fall, Jesus will pick us up and help us the rest of the way.

If we sin, He will forgive us so we can start again. We have not yet obtained the glory crown, but we are still running.

Oil for the Lantern
September 8

One day while camping in the mountains, we needed a few things from the store. It was almost dark and the food market was about half of a mile away from our campsite.

If we took a shortcut along the mountain ridge, it would not take near as long. One man decided he wanted to go down the rocky trail. We told him it was too dangerous.

An oil lantern was hanging on a tree branch nearly empty of fuel. This man took the lantern and started walking through the woods.

A short while later, he arrived at the store and bought the necessary supplies. It was really awkward for him, carrying a bag of groceries, water, and the oil lantern.

The storekeeper offered to take him back to the camp in his truck, but he refused. Back at the camp his friends were anxiously waiting for his return.

Their worst fears were realized when they picked up an empty lantern from a rocky ledge. He had fallen to his death. His lamp had gone out, no oil in the container.

As we travel through this life, how can we make it home if the lantern of faith has gone out? The weight of our sins was lifted at Calvary and Christ fills the heart's lantern with glory. When Jesus comes will He find the fire burning?

Throw out the Lifeline
September 9

Our travels today will take us far out to sea. This will be a voyage on a cruise ship. We were out on the deck one day and the warning system alerted the crew that a man had fallen overboard.

He was a good swimmer, but even the best have died at sea. We saw him struggling in the water.

A lifeboat was quickly lowered into the raging sea. We could hear his frantic cries for help. Every time he went under, his resurface time was longer.

The two rescuers could not put anyone into the water because the sea was too rough. They knew there was a strong possibility of dying themselves in the turbulent waters. It took both men to maneuver the boat.

There was only one chance to save this man's life. If they could throw him a life preserver, he could be saved. But was it too late, the man was under water longer this time. Finally he emerged and was rescued just in time.

Throw out the lifeline; souls are daily sinking in their sins. Their only hope is in Jesus. He will use all of His life-saving abilities to rescue the perishing.

It just takes a little faith to hold on to His nail-scarred hand and receive life. He is the one with the strong grip and He will not let go.

A Thief in the Home
September 10

All was quite in the neighborhood as everyone had gone to sleep. There was one family that lived in the country. Recently they loaded up the van and went on a vacation.

They were unaware of some crooks that had been watching the family. These men were waiting for the right time to break into the home and steal the valuable merchandise.

Most of us have special things in our homes that are very sentimental to us. We care deeply about our personal possessions that were given to us by family members.

When a thief breaks into someone's home, they do not care what they destroy or who is hurt in the process. Their main objective is to rob and to kill if necessary.

These thieves are already in the home, tearing the place apart. Looking for jewelry or anything of value, they will not stop until the home is completely ravaged.

Our enemy (Satan) uses the same tactics to steal from our personal lives. The Bible even warns us about him. "The thief cometh not, but for to steal, and to kill, and to destroy" (John 10:10).

There is a whole lot of difference between him and Christ our Lord. Jesus is come that we might have life and have it more abundantly. Thieves ransack our homes, but our souls are kept by the mighty power of God. Our eternal possessions are always safe in His hands.

Foxes Spoil the Grapes
September 11

Grapes are ripe and ready for the laborers to harvest this fruit of the vine. This vineyard is not very large, as a small family owns it. They went home for the evening.

First thing in the morning, the grapes would be picked and taken to the markets. This crop would be used to buy groceries and pay the monthly rent.

No one was aware of the little foxes that lived in dens a short distance away. While this family was sleeping, these little creatures came out of their hiding places.

All through the night, the little varmints were destroying the vineyard. It is hard to believe these little foxes could cause so much damage.

The farmers woke this morning and they were real excited about the harvest of many grapes. They could hardly wait to get started. Soon their joy would turn into frowns of dismay.

Mangled grapes were hanging on the vines. The crop was completely ruined. Although this family was disheartened, they did not give up. A strong fence was built that kept out all intruders, as long as the family lived.

We need to be aware of the little sins that are hidden in our lives. These little ones could not possibly do any harm to us.

It really depends on how much we feed them. It does not take very long for small innocent sins to corrupt pure hearts and destroy lives.

Search for God
September 12

Our journey today will take us on a flight into the regions of the unknown. We will have to use a little imagination mixed in with the truth of a jetliner, missing at sea.

The airplane took off at the scheduled time. No one was aware of any danger. The communication lines were open between the plane and the airport tower. Everything was working properly, at least for the first hour in flight.

It was required of someone in the cockpit to contact the flight navigation team every hour for security reasons. This was a regular routine for all aircrafts. Safety of all passengers was the highest priority.

The signals from inside the plane to the command tower were essential in guiding the plane to its destination.

Somewhere this flight lost all communications. This airplane with 239 passengers disappeared without a trace in March 2014.

There is danger in our lives of being lost eternally by lack of communication to our heavenly Father. He knows where we are at all times.

If we do not approach the throne room of grace, our fellowship is broken until we seek Him with heart, soul, and mind. We will find Him when we search for Him with all of our hearts.

Walk Away
September 13

There comes a time in life when we have to walk away. An airplane crashed in the field and there were not any casualties in this terrible accident, at least not yet.

A rescue unit was on the way. Hopefully they would get there in time to save everyone from this horrible crash. The pilot was trapped in the plane. His leg was broken and held fast in the wreckage.

Three other passengers were injured but they managed to climb out of the plane and walk to a safe area. They had severe wounds that had to be treated immediately.

The first responders arrived on the scene and gave medical treatment to the woman and her two sons. Other men from the recue unit were trying desperately to save the woman's husband.

Finally the twisted metal was cut loose from around his leg and they freed him from the plane. They were all taken to the hospital for treatment. Later they were released and they all walked away, praising God for sparing their lives.

As we go through life, there are sins that will hold us fast and not let go. They will be fatal if we are not released from the death consequences.

We cannot free ourselves; no matter how hard we try. Nothing but the blood of Jesus will set us free. When we call upon Him to forgive us, then we can walk away, praising God for life and liberty.

Our Best is not a Fraction
September 14

The corn is ripe and everything is ready for the harvest. This will be a day of hard work for the farmers. The old wagon has already been hooked up to the horses.

It will take all day to gather in this crop. So we began early this morning. It is very important to pick all of the corn today, as it is supposed to rain the rest of the week.

We were using a team of horses that had recently been broke to harness. They were fast walkers and we had to work faster to keep up with them. We were about half way through the field, but the wagon was nearly empty.

The corn was in abundance, but we were just working too fast and always trying to catch up to the wagon. Let's slow down and pick more corn.

If we work at a slower pace, the corn will be ready for the market. The sun was starting to set and the truck was rolling down the highway with a fresh crop of corn.

Sometimes in life, we are just too busy and we cannot get very much done. There are so many activities that we just cannot do them all.

We are so fast that our labors of love are like the empty wagon. Give a little here and more over there. How can we give our all, when each job requires our best and only receives a fraction of it?

Walk in the Dark
September 15

Our journey today will take us along a mountain ridge. This will be extremely dangerous, as we will not have a light to guide us. There will not be any light sources on this journey.

I feel like a warning is necessary for this rocky ledge endeavor. Most of us who venture down the treacherous mountain trail will not make it back home.

Only those who fall to a safe ledge or hang on to a tree branch might survive this nightmare experience. There will be plenty of new graves in the valley.

I see some of our good friends have already turned around and speeding away from this horrific event. This will be a normal walk in the dark, except for the life threatening dangers of a perilous fall over the cliff.

The crowd is gradually disappearing and soon everyone will be gone, including me. Is there one person here who can walk in the dark and make it safely over the mountain? There is no one here. Let's all go home.

Let's go back to a real life situation. When we walk in the darkness of sin, we will stumble and fall from grace.

"Walk in the light, as he is in the light, we have fellowship one with another, and the blood of Jesus Christ his Son cleanseth us from all sin" (1 John 1:7).

Is there anyone here who would like to take a faith step into the light? "Praise the Lord!"

A Fall From Grace
September 16

Each of us has a responsibility to help those in need. If we are walking at the park, a person accidently falls to the ground. Our response should be to offer assistance.

Sometimes a fall has caused serious injuries. Perhaps the help of an emergency unit is needed to transport the person to a hospital. A bicycle accident has caused injuries that require doctors to perform surgery on the affected areas of the body.

A really bad fall would be the one where death claims the victim's life. Occasionally a person will be walking a mountain trail, slip on a rock and go over the cliff. A grave will be the final resting place.

There are many ways that falls influence our lives: A casual fall where no harm is done or an injury that requires a doctor's care. The last one is a death fall; it is too late for help after this one.

I believe the worst fall is from grace. A little bit of assistance will get us back on our feet. If our descent is more life threatening, a spiritual touch can restore us to life.

Since there is no help for us in the grave, we should make things right with God while we are still alive. A death fall will occur for our bodies, but our souls will live on in eternity if Jesus is our Savior.

In the Lions' Den
September 17

We are to going to a place today where our chances of survival are very slim. Many of us have been to zoos where wild animals are kept. There are lions and tigers enclosed in cages or running free in a fenced in area.

Today we are going to be on the inside of a den. Hungry lions will be there with us and it has been days since they had a good meal.

If it will make everyone feel more comfortable, Daniel will be the main character in this drama scene. We will be more like invisible spectators in the lions' den. It is easy to be brave when we do not have to confront the wild beast.

Daniel was cast into the den because of a petition that was signed by the king. No one should pray to any God or man for thirty days, but only to the king.

Daniel is with us in the lions' den because he prayed to God, disobeying the king's orders. All through the night hungry lions were walking around. God delivered Daniel from the lions' den.

Satan is as a lion walking about seeking whomever he may devour. He is not in a cage, but is on the outside with us.

We have the same protection as Daniel when we obey God. He can stop hungry lions from devouring a man. Our God will deliver us from all of Satan's evil powers. Keep praying and be very courageous for thy enemy is a defeated foe.

Adopted into the Family
September 18

Today we will be running in a race for a special project. The money raised for this outdoor activity will go to build an orphanage.

The winner's will be the children who do not have any guardians. These little ones need someone to take care of them; a home they can call their own. They need parents to love and hold them.

An administrator of the old orphanage was at the race with two orphaned little girls. We saw them standing there with joy in their hearts. Their hopes for a new life were seen in the tears that trickled down their cheeks.

Finally the race was over and enough money was raised to begin the building process of the new orphanage. The donations and state contributions would be enough to pay for the final cost.

My imagination couldn't resist an opportunity to help the two girls. They were adopted that very day and a short while latter they went home with their new parents.

There is another charity project going on. This one does not involve any money. This is a love endeavor to help the homeless, the outcast, and all of us to have a home in glory.

Please don't leave just yet. God will adopt each person who has a repentant heart. We will become His children and He will be our heavenly Father.

Oil in the Lamp
September 19

A small flickering flame will only give light for a short distance. When the wick is low, the shadows of darkness creep closer. The dangers increase by each passing hour.

A little oil in a lantern will not help a struggling fire. There is no way to see in the night if the oil lantern is no longer burning. The lighted pathway fades away into a dismal day.

Those in the camp are in a distressful mood. Their bright hopes all vanished when the flame was no more. An empty lantern is a sign of neglect.

On the other side of the camp, the campers are rejoicing in pure delight. The flames of hope are glowing, dispersing the shadows far and wide.

A dangerous trail has lost its anger in a gentle glowing light. The lighted pathway gives comfort to the campers from a distressful night. There is oil in the lantern, peace all along the way.

The signs of neglect are nowhere evident. No one is stumbling in the dark or falling by the wayside. The flames grow stronger as the wick is raised higher. Those with oil in the lamp are safe and secure all the night.

We have a lantern that is supplied from the throne room of grace. It is empty at first, with no fires burning. When we give our hearts to Jesus, He ignites the flame of love that is all enduring. The lantern of hope shines brighter still, when we live by faith according to His will.

The Rails of Faith
September 20

Our travels today will have us on an old train, going down the railroad line. The passengers have come from miles around to go on this adventure.

The conductor at the station was calling for the people to load the train. "All aboard." Soon all of us were in our seats ready for the journey. After hours of riding and visiting the tourist attractions, it was time to go home.

We were going down the mountain and leveled out in the valleys. Some of the rails were loosened by a huge rock that rolled over the tracks into the ravine.

It is a good thing we were going slowly when the train jumped the tracks. No one was hurt and all made it home safely.

While traveling the faith rails, occasionally we get derailed from our original course. Everything is going good, when all of a sudden we are off the rails and unable to continue our journey.

We can be derailed by sin or like these passengers it was no fault of their own. Whatever the reason, we cannot go on unless our lives are on the rails of faith in Jesus Christ.

Lion on the Prowl
September 21

An urgent warning has just been announced over the airwaves. A lion escaped from the local zoo.

Everyone is advised to use extreme caution in all outdoor activities.

Please warn the neighbors to stay off the streets and be vigilant to avoid the danger. Only go outside if it is absolutely necessary.

A concerned citizen called the Police Department to inform them about a family picnic at the park. A man and his wife are there with two children. They do not know a lion is on the loose. "Please warn them!"

I hope it is not too late, as the lion moves closer to the unsuspecting victims. This predator is in the underbrush waiting for the right moment to attack.

All of a sudden he springs forward, but no sooner than he leaps, a shot from a rifle drops him to the ground. The family is saved and the community is safe.

There is danger in our lives as Satan goes about as a roaring lion, seeking whom he may devour. Use extreme caution and avoid the sins of a corruptible life. This is where he feeds.

Our best defense is to plead the blood of Christ. Stay close to Him for divine protection. He will not let any harm come to us. Just believe and speak the name of Jesus. Satan will flee back into the jungle of defeat.

Thin Ice
September 22

This year winter came a little early and the temperatures have already dropped below freezing. A fresh coat of snow is on the ground. It was a strong storm that came through last night.

One young man was more concerned about a frozen lake. He thought this would be a really good time to go skating. Without telling anyone where he was going, he headed for the water source.

Since winter came in so early, the lake would not be frozen solid. It is really dangerous to go on a thin layer of ice. Along the edges of the lake, the ice is thick, as the water is shallower next to the bank.

This young man is all by himself and going skating on thin ice. It certainly looks like a terrible accident is just waiting to happen.

The danger signs were all around, but he did not heed any of them. When he was about a fourth of the way across the lake, the ice gave way and he could not save himself. On a lake of thin ice, death will come without warning.

Sin is like the frozen lake; it lures us past the shallow areas with sinful pleasures. When we are too far from shore, the ice breaks and we struggle to stay alive.

Living for Jesus will keep us away from the thin ice. If we do go to far into the deeper areas of sin, Jesus will save us if we let Him.

God Never Abandons
September 23

The family is gone and the old house on the hill has deteriorated over the years. No one lives there now, as it as been condemned by the property inspectors.

There is no glass in the window sections and the doors are barely hanging on. The roof with rotten rafters has collapsed into the interior of the home.

This dwelling was abandoned many years ago. There is no hope of restoring it. The decay has gone deep into the timbers.

A home that is forsaken will not last very long. At one time this old house was new and strong. When the family left, there was no one to take care of it.

An old house on a hill no longer stands. There is a new home that has taken its place. Some of the family members who deserted the old structure have come back to start all over again.

I am so glad that when our lives were in decay, God did not give up on us. There was no fellowship with Him. We did not know Jesus as Lord and Savior. Our sins were corroding our lives away.

Now that Jesus came into our hearts, new lives replace the old. This newness of life will still be strong as the years pass. Our God who loves us so much, He will never abandon His adopted children.

Too Close to the Edge
September 24

We were standing near a mountain ledge, enjoying the scenery. Pictures were taken of the beautiful landscape. Everyone was having a really good time.

The tourist guide had warned us not to get close to the edge. We were following his instructions, at least for a while.   More attention was going to the photography than to the safety of our lives.

It was really a remarkable day to take pictures. The sky had a beautiful array of colors. We were so enthused by the glorious display of light; we did not realize how close we were to the edge of the cliff.

We were only going to take one more picture. There was only one more step to the abyss below. The photographer was just getting ready to move into position. He took the step and began to fall from the cliff.

No sooner had he started to fall, when the guide grabbed hold of him and pulled him back to safety. His life was spared just in time.

There are times in our lives when we might stand too close to the cliffs of sin. We could be so involved in the corruptible things of life that we cannot see how far away from God we have gone. How close are we to the edge?

Back away before it is too late. Repent! One step could be our last or our first one in life eternal with Jesus.

Self-Inflicted Wound
September 25

A self-inflicted wound takes time to heal. I admit my guilt of using a false impression. Deep down in my heart, all I wanted to do was honor the veterans on Memorial Day.

Some of the church members were putting together a video. They wanted a picture of each veteran for this time of honor.

At the time, I did not think I had a picture, so I created a self-portrait using some of my military photographs. Computers are really remarkable for photo creations.

My mistake was creating a self-image that portrayed me as a larger person in the military. It did not show a good profile of the actual time. My intentions were good, but my proportions were terrible.

This was my self-inflicted wound. I was very sorry for my false impression. The following year I gave them a real photo to replace the old picture.

The injury I inflicted was my own. My good intentions turned out to be a lie. The veterans were still honored, but I had lost mine.

Jesus saw that I was hurting on the inside. He came by and wrapped up the wounds in bandages of love. Since then my honor has been restored and I stand proudly with the other veterans of America.

Open the Floodgates
September 26

Our adventure today will take us to a location where a dam is needed to prevent the valley from flooding. We do not have much time, so we had better hurry.

A small valley with thousands of people who live there are unprotected from violent storms and strong currents of rushing water.

A committee decided the best way to prevent this catastrophic event was to build a reservoir. Some of the members were angry because they had to sell their homes, farms, and all property rights to the land.

The vote was cast and the debate was over. Construction would begin immediately. The disgruntled citizens sold their assets and moved out of the valley.

The dam was built and the floods came with a vengeance. Homes in the valley were alienated and people lost their lives.

Worldly cares and sins of our lives are like reservoirs. They let the corruptible sins pass through the gates until our lives are completely ruined.

Our best hope of having a pure heart, undefiled, is to have Jesus' precious blood flowing through the floodgates of our lives.

All of the corruptible sins are washed away. God is longsuffering, not willing that any should perish, but that all should come to repentance.

Escape, Sparks of Sin
September 27

The more wood that is added to a fire will cause the flames to grow higher. If we are standing real close to the heat source, we will be burned.

There are some safety requirements that we need to follow to keep from having severe injuries. Fires are very dangerous and they have caused many casualties.

A good way to avoid these life-threatening experiences is to stay a good distance away from the flames. There are times when we have to get closer to the fire.

It is about to go out and the only way of keeping it alive is to add more flammable materials. A good water source will help prevent wildfires that consume everything in sight. These instructions came too late.

The underbrush is a very dangerous place for a runaway fire, as it will ignite a huge blaze that will consume an entire forest if not controlled.

Sparks drifted off into space and some of them fell into the brittle brush. A wildfire had developed and all the people were running for their lives. Finally the fire department put out the flames with water from the truck.

When sins are drawing us closer to the flames, only the blood of Christ will save us from a burning inferno. How can we escape when the sparks of sin surround us? We need to run for our lives, straight to the throne room of grace.

Drifting on Waves of Sin
September 28

Remember the days when we were on the peaceful shores of God's grace and mercy. Time has gone by with the precious memories left behind.

We do not have time to pray, go to church, or have fellowship with Him anymore. Our joyful days of serving Him are special moments of the past; they also are gone.

There were no goodbyes as we just gradually drifted out to sea. We followed the deadly currents of sin and our ship was tossed to and fro in the corruptible waves of life.

The peace we once had with God is no longer the anchor of our souls. Drifting away more everyday, far out to sea in the darkness of despair with no hope of heaven anymore.

The fulfillment of a sinful life will bring us to ruin as our ship drifts more out of sight. Our ungodly living will bring us closer to the grave, eternal separation from God. It will be too late to return to His love and mercy when death seals our fate.

A person who died at sea with sin as his burial marker left those words in a note on the ship. The captain, who was on the same destructive course, broke down in tears after he read them.

He ordered the men to turn the ship around. "Where are we going, they asked?" "We are going back to the peaceful shore of God's grace and mercy."

Unexpected Grace
September 29

The campers were warned about the danger of having fires. Warning signs were posted throughout the area and the forest ranger came by on a regular basic to enforce the restrictions.

A few dark clouds had formed in the sky. There seemed to be a relief from the drought. A thunderstorm was forming a short distance away.

The forest ranger was even more worried than before. He spent a lot of time in the lookout tower, watching for lightning strikes, small fires flaring up.

His worst nightmare was about to take place. Lightning had struck a dead tree and quickly ignited into flames. The fire was growing at a rapid rate and moving towards the camp.

God was evidently watching over us, as the storm clouds hovered above, it began to rain. The fires went out and our lives were saved. It continued to rain all week.

Sometimes when we least expect it, God brings the showers of blessings to satisfy our spiritual needs. We may be going through the fiery trials; He knows how to extinguish the flames. My God supplies all our needs according to His riches in glory.

Never Castaway
September 30

Our story today is told of a runaway who left his family. His travel adventure was far more life threatening than the home he left.

Flying on a plane is probably the fastest way to get to a certain location. His transportation methods were not the best. Since he did not have a ticket or boarding pass, there were not many options left.

Things are not going very well for this young man. At first he was a runaway, now he is going to be a stowaway. He has chosen a place on the plane where no one would find him.

I would have thought a good place to hide would be in the storage dept. with the luggage. We can eliminate that area, as he is not on airport property yet.

He waits to dark and then scales the fence. An airplane is already fueled and ready to go. This young man heads toward his layaway confinement space. He will be unnoticed the entire journey.

This young man is determined to get on this flight. He climbed up into the wheel well and stayed there until the plane landed. He is very fortunate to be alive. He passed out several times in flight by not having oxygen.

Our adventures will cause us to run, stow, or even layaway, but they will never take us away from God. His love is great toward us, and we will never be castaways.

SOS, Help is on the Way
October 1

There were four fishermen in a boat and they were having difficulties getting to shore. Finally they had to swim for their lives and eventually they all made it to a safe haven on land.

This was a deserted island; no one lived in this remote part of the country. Their chances of survival were slim as the damaged boat drifted upon the rocky shoreline.

When these four men set out to sea on a fishing trip, they did not tell anyone where they were going. Here they are on a desolate island, starving and growing weaker by the day.

If they do not find help very soon, they will perish in a strange land and be buried in shallow graves from the wind blown sand.

Before these men had this boat accident, they had just passed a sandbar in the ocean and it was not very far from their present location.

This could be their only way of escape. One of the men swam to the sandy area and wrote SOS in large letters on the sand. All four men were rescued.

We have the blessed assurance that whether we are in perilous conditions or in peaceful circumstances, we can call on God and He responds immediately to our prayer request.

Call upon God in the day of trouble and He will "Answer thee and show thee great and mighty things, which thou knowest not" (Jeremiah 33:3).

Abundance of Grace
October 2

An old well has supplied water for a family many long years. The old well was running dry and a new one was in the process of being dug.

The well diggers were having doubts about any more water being found in the area. They were thinking about giving up.

One morning the old farmer and his family woke up to find there was no water. The old well had gone dry and the nearest water supply was about a mile away in a lake. Tankers were used to transport water to the farm, until the trucks broke down.

There was one problem after another and the family could not survive without water. No one would buy a farm with a dry well on it.

The farmer told the well diggers to try one more time. Soon a fresh supply of water was flowing from a full well.

There are times in life when the well will go dry and the problems mount up by the hour. Don't give up; just keep digging and believing.

The Bible tells us to cast all of our cares upon God. He cares for us. We have a dry well today; by faith in Christ we will have a full one tomorrow, an abundance of grace.

A Reflection of Christ
October 3

If we could travel back in time, to the days and years gone by, what souvenir of the past would we find? We are looking for one that has precious memories.

This object is old but it contains the new. Please walk with me down memory lane and I will give a few clues along the way.

We will visit the antique shops and walk through the flea markets. Some of these items are skillfully crafted with hand carved displays.

Our favorite songs were broadcast over the airwaves. As the years passed we had many talented singers and new songs along the way.

Let's continue our treasure hunt and see if we can locate an object that is old in appearance but has the new on the inside.

These things are collector's items and we had them even before a TV was invented. We have gone far enough. An old radio is the souvenir of the past. It is old on the outside and new songs are played on the inside.

Let's us take a close look in the mirror of our lives. Our appearance has changed, but our old sinful lives reflect an image of the past. When our sins have been cleansed on the inside by the blood of Jesus, a new image will appear. This one is a reflection of Christ.

Tear the Old Fence Down
October 4

Cattle on a ranch in Texas were gradually disappearing. It was discovered that the old fence needed some repairs. The strands of barbed wire were broken in several places.

A few ranchers were sent out to check the fence line. They noticed that there were places where the cows could easily wander into other grazing areas.

Some of the other farmers had also lost livestock. There was a lot of contention between the landowners and even bitter arguments.

A meeting was held between the ranchers and farmers about the bad fences. This fence line separated the two groups, but they decided to work together to repair the fence. Immediately the fence was torn down and a new one built.

After a short while the new fence was used to secure the livestock. The best thing about this situation was the ranch-hands and farmers became the best of friends.

There is a fence in our lives that separates us from God. This one is not made of wire, but there seems to be barbs of sin that keep us in alienation.

We can have fellowship with God, but we have to tear the old fence down. Jesus will help us, as our best friend. We will have peace with God and all of us will have praising rights.

Prepare to Meet thy God
October 5

There is still a little time to get ready. The final sunset will disappear into the horizon of the night. It will be too late to make peace with God when there are flowers on the grave.

No one knows when death will make an unexpected visit. There will be no announcements to warn us ahead of time. Special notices will not be sent out in the mail.

Our death hour will have no special warning. Who would give it? We cannot rely on our friends to warn us, their life expectancy may be shorter than ours.

None of us know when it is time to go. If we did know, we couldn't prevent it. There is no way we can turn back the clock. The hour of death is unknown.

We know it is coming, so we had better be ready before the grave is adorned with flowers. The time of our departure is near.

Preparation will save us from a life of despair. "What must I do to be saved?" This question has been asked down through the ages. The answer is always the same. "Believe on the Lord Jesus Christ and thou shalt be saved."

When it is time for the funeral, close the casket and bring on the flowers. A soul was saved just in time. Peace was made with God before the death shadows, now there is life forevermore.

Search Diligently
October 6

Please go and search one more time. This is a life or death situation. A person is dying and she wants to make things right with God before it is too late.

My imaginary friend wants to meet Jesus before she leaves. Anyone who knows where to find Him, Please tell Him that He is urgently needed in the hospital.

Her family members have joined in the search. Her friends and neighbors are also searching diligently to find Christ before her eyes close in death.

Now our pastor and all born again Christians know exactly where to find Jesus. Let's all go back to the hospital; Jesus is already there, waiting for us.

We walked into the room and the girl seemed disappointed, as she did not see Jesus with us. The pastor assured her that God is a spirit and those who worship Him must worship Him in spirit and in truth.

She still did not understand. The pastor asked her if she would pray with Him. She agreed, "Lord Jesus, come into my heart. I believe that you died and rose again. Please forgive me of my sins. I right now accept you as my Lord and Savior."

Right before she died, a smile came over her face and she said, "I see Jesus standing at the Father's right hand." We can find Him when we search for Him with all of our hearts.

Break the Bonds of Sin
October 7

One dark night the peaceful tranquility of a family would end in a disastrous situation. There had been a number of break-ins the past couple of weeks.

There were a few homeowners who lived way out in the country. It was a man and his wife who lived in one of these isolated homes. Their children lived in other parts of the state. The mailman was the only person who came by on a regular basis.

Later that night a thief had broken into the home. The couple was awakened by the intruder and confronted him. A fight resulted and the thief subdued the man and his wife. They were tied in chairs and left to die.

The mailman came by that day and noticed the glass in a window had been broken. He discovered the two people tied up and he released them. Later the thief was caught and arrested.

There are times in life when the trespassers of sin will subdue us. We will be overcome by their crafty devices and be bound by deceit and false truths.

Jesus knows when we are in a perilous condition. He breaks the bonds when faith is restored and we commit our lives to Him. When the Son of God sets us free, then we are free indeed.

A Runner has fallen
October 8

The time has gone by and we have endured many things in our lives. We are approaching the finish line of the last mile of the race.

There is not much longer until we pass over onto the other side. The glory land is in sight and soon the gates of heaven will open for the redeemed.

Our hopes of eternity will materialize when we finish the race and a crown of glory is won. Please don't give up; we are almost home.

While running in this race, a runner had fallen. He was so close to the finish line but he was unable to keep going. His injuries were not of the physical kind.

He had fallen from grace. Some of us stopped running to give assistance to our fellow runner. We helped him to his feet, but our efforts were not sufficient to get him back on life's track.

Sins were too many and they were holding him back. We told him about the times in our lives when we too had fallen and God still had mercy on us.

"God is faithful and just to forgive us our sins and to cleanse us from all unrighteousness." This man was revived in spirit and restored to grace.

We all continued the race for the glory crown. God's grace is sufficient to keep us unto life eternal. Let us run with patience and endure to the end. We are almost home.

In God we trust
October 9

We have a very special project that we are going to be working on today. If anyone has any good wood carving tools, please bring them to the woodworking shop.

We are going to be carving a wooden nickel. Some of the more intricate details will require a flexible shaft tool with small grinding bits.

Let's get started. The first word to be carved is, "Liberty." This refers to our freedom, "one nation under God, with life, liberty, and the pursuit of happiness for all."

Our forefathers had the right idea. All the battles that were fought and all the blood that was shed reveal our heritage. This carved word is the symbol of our freedom.

Let's move on to some more words, "In God we trust." This is a wonderful thought that the whole nation will recognize our true existence is in God, the creator of the world. He is the one who has complete authority and rule over us. "God bless America."

We trust Him with our lives for He has all power in heaven and earth. He is our deliver, mighty fortress, and everlasting Father.

When God is for us, who can be against us? The wooden nickel we just carved tells the entire story, "In God we trust." We all said, "Amen!"

Unbreakable Cords of Love
October 10

We will need all of our survival skills to make it safely home. Stranded in the mountains when a bear approached the camp and scared the horses away.

One young man was injured by a fall when he tried to escape the wild animal. He suffered severe lacerations from the bear attack. His broken leg was put in splints and his severe wounds were bandaged to stop the bleeding.

The bear was killed and they did not have to worry about any more vicious attacks. Their main concern now was to save the life of this young man.

A trip back down the mountainside was just too dangerous. There was only a slight hope that he would survive this ordeal.

An old wooden raft was seen in the raging waters below. These men pulled it onto the bank and took the rope and bound the logs tightly together.

This was their only chance to ride the rapids to one of the main base camps. There were times when all of their lives were in danger, but they survived and the man was saved.

When we are on the strong currents of life, drifting in the raging waters, we are safe and secure by our faith that is in Jesus. Sometimes He holds each of us a little closer to ensure we escape the turbulent trials of life.

His bond of mercy will never fail. The strong cords of His love cannot be broken.

Home Fires Burning
October 11

We are expecting the Lord to come in the clouds of glory. When He comes will He find the home fires burning and oil in the lantern?

There is still a little time to trim the lamp and gather more firewood. Please don't take too long as He might come today. No oil and a fireless faith will not be a welcome sight.

When the flame is flickering, the fire is about to go out. We do not know the day or hour when Jesus will come.

A strong flame burning is a good indication that we are looking for Christ to come and believing He will very soon. When He does we will be ready to go with Him.

If the fire of life is burning low, the faith flame is about to go out, go quickly to the throne room of grace. He will restore a fading life.

There are some people who never built the fires of faith and still others who let the fire go out. Please don't despair, Jesus' love and concern is for all. Just go to Him for a fresh supply of grace.

Soon the fire will be burning and all of our hopes and expectations will be realized when Jesus comes again.

We still have the same warning; keep the home fires burning and oil in the lantern. Jesus is coming, ready or not.

A Shortcut to Heaven
October 12

Finally the big day of the race had arrived. Awards and cash prizes would be given at the finish line for first, second, and third place winners.

This was a cross-country marathon and all runners were required to stay on the designated course. However, there were three men in this race that was determined to win, no matter what the consequences.

They were familiar with this area and they knew of a shortcut that would eliminate several miles and about two hours off of the finish time. Their plan was to start out last and then they could easily disappear from sight and reappear in front of the other runners.

The race has begun and about four thousand runners were participating. The men took the detour as planned and then came back into the race at the precise moment.

They had just crossed the finish line to claim all three prizes. The policemen were there to present the awards. All three men received silver metals, bright shiny handcuffs and a special escort to the county jail.

As we journey towards heaven, there are some shortcut runners in our midst. They use kindness, good deeds, and many wonderful works, but the blood of Christ is missing. He will tell the imposters, "I never knew you." Depart from me, ye that work iniquity" (Matthew 7:23).

Glory-Land Express
October 13

Let's go back in time to settlers having new lives and building new homes. They moved west with the other pioneers. They were determined to go all the way.

They had already made many sacrifices in this journey and they were not going to turn back. The weeks of travel turned into months and even years for some of these wagon train riders.

The weather conditions were extremely hazardous. Snowstorms and freezing temperatures caused the pioneers to build temporary homes.

When the first signs of spring appeared, the wagons were loaded and these committed pioneers began their journey again.

They traveled over rocky terrain and crossed rivers. Finally the last mountain was crossed and these settlers, each of them began a new life.

We also are on a journey; the old sinful life is left behind. Our new life in Christ began when Jesus came into our hearts.

If we are committed like the pioneers of old, someday soon we will be in our brand new homes in heaven. We will not be leaving on a slow moving wagon train, but on the glory land express flight.

Fervent Prayer
October 14

The drought continues in a local community and there is no forecast of rain in the near future. Grass has changed from a bright green to a hazy brown.

The beautiful landscape has deteriorated from lack of moisture. Everything is beginning to die; crinkle leaves hang lifelessly from the branches of the trees. The people also will perish if there is no rain.

Something is really amazing as the people are kneeling down to pray. It is not just a few residents of the valley. It looks like the whole community is bound together in prayer. The cries for rain ascend to the throne room of grace.

God cannot turn away from the sincere heartfelt pleas. "Call upon me, and I will answer thee, and show thee great and mighty things."

A sound of thunder rumbled in the air and everyone ran outside. Dark clouds hovered above and it began to rain. Soon the lakes were full and the streams flowing again.

Life was restored to a lifeless community. God answers prayer even if it is just from one person. "The effectual fervent prayer of a righteous man availeth much" (James 5:16).

Stir up the Coals
October 15

The coals of a fire have not been turned in a while. It is cold in the room; more heat is required.

There is a little doubt of the flame still burning. The residents would say it is completely gone out.

When we see all the people shivering and trying to get warm, we would probably agree, there is no fire. If our hands were cold and we had to wear coats on the inside, the evidence would show a fireplace that had grown cold.

Let's all walk over to the coals and see if we see anything that reveals life. While we were standing there, no flames were burning. It was starting to get a little colder.

All of us were not convinced that the fire had gone out. One person knelt down and stirred up the coals. Immediately sparks flew into the air and they slowly faded away.

Then we all saw the bright embers beneath the coals. After a few minutes, the flames were burning higher and more lumps of coal were added. Now we have a really nice fire and everyone is comfortable in the home.

If in our lives the coals of faith have not been turned, then our fellowship with God will grow cold. Faith is the flame that keeps us believing all things are possible. Without faith it is impossible to please God.

If we are still shivering and cannot feel the warmth of His love, it's time to stir up the coals and draw near to Him.

Unload the Wagon
October 16

Several years ago wagons and horses were used to transport the produce to the markets. The farmers have been working in the fields, getting ready for the trip to town.

It was a peaceful day, as the farmers ride down the dusty road enjoying the scenery. The horses were pulling a really heavy load and it was hard for them to get the wagon of melons over the hills.

After struggling on this rocky terrain, finally we were past the rough hills and the rest of our trip would be on good level land.

The market place was about a half of a mile away. We stayed there all day and sold all of the melons. Our return trip home would be a lot easier without the excessive weight to slow us down.

We are on a journey to the glory land, across the hills and through the valleys. If we are carrying the heavy weight of sin, we cannot get over the mountain.

It is time to lighten the load. Jesus bore the weight of our sins on His shoulders at Calvary. Since He took the burden and set us free, there are no sins to carry. The wagons of our corrupt lives are empty and we are going home through the valley of repentance.

Slippery Slopes of Sin
October 17

We had better stay inside today, as the weather is too bad for us to get outside. The roads are too slick to drive on and most of the shopping centers will be closed for the day.

State trucks were on the highway late last night, putting chemicals on the road. Snowplows were also utilized to keep the asphalt surface clear.

A father and mother were deeply concerned about their son who had left his state of residence to come for a visit. He lived along ways off and had been traveling for hours.

His parents kept looking at the clock and staring out the window. They were worried deeply about the safety of their son. He was already four hours late.

This family feared the worst, but they were overcome with joy when they saw their son walking up the driveway. He was all right.

When we live in the hazardous conditions of sin, Our Farther is deeply grieved about the sinners who have not made peace with Him. They are on the slippery slopes of disaster.

There is joy in heaven when we come walking up the highway with Jesus, as our Lord and Savior.

Wait on the Lord
October 18

It was a beautiful day as the hikers followed the trail through the mountains. A young couple failed to see the direction marker and they wandered from the group.

The sun was beginning to set on the horizon. Soon it would be dark. All of the other hikers had made it safely to their destination and they set up camp for the night.

When the sun came up, they realized the couple was nowhere to be found. Immediately a search party was formed.

A forest ranger was called to help find the two individuals. He brought with him a couple of bloodhounds for the search.

After several hours of walking through the mountains, the dogs picked up the scent and were hot on the trail. The couple was found in a rock shelter, waiting for someone to find them.

Whatever situation we have in life, our best source of action is to pray and wait for help. Whether we are lost in the forest or facing one of life's battles, we will prevail if we wait.

"Wait on the Lord: be of good courage, and he shall strengthen thine heart: wait, I say, on the Lord" (Psalm 27:14).

Stay on Course
October 19

Our adventures will take us to many wonderful places. We are going to be sailing across the ocean and each of us will be in our own vessel of life.

Our main objective is to stay on course, never wavering or losing sight of our eternal destination. Let's begin our heavenly journey.

The sails have been unraveled and the anchor is back on deck. A strong wind is blowing. It will not be long till we cross over to the other side.

There are many things along the way that will interfere with our eternal plans. Pleasure seeking towns will try to lure us into corrupt situations. It is really sad, but we have already lost many in the fatal waters of unrighteousness.

Remember we must stay on course and be on time. Those who have turned aside have to catch up, but first they have to forsake all sinful conditions.

The flag of truce is waved and some of them rejoined the fleet to the glory land. We have not yet reached the shore of eternity, but by God's grace we are still pressing on.

It will not be long now. We are traveling through this world and there are many things that will corrupt our lives, but our love for God will sustain us unto life eternal.

Don't Give Up
October 20

A baby bird had fallen from the tree to the ground. It had not yet learned how to fly. A person came by and gently placed the bird back into the nest.

The disturbed mother was fluttering all about. Finally she calmed down when her baby was resting peacefully in the nest. She was probably more fearful of us than the fall.

We thought the bird was in danger, when it could have been the first flying lesson. Sometimes we interfere with nature and slow the learning process down.

A day or two later, the little ones courage had returned. It walked out onto the limb and spread its wings wide to fly. After a few tries, the bird was flying across the land. Before this bird could fly, it had to go out on the limb.

There are times in life when we are just beginning a new job or a special task; we need special training or a little more encouragement for us to be successful.

Remember that first bicycle ride and the falls from it, or a horse back ride and more falls. Each time we fell, we had to get back up and start again.

There are some falls when we couldn't get back up by ourselves. Our heavenly Father reaches down and gently picks us up and gives us courage to try again. Don't give up!

Cougar Attack
October 21

We started to go for a walk, but we found out the park was temporally closed until further notice. The park ranger came by and told us about a cougar attack.

Earlier this morning the encounter took place. This would have been the scene of a horrific tragedy had it not been for a brave young man who almost lost his life.

A young woman was riding her bicycle at the recreational area. All of a sudden a cougar sprang from the underbrush. The woman was knocked off of her bicycle and the wild animal tried to kill her.

Another person on a bicycle saw this brutal attack. He dismounted from the bike and found a big stick and began beating the mountain lion.

The woman was able to escape, but now the man had to fight for his life. He quickly grabbed a few rocks and hurled them at the beast, hitting it in the face. The puma ran away and was killed later that day.

The man risked his own life to save the girl. How much more did Christ do for us to save us from our sins? He died so we could live.

He took our place, became our substitute, and died on an old rugged cross for us.

Grounded in Jesus
October 22

The storm is passed and the old tree is still standing. Down through the ages in all kinds of turbulent weather, the forces of nature could not make it yield.

Today it stands strong with roots in the ground; they go deep into the earth and hold fast to rocks. The strength of the tree must be in the roots that spread out underground. They have a strong hold and they will not let go.

Severe storms have lifted houses from their foundations, but this old tree is steadfast, unmovable, it defies the elements with enduring strength. Once it was a little thing, swaying in the wind.

The storms came with a vengeance, but they could not loosen the hold of this young tree. Over the years it continued to grow and fight many hard battles. The tree is older now; its age is beginning to show.

There is no weakness in the tree as it became stronger with each passing storm. A tree that stands strong in the field with limbs of praise to the creator will not falter or disengage the roots of a sure foundation.

Oh, that we would become as strong as the tree with our lives grounded and settled in Jesus. We are constantly growing, always praising God with arms lifted high to our creator.

When the trials of life are over, we will still be standing on the rock of ages.

Force the Door Open
October 23

An elderly man, John was taking care of the farm. He lived by himself out in the country. A friend of his came by every once in a while and talked to him about Jesus.

They always had a good conversation and the two would part company. The Holy Spirit had brought conviction upon John, but he would not ask Jesus to come into his heart.

One day John was working inside of his home and the doors were locked. He was upstairs painting the ceiling when all of a sudden the stepladder shifted and he fell to the floor.

His leg was broken and he could not get up. His friend, Jim came by and stood at the door, knocking, but no one came. He started to leave when he heard the cries for help inside.

Jim forced the door open and then he saved the injured man's life. Later when the two were visiting, somehow the conversation went back to the locked door.

Jesus is knocking at the door; He will not force His way into any one's life. The Holy Spirit was drawing

John again, but this time the door was open and Jesus came into his heart.

Christ stands at the door, patiently waiting. He wants to save us from our sins, but we have to open the door.

Flames in the Night
October 24

On a cold wintry night an airplane was flying over the mountains and the plane crashed. Four passengers and a pilot were on board when it went down.

Immediately they had to find shelter or they would freeze to death in the bitter cold temperatures. One of the passengers found a cave and everyone gathered together on the inside.

A box of matches was found in the emergency pack. Soon a small fire was heating up the room and keeping the people alive.

All through the night small branches were placed on the fire to keep it burning. If the fire died, there would be no chance of survival for those who were on the plane.

Helicopters had been spotted in the area, but the recue unit could not see the people in the cave. It appeared as though they would die unless they could get a fire started outside of the cave.

The fire was blazing in the middle of the night when the helicopter crew found the people and rescued them. Lives will be saved when the faith fires are burning bright.

Those who are still in the darkness of sin will find a rescue is on the way when we let the flames in each of our hearts reveal His love. No one can see a light in a cave, but place it outside and souls will be saved. "Ye are the light of the world."

Fresh Supply of Grace
October 25

While working on the farm, sometimes we have to go on errands to the mall. We have a supply list of all the things that are needed. The buckboard wagon is ready to roll.

This is our regular shopping time. All of the necessities for daily living will be acquired on this trip to town. We will get enough food supplies to last the entire month.

Today is Ralph's birthday and the family has decided on the gift they want to buy him. So Amy and Jill headed toward the hardware store. A nice plow was in the building next to the display window. The purchase was made and it was loaded onto the wagon.

Ralph would be really surprised and overjoyed with this new piece of hardware. Since his old plow was worn out and broken down, this new one would be a great replacement.

Soon the garden was plowed and a short while later fresh produce was in abundance. A new plow and hard work brought forth a good crop.

God supplies all of our needs according to His riches in glory. He blesses us abundantly on a daily basis and He is not hesitant about giving a special gift to help us prosper all through life.

The bounty of His love extends into the future and we are always nourished by a fresh supply of grace.

Big I and Little u
October 26

Many battles have been fought over the years with casualties of men and women in all wars. We are going to go back in time to a major battle of the "Big I's and little u's."

This is a war where humility meets pride, and the final winner will prove that there is a living God who is able to deliver.

Let us look at the profile of these two opponents. The first one appears to be weaker in strength. He is just a youth, not even old enough to be in the military. His qualities are meekness, gentleness, and kindheartedness. This little u represents humility.

I know there are spectators among us that are wondering if this is a real battle with blood shed and the loss of lives. Who would send a boy to war? In a few minutes we will find that one opponent will die.

The other profile is a man of war from his youth. He is a man that takes pride in his size. His main features are arrogance, conceit, and superiority. We call him the "Big I," and he is looking down at this youth-humility.

Let the war begin. David, the "little u" places a stone in the sling and hurls it to the giant's forehead and kills the man of pride-the "Big I." I wish I could be more like you!

Self-Sufficient
October 27

A ship out at sea was taking on water and sinking rapidly. All of the people on board would be saved, but they had to let the lifeboats go. Paul promised them life.

Since it was Paul who told them to release the boats, they obeyed this man of God. The ship was going down, water overflowed onto the deck, and the people were swimming for their lives.

Lifeboats drifted away and planks from the ship were floating in the water. Some of the men were holding onto pieces of the wrecked vessel, struggling to get to shore.

Finally they made it, and the people on land took care of them. The promise came true, as no one lost his life. Shelter and food was also given to the survivors.

God has promised us life eternal in Christ Jesus. Keep holding on, for God is faithful. The lifeboats of our sinful lives let them go, or we will crash on the rocks of destruction.

When we are in the troubled waters of life, trials all around us. Keep holding on to the promises of God who never lies.

Sometimes we have to let go of our self-sufficiency before we will trust Him to deliver us. Let go of sin and take hold of His hand. Soon we will be on heaven's shore.

Faith Lines Open
October 28

The home is a desolate place when the water stops flowing, no fresh water to drink. It was on a cold wintry day when this disaster took place.

My home was not the only one affected by this calamity. There were many unfortunate victims in the neighborhood. Cold temperatures had brought the feelings of frustration and anxiety into our lives.

The problem actually started with a deep freeze. Water lines had frozen and many homes were affected by the cold weather. Sometimes it takes hours to thaw out the pipes.

Normally the water flows through the lines and waits patiently at the faucet. When the handle is turned, fresh water begins to flow.

That was not a very interesting day, as we had to go outside in the bitter cold and thaw out the lines. No wonder there was frustration throughout the community.

After hours of working on the line, the water began to drip and then there was a full stream. Fresh flowing water satisfies our thirst and removes all anxiety.

Faith is like an active faucet, giving life and restoring our fellowship with God. If there is no motion, no activity, we may die of spiritual thirst.

Let us keep the faith lines open. Thaw the lines if we must, but never leave them dormant. When God turns on the faucet, will He find us available for service?

Meet Me at the Cross
October 29

A special meeting is planned for today. It is not very hard to find this place. When we tell someone else about a certain location, we tell him or her how to get there.

Sometimes a map is drawn with instructions. We all know GPS is an excellent guidance system and it is used worldwide in travel situations.

Leave the maps and high tech instruments at home. They cannot show us the course of action to take for our spiritual journey. We are going to meet at the cross.

There may be some concerns about the travel arrangements. Since this invitation is going out to people around the world, what source of transportation should we use?

If we were traveling overseas, then a recommendation would be an airplane or a ship. Motor vehicles would be an excellent choice for local residents.

This special meeting place at the cross does not require any of those things. Cancel all flights, voyages, and any other means of transportation.

Jesus will meet us at the cross when we are ready to see through the eyes of faith an empty grave and believe He has risen from the dead.

We will meet Him daily at the cross when we believe for us He bled and our sins are forgiven. A good place to meet Him is in each of our hearts.

Follow Jesus
October 30

We need to be careful whom we follow on the pathway of life. Many lives have been swayed by the influence of actors, movie stars, and professional entertainers.

It is possible that we will imitate a special character on TV and pick up some habits that will cause bodily harm later in life. Occasionally the false impressions of someone's life will lead us astray.

Sometimes we hear on the news about a famous person who overdosed on drugs. We are sorry for them, and we are fearful of the followers who are walking in their footsteps.

We only have one life to live, let us be careful with the person who we choose to follow. There are good role models in the entertainment business, but we need to proceed with caution or our lives will be ruined.

The best choice we can make in life is to follow the Son of God. Jesus will never lead us astray or give us a false impression. There is nothing fake about Him; He is the Christ, the Savior of the world.

Those who follow Him will not walk in darkness, but will walk in the light and we will have the hope of life eternal. One life, whom are we going to follow? Jesus said, "Follow Me."

Fox in the Hen House
October 31

One of the hired employees met Bill in the driveway and told him about the disappearance of several of the chickens. Also a lot of the eggs were destroyed.

Days went by and there were no disturbances in the barnyard. Bill called off the watch and the farm hands returned to their daily routine.

After a while the criminal activity continued and the villain always left clues on the floor of the hen house. There would be broken eggshells and chicken feathers lying all around.

One day the culprit trapped himself and was caught trying to escape. This would be his last free meal. A fox was trapped in the fence.

All of those delicious chicken meals increased the size of the fox. He became so big that he could not get through the small hole in the fence.

The Bible tells us very plainly that our sins will find us out. We tend to think that our little sins are not very important.

It just takes a short while of indulgence before the small sins become larger ones. Our way of escape is hindered by our increase in sinful activity. One sin when fed equals many.

Wet Matches Burning
November 1

A man is stranded on the mountain and the snow is coming down. Ice crystals hang from the tree branches. It is hard for Steve to stand on the slippery slope.

He prayed that God would provide a shelter from the bitter cold. A short while later, Steve was standing in a large cave.

He only had a few matches and they were wet from the sleet and freezing rain. Without any heat to keep him warm, he would probably freeze to death in this cave.

While Steve was shivering in the cold, he thought of a scripture. "What things soever ye desire, when ye pray, believe that ye receive them, and ye shall have them" (Mark 11:24).

He knelt down in the cave and called upon God. He told Him about his family, his little girl and son that needed a father.

Tears were flowing down his cheek as he mentioned his wife's name. "Please God, I want to see my family again; I want to live."

Steve took out the wet matches and believing God would ignite the fire, his faith was rewarded with a burning flame. A short while later, he was at home with his family.

"All things are possible to him that believeth." Ask and we shall receive. There is no room for doubt when God says, "What things soever ye desire, believe."

Sneak out the Backdoor
November 2

The mountains have fresh snow and the ski slopes are already open. After driving all day, we finally arrived at the lodge. During the night, the snow continued to fall.

There were four of us in our group and we were warned not to go out into the snow, three of the men sneaked out the back door and started up the mountain on the faded trail.

None of us had snowshoes and somewhere along the way, we got off the trail and were knee deep in snow. No one was there to help us. The temperature was dropping and if we stayed there much longer, we would all die.

Back at the cabin, the fourth man had told the resort owner and soon a rescue unit was searching for the three men. Finally the men were found and they were barely alive.

We have been warned about the consequences of sin. When we sneak out the back door, sin is hiding in the shadows, waiting patiently for us.

Our only chance of survival is the precious blood of Christ. When we are deep in sin, God's grace does much more abound. But if we wait too long, will it be too late?

One Call for a Bailout
November 3

Several years ago a young man had a bad habit of visiting the county jail. It was more like a free room and board. He didn't come to see anyone special, but he was real familiar with the jail keeper.

Most of the time it was for minor offences like fighting or disorderly conduct. Randy would usually stay a day or two and after he sobered up, the sheriff would let him make one call.

This jail visit usually occurred on Saturday nights and Sundays. The only time Randy would call his parents was when he needed someone to bail him out of jail.

The crimes seemed to be getting worse and jail time was even longer. Tom and Mary would not give up on their son. Every night they prayed for him and on Sundays requested prayer in church.

One night the phone rang at Tom and Mary's home, they expected the worst. It was Randy on the other end and he told them they would never have to come and get him again.

He also told them that Jesus came into His heart and saved His soul. When Christ comes into our hearts, there will not be any more jail time, unless someone else makes a call to Randy for help.

Call Jesus first and the jail cell will be empty.

Life Expectancy
November 4

Life expectancy, who can count the days, how long on earth will we stay? Each of us has a different life span. A few years or many it is not in our control.

Death is no respecter of who is laid in the grave. A small child or an adult will not be turned away. A coffin is made in all sizes and it will fit the poor or the rich.

We are just passing through; our time on earth is limited. All the good we can do, we had better do it now. There is no time to waste; we will not pass this way again.

Our existence here is only temporary. We will not be granted an extension to prolong our lives into the future. Live for today, tomorrow may never come.

It is time to stop worrying about our life expectancy. Death is also a temporary place that will not hold us very long. When Jesus comes in the clouds of glory.

"The graves will open and "The dead in Christ shall rise first: then we which are alive and remain shall be caught up together, to meet the Lord in the air: and so shall we ever be with the Lord" (1 Thess. 4: 16,17).

We are just passing through a temporary life span to one that is eternal. The gates of heaven will open wide for the believers. All the good we can do will last for eternity.

Shelter of His Love
November 5

Frank and his wife Jane were lost in the mountains. They were hikers who loved the great outdoors. Every year they would choose a different location for their journey.

They were hiking and left the main trail when a bear and cub appeared suddenly from the brush. The mother bear quickly became aggressive to protect her cub.

She stood on her hind legs and was growling furiously at Frank and Jane. The mother bear did not attack, but that could change any moment.

The terrified hikers began walking backwards very slowly and watching the bears every move. They had not gone very far when the mother bear decided to defend her cub.

Frank and Jane were now running for their lives. Their only hope of survival was to cross a narrow swing-bridge to a shelter on the other side. They survived the attack and this is where they were found.

When God looks down from heaven, the best place for us to be is on the straight and narrow path, following Jesus. If we are in the shelter of His love and grace abounds in our hearts, we will not be hard to find.

There will be rejoicing in heaven when we are at home with Jesus.

See You in the Morning
November 6

The saddest words are spoken at the end of life's journey. Tears roll down the cheeks of the parents as they say goodbye for the last time to a wonderful son or daughter.

A short while later the Pastor comes by to offer his sincere condolences and to lead the family in prayer. "Our Father and our God, we come into your holy presence in the name of your Son Jesus Christ.

We pray that you will lay your holy hand upon the family. Comfort their hearts and give them peace. Hold them close to you with a loving embrace. Bind each one together with the blessed assurance of being united again in heaven, in Jesus name, amen."

Rest in peace, it won't be long till Jesus comes. A glorious day that will be when our Savior takes us home to be forever with Him. We do not know the hour of His coming; before He comes, we may be at the bedside giving our final farewells.

Goodbye is one of the saddest words on earth. We are not going to let that word be the final closure of a dying loved one. "See you in the morning." Our hope is in Jesus and our home is in glory. He is coming soon.

No Turning Back
November 7

The athletes from around the world have gathered on the track. Everyone is waiting in anticipation for this sporting event to begin. The signal is given and the men and women begin the race.

After a while some of the participants are lagging behind. They are running at a slower pace and a few of them have dropped out completely.

What happened to their motivation? Somewhere along the line, they lost their enthusiasm and determination to win the prize. Let's take a closer look at their lives.

They seem to be looking back for something and they are not focused on the race at hand. The excitement of the race has faded and the glory crown is not in sight.

The cares of the world and the corruptness of sin are luring the runners back into sinful pleasures. They prefer the temporary enjoyments of sinful living and cannot see the permanent things of life eternal.

The glory crown is just ahead; keep running to the finish line. Never turn back to the old sinful ways. It is really hard to win a race if we are looking back and not forward.

If we turn back to our sins, how can we win the crown of righteousness, if our hearts are impure? We cannot win unless Jesus' precious blood purifies our hearts again.

Tragedy at the Circus
November 8

Thousands of people went to the circus that day. A terrible tragedy took place in the arena, as nine acrobats were injured from a fall.

The apparatus that was holding them broke loose and these professional entertainers fell about forty feet to the ground. All of the injured were expected to make a full recovery.

There are some things in life that we would trust to hold us, especially if we commit our lives to them. The acrobats had full confidence in the metal framework. They did not have any doubts about this strong metal structure holding them.

It is possible that strong chains were also used to support the apparatus. The circus was closed until an investigation would reveal the cause of this tragedy.

There are many situations in life where we have to hold on until someone can rescue us. The object we choose may not be the best choice, but if it is a matter of life or death, we will take whatever is available.

When it comes to spiritual matters and there is a possibility of us falling. We can have full confidence in Jesus that He will never loosen his grip on our lives.

When we commit our souls to Him, He is able to keep us unto life eternal. Keep holding on, He will not turn loose.

A Wild Man's New Life
November 9

Today we are going to visit an imaginary character; a person of interest that we would like to meet. He was well known around town and throughout the community. All of his neighbors spoke well of him and the little children loved to be with him.

A day would not go by without him helping someone along the way. No matter if it was a little child or an elderly person, he loved each one and was always doing good deeds.

Every Sunday he would be at church worshiping and praising God. We just imagined the life of this man after he met Christ. Let's see what kind of man he was before he met Jesus.

His name was Legion because he had many devils. No one wanted to be around him for he was a wild man. Little children were scared of him and the people would go out of their way to avoid being in his presence.

He didn't live in a house, but in tombs. They bound him with chains and he would break the fetters. Jesus cast the unclean spirits out of the man and gave him a new life.

Oh, it is a blessed day in our lives when Jesus walks by and touches us. He gives us peace and forgives our sins. Our wild sinful nature is replaced with loving-kindness.

Old Sins and Divine Grace
November 10

The old things fade away as new ones take their place. Many years ago farms had no electricity or running water. Candles and kerosene lamps were used as the main light source.

Wood was used as a good source of fuel to heat the kitchen stove. Other rooms were heated with coal stoves. This was a comfortable heat and it kept the rooms warm.

The old things have gradually disappeared, we think about the horse and wagon days. This was the main type of transportation to town, church, and other places of interest.

There have been many changes over the years. Vehicles move up and down the highways. It is a rare occasion to see horses and wagons on the roads. They have been relocated to pastures and farmland.

We can see a lot of changes in our surroundings, but what about the people? The old sins that existed from the beginning of time are still the same.

Our personal appearances have changed over the years and the blood of Christ has purified our hearts. Once we were in bondage to the old sins; now Christ reigns in our hearts by faith and we are free. Sinful living is replaced with righteousness and divine grace.

God Bless the Veterans
November 11

This is a special time in our lives when we honor the veterans of our great country, America. These brave men and women answered the call to serve and fight for our liberty.

Many of them never had a chance to return home and hold loved ones in their arms again. They fought for our freedom and some of them paid the ultimate price.

We hold in our hearts deep respect, love, and the utmost appreciation for our men and women of the armed forces. May we never forget their commitment to serve, live, and die for their country so we can have a better life and be free.

America is the greatest country on earth and it is because of the men and women who gave all they could give for life, liberty, and the pursuit of happiness for us.

Their faithfulness and dedication continues today. These brave veterans never give up and we will never stop honoring them. One thing is for sure; freedom is not free.

Today we honor each veteran for his or her loyalty and commitment to the United States. Their love for America is so strong that they will stand beside her, live to protect her, and die to save her.

We want to thank all veterans for their service to our great country. "God Bless the Veterans of America."

How much do you love me?
November 12

We have a very important question that each of us would like to ask Jesus. "How much do you love me?" Let's travel back in time and see how the answered is revealed.

He was beaten with a whip (a cat of nine tails) thirty nine times. Many of the victims died before they even got to the cross.

He was placed on the cross with His arms spread wide and spikes were driven into His hands and feet. He was dying on the cross for you and me.

A crown of thorns was forced upon His brow and blood was flowing from His wounds. He was being crucified for your sins and mine.

Jesus is revealing His great love for us by giving His life to save us. When Jesus was on the cross, we were on His mind. He was thinking about us.

If it were not love, would He have stayed on the cross? "Greater love hath no man than this, that a man lay down his life for his friends" (John15: 13).

If it were not love, would God have given His own Son to die such a horrible death? "How much do you love me?" Jesus spread His arms wide on the cross. The answer is plain to see, this much and He died for me.

Closer to Home
November 13

We are on the highway of life, traveling toward our destination. There are many miles to go, but each one we are a little closer.

Soon the lights of home will appear when we drive through the gate. It won't be long, so keep driving. The hours slowly pass, after a while the days turn into weeks and months into years.

We are driving down the highway and enjoying the beautiful scenery along the way. This is a lifetime adventure, but we are closer everyday to our new home.

A hitchhiker is just ahead, trying to catch a ride to a place unknown. Normally we don't pick up strangers, but this one time wouldn't hurt.

He was a well-dressed young man and he just looked like someone we could trust. It was not long before we were going in a different direction.

He persuaded us to take him to sin city. Once we were there, the cares of the world took us deeper into sin. We were a long ways from home and we were not getting any closer.

The directions in life are easy to follow, but if we take our eyes off of Jesus we will perish. It is not too late to turn around. God's grace abounds when we forsake our sins. Just ahead are the lights of home. No more distractions please.

When We Fail to Pray
November 14

Early in the morning when the sun is just beginning to shine, we are starting a new job. A couple weeks ago we had an interview with a clothing company.

The personal manager talked about absentees and people who are late coming to work. One other thing he mentioned was the personal appearance of the employees. Their dress codes were of the highest standards. Everyone was required to look his or her very best.

Today is the first day of the new job, but we slept a little longer than usual. A fresh pot of coffee was on the stove, but we accidently spilled it onto our new uniforms.

There was not enough time to change clothes or finish breakfast. So we hurried out the door and the glass broke on the way out.

Once we were outside and about to get in the car when we noticed a flat tire. Our dirty hands and soiled uniforms were not a very pleasant sight. We were fired that day.

There are many dramatic things that can happen in our lives. If we fail to take the time to pray, our journey through the day may be a disaster.

If we prayed, those terrible things might not have happened. Even if they did, we would still have peace with God.

Exalted Above Humility
November 15

There are certain events that happen in our lives that leave us with an unsolved mystery. We are faced with a reality and a dream that seems so lifelike that it is hard to distinguish the real from the fake.

Whether it was in the day, this live event took place, or in the darkness of the night an illusion is formed in the mind, we do not know.

Our story begins with a high-level position offered to a man or woman. The consequences could be fatal if either one is incapable of fulfilling the obligations.

After a few days of considering the benefits and thinking about the job requirements, a decision was made to take the career advancement.

A short time later, the burdens seem to be too heavy to bear. The responsibilities were more than expected. Those involved in the promotion were not ready to be exalted into a more reliable experience.

If they continue with this high level position, deep sadness will occupy the mind and discouragement will bring sorrow and grief to the affected victims.

A dream or is it real, we want to know. The mystery is unsolved when each of us take on a position that is higher than we are capable of performing. We are not to become so highly exalted that we loose our humility along the way.

Jesus is too Far Away
November 16

How strong are our affections to win the glory crown? The race will be difficult at times. Occasionally we will have to slow down to adjust our pace.

If we go too fast and get ahead of Jesus, faith and hope will not respond and our heart's desire will be like a fire that has gone out. Our motivation to win will fade when Christ is no longer in sight. If we cannot see Him, then we have gone too far for grace to keep us.

Discouragement and despair will weigh us down and take us to the side roads of desolation. Without Jesus as our constant companion, we will be as those wandering in the wilderness or the blind stumbling in the dark.

It will really be a disappointing time if the crown of life is just ahead and we fail to finish the course. It is hard to claim the prize when we cannot find the way.

If we are going to fast, it is time to slow down and restore the fires of faith with Jesus in the lead, follow Him. Adjust the pace, slow down if we must, but never give up. There is only one way to win this race;

follow Jesus and the light of His glory will show us the way.

If we are too far in front or too far behind, our hopes of glory are obstructed because we cannot see Him and the fire of faith goes out. We cannot win if Jesus is too far away. When we draw near to Him, He draws near to us.

Strong Current of Sin
November 17

Two fishermen were going fishing at the river. This time of year the current was stronger than usual and the water more turbulent as a result of strong winds and excessive amounts of rain.

These fishermen had a fairly large boat and they thought it was safe enough to use in the water. So they loaded it up with their supplies and fishing gear.

Early that morning they were going down the river to a more peaceful place where the water was calmer and the fishing trip would be more enjoyable.

The wind was not as strong now. There was still one more place in the river that had strong currents. This is where the accident happened. The boat turned over and the two fishermen climbed on top of the hull. Eventually the boat floated free from the current and the men were rescued.

We are traveling through this life and not necessarily going fishing, but there are some places we need assistance to get through the rough places of turbulent times.

The worst conditions are sinful living. This is a really strong current that will cause us to perish, unless we are rescued by a first responder, Jesus Christ.

Earthly Riches
November 18

It won't be long now, so dig a little deeper. This drilling process has been an ongoing operation for many years.

The cost was tremendous as a family of five invested all of their life savings to bring this valuable resource to the surface. The banks have refused to loan any more money.

As a matter of fact, the foreclosure papers have been written and tomorrow is the final day. Eviction notices will be given and the family members will be homeless.

Early the next morning, the bank officials met at the farm and were starting to sign the paper. All of a sudden there was a lot of commotion in the field; horns were blowing and men shouting.

They ran outside and saw oil gushing out of the ground. It would certainly be a wonderful thing to strike oil, pay off all of the debts, and have money to spare.

All of the money in this world cannot buy the one thing that is needed the most in our lives, peace with God. *"What shall it profit a man, if he shall gain the whole world, and lose his own soul" (Mark 8:36)?

We can have earthly riches and still be poor in the sight of God.

Locked in the Past
November 19

There seems to be no escape from the dark ages of the past. The days and years are gone, but the memories remain. It is a terrible thing to be locked in this confinement area.

Everyday we try to escape the thoughts that cannot be erased or eliminated from our minds. It is a cruel torture that will not let us forget.

Our heart's long for the day when we don't have too look back over our shoulders and see if we are being followed.

We have had some days where we almost escaped and we were running for our lives. It seemed as though we were being tracked by a GPS system.

The violator of our conscience was always on our trail. No matter how fast we ran or tried to hide. We were always found and placed in the chains of eternal regret. This culprit who has been after us for many years is the past.

When we keep looking back, we see the things behind us. Look straight ahead to Jesus and there will be no image of the past. When we see Jesus, the past is a forgotten memory.

Water is contaminated
November 20

A chemical had leaked from storage containers. The river was contaminated and no one was allowed to drink the water. There was one family that lived out in the country and they did not know the water was polluted.

That morning the cistern handle broke and Bill took it to the tool shed to weld it. Meanwhile back in the house, Sarah, Bills wife went to the river to get some drinking water; she had not been warned of the contamination.

The cistern was fixed and fresh water was taken into the home. But was it too late as Sarah was very sick. First responders came by and told Bill about the water.

While they were there, Sarah was given assistance for her condition. It was not known if she was going to live or die.

A short while later she was feeling much better and she told her husband that she had eaten some berries that caused her illness. No one in the family drank the water. My imagination gave a sigh of relief.

The contamination of our hearts is caused by sins that flow like a river, polluting our physical and spiritual lives.

A thorough cleansing requires the blood of Christ. When that happens we can all say, "We are feeling much better now."

An Empty Bucket
November 21

The master of the house wants two men to go on an errand. Jerry and Frank are given empty buckets. They are told to go to the river and fill up the containers and bring the water back home to him.

Jerry, he quickly filled up the bucket, but Frank left his empty. The master was not pleased with the results so he sent them out into the fields to work all day in the scorching hot sun. Neither of them was allowed any water.

The next day the master gave two empty buckets to the men and told them to bring the containers back full. Jerry filled up his bucket just like before and brought it to the master's home.

Frank had a change of heart since the last time. He filled up the bucket and was delivering it. There were some children along the way that were very thirsty. Frank gave each one a drink and his bucket was empty again.

He thought the master would be angry, but instead he was well pleased. Many lives were blessed by Frank's kind deeds. His bucket was empty but the fullness of his heart was filled with love and compassion.

It is better to have an empty bucket when our talents are used for God's glory than to have a full bucket of selfish conceit.

Jerry had enough water for himself, but no one else. God gave him one talent and he did not use it.

A Divine Connection
November 22

A powerful storm moved through the area and it left a terrible path of destruction. Snow mixed with freezing rain and sleet continued to fall. Robert and his wife Jill lived with their two children in a cabin in the mountains.

They had lost power and were dependent only on the fireplace for heat. The wood supply was slowly dwindling away. After a while the fire had completely gone out.

Strong winds had caused the snow to drift up against the doors and fallen trees also blocked the entrance. The family could not get to the woodshed and bring more wood inside.

Finally the storm was over, but Robert and his family were freezing in the bitter cold temperatures. If they did not receive heat very soon, they would die.

The power company was busy restoring the electricity to the community. A rescue unit was trying to get up the mountain to the family, but the sleet and ice made it impossible to reach them.

There was only one chance of saving their lives. The power line was connected miles away from the home and a miracle took place; the family was saved.

There is only one way for us to be saved in this life. Jesus will make the divine connection between God and us. He is our intercessor who restores the broken lines of faith. Christ removes all barricades and obstacles of sin that separate us from God's grace and mercy when we ask Him.

Bloodhound on the Trail
November 23

A young girl has disappeared from the neighborhood. Ronda lived with her parents in a home in the country. She was eighteen years old and loved the great outdoors.

It was starting to get late as the sun was beginning to set on the horizon. The parents were more worried this time because the family had planned on going to a wedding of a close relative.

A call was made to the police department to report a missing person. The mother was frantic and convinced the officer to bring a search team to look for their daughter.

Shortly a K9 unit arrived with bloodhounds to follow Ronda's trail. Immediately the scent was picked up and the dogs were running through the mountains.

They came to a creek and the dogs lost the scent. It was dark now and the policemen were thinking about calling off the search until morning.

Just as they started to leave, they heard Ronda's cries for help. Her ankle was sprained from a fall. Soon she was at home with her family.

When it comes to our sins, we leave a really good trail. We don't need bloodhounds to track us down. Our sins will eventually catch up to us, unless we are in the stream of God's love and mercy.

God's Power Over Sin
November 24

Throughout the neighborhood crimes have been on the rise. A day does not go by without someone being affected by the sinful conditions.

The police are active in the investigation and they are trying to control the daily occurrences of corruption. There are some reports that some of the policemen are involved in unlawful activities.

Thieves have broken into homes and stole jewelry and other valuable items. These crooks are under the influence of a gang leader that is very ruthless and cunning.

Some acts of violence have been in the daytime, people's homes, and in public places. The courtrooms are full of couples seeking divorces.

There have been numerous arrests, but the administrator of all these disgraceful acts is still on the loose. No one has been identified as a suspect.

Even the people in church suffer the consequences of past circumstances. They have suffered affliction and terrible scars from their encounter with these villains.

We know now who is responsible and it is "Sin." Where there is sin, there is also grace and it nullifies all sinful conditions through the blood of Christ.

Sin is not a superior force that cannot be controlled but is under subjection of God's mighty power. "Go and sin no more."

Faith's Battery Recharged
November 25

Lately we have had a lot of trouble starting the car. Early the next morning the car was packed with camping gear. The family was ready to go.

Today the old car started, but no one noticed the dim dashboard lights. After a while we arrived at the campsite.

Soon this camping trip would have us struggling to save our lives. A storm had set in overnight and it rained for three days.

The camp official came by and told everyone to get out now. Mudslides are forming and it is too dangerous to stay. As usual we were the last ones to leave, but this time the car would not start.

The battery was dead. Quickly the battery cables were hooked up to my car and to the boat. The engine started and we drove to a safe area.

There are times in our lives when we have difficulty escaping the problems of life. It seems as though we are in the mudslides about to be overwhelmed by the forces of destruction.

We need to keep our spiritual battery charged at all times. If we are weaker than usual, than we need to have faith's battery recharged so we can go home.

Second Chance
November 26

Two men and a dog were on a fishing vessel in the ocean. Dark storm clouds were starting to form overhead as the wind was getting stronger.

The large boat began to sway back and forth in the turbulent waters. Finally the storm was over, but the boat had significant damage.

The men had to abandon this sinking vessel. They tried to release the lifeboat, but the mechanism was jammed. There were no lifejackets or a raft to save the men.

A short while later, the fishing boat had disappeared out of sight into the depths of the sea. It seemed as though the men and the dog would die in the ocean.

One of the men who didn't really believe in miracles, prayed anyway. He asked God for a second chance. A short distance away there seemed to be a cross on the horizon. It was the staff of a ship. All three of the survivors were rescued. The name of the vessel was "Second Chance."

As we travel through life, it is always good to have a first chance, especially when we are trying to make peace with God.

He may give us a second or many more opportunities, but we never know which one is the last. If there is one life preserver, don't give it up and wait for another.

Thanksgiving Day
November 27

Many years has gone by since the proclamation of Thanksgiving Day. This was a time when the Pilgrims and the Native Americans gave thanks to God for His divine providence and care.

He was recognized as the sovereign creator, a God of goodness and mercy. The bounty of His love was seen in the harvest of crops, abundance in food supply, and the people worshiped Him with heart, soul, and mind.

Somewhere down through the ages, attitudes have changed and some of the people's visions have become distorted; the same reverence is not shown to God.

If our vision has been blurred, we need to go back to the years long ago, and sit down at the table with the Pilgrims and Native Americans, give thanks unto God.

Since it is not possible for us to travel back in time, God will restore our vision when our hearts are made right with Him. If we cannot see God's loving kindness, Christ precious blood will purify our hearts so we can see clearly.

This Thanksgiving Day, bless God for His abundant mercy and goodness which continues throughout the ages. Love Him with heart, soul, and mind.

Thank Him in all sincerity for divine grace. Blurred vision, it is time for a heart checkup.

Too Late to Pack
November 28

The days of our lives fade with each passing hour. When the sun sets on the horizon or it rises at the break of dawn, no one knows the time of our departure.

Life is so precious; hold onto the memories of loved ones passed away. Live each day as if there were no other. Love God with heart, soul, and mind.

Soon we will cross the river onto the shores of eternity. Until that day comes, keep holding on to the blessed assurance of life everlasting.

Let's all go for a walk and see what the day has in store for us. It was a peaceful time at the park; we enjoyed the scenery and then we all went home.

During the night when everyone was asleep, a tornado came through the neighborhood and homes were destroyed. This was the final hour for some of the residents. There would be new graves on the hill.

The storm came so quickly that no one had time to prepare for the devastation. There were no warning signs. It was too late to pack personal things and leave.

Jesus is coming in the clouds of glory. Wait patiently for His return. The day is quickly approaching. We do not know the day or the hour.

If we have made peace with God, anytime is acceptable. Many warnings have been given, but how much of the faith baggage is packed?

Overcoming Hurdles
November 29

All along the pathway of life, we will have many obstacles that we have to overcome. Athletes from around the world have had these experiences.

The race has already begun and the runners approach the first hurdle. A young girl, Sharon accidently fell when she was going over the obstacle.

She quickly rose to her feet and continued down the track. There was still a possibility that she could win the race, but it seemed like her chances were slim.

If she gave up at the beginning of the race, this failure would hold her back in life until she could overcome the emotional stress of giving up.

Some runners have fallen and accepted defeat; they never raced again. One hurdle and a fall, but it was too many to get back in the game.

Sharon went on to finish the race; she still had a good score, but it just wasn't good enough to win. However, that did not stop her from entering other races. She won some and lost others.

When we walk away or call it quits. We have higher hurdles to overcome than if we stayed in the race. Discouragement causes us to lose our motivation and enthusiasm to try again.

Discouraged in life, but not defeated. We can do all things through Christ, which strengthens us. Encouragement will turn a fall into victory.

Arise from the Shadows
November 30

We are going far away into the mountains where the eagles build nests and raise their little ones. This will be an adventure that will help us to rise above the shadows of despair.

When the eagle is hungry, she will descend to the lower heights so she can see a rabbit, playing in the field. This mother bird has a family to feed.

Sometimes it will perch on a tree and look out across the land. If there are no animals to be found, a flight over the water may produce a salmon. This eagle found that it was a good day for fishing.

Returning to the nest with the catch of the day, but to the eagle's dismay, an eaglet was missing from its resting place. Quickly the eagle searched all around and soon saw the little one on the ground below, hiding in the shadows.

The baby bird was not hurt, but it way crying for it's mother. A rescue took place and the eagle lifted the little one out of harms way and flew back to the nest.

When we are in the dark shadows, no way to escape, Jesus will lift us to higher ground. There is peace and safety in the glory of the Son. Please don't despair; soon we will meet Jesus in the air.

The Wagon Trail of Sin
December 1

We are going to travel on a wagon train to go out west and build homes in the valleys and on the mountains. There will be rivers to cross and rough terrain along the way, but each of us has a strong desire to begin a new life.

Traveling in the summer time was difficult, not knowing when the next rain would come or where to find the next river. We never gave up, as the hopes of a new life kept us going.

Autumn was the best time to travel, but the terrain was really hard on the wagons. We had to fix broken wheels ever so often, but nothing would stop us from our quest of having new lives.

Wintertime came and we had to stop for a while and live at the fort until the weathered cleared. Winter was just about over when we started again on life's adventure.

At the beginning of spring everything was coming to life. We all rejoiced as we crossed onto the land where our new homes would be built. It is a blessed day when we can have a fresh beginning, start all over again.

So it is in our lives today. When the old sinful ways are left behind, the journey ahead is glory divine. We would like to know, when does life begin?

The day and the year for each of us is different, but we would all agree, when Jesus came into our hearts and set us free. Where the wagon trail of sin ends, life begins.

The Candle of Faith
December 2

A little candle is in the window and the flame is burning low. The small fire struggles to stay alive. It gives just a glimmer of light to keep the dark shadows away.

The hours slowly pass and very soon darkness will control the night. At one time the candle was tall and strong, but the hours have passed, leaving a weakling to fight life's battles.

The shadows become a little braver and get ready to attack; they are just waiting for the right moment. They have already grown in size, as they are much larger than the small glimmering light.

Even a sparkle, a little light from a dying candle will keep us from stumbling in the night. We are the suspected victims.

There have been many falls in the darkness and they have caused serious injuries. When it is dark, we cannot find our way.

If this small flame goes out, an elderly man at the top of the stairs may miss a step and fall to his death. All of a sudden the flickering fire is brighter, as a new candle replaced the old.

The dark shadows will come again, but if the faith candles are burning bright, we will not fall from grace. A flickering flame grows stronger still when Jesus is near.

Keep our Eyes on Jesus
December 3

It was a normal day at the park; athletes were practicing for a soccer match. One person there seemed to be having more difficulties than the others.

She would kick the ball, but it would not go in the intended direction. Janice tried a few more times and she was getting more frustrated with each attempt.

Finally a coach, who was standing by gave Janice some encouraging words. He saw that she was very nervous and took her eyes off of the ball right before she kicked it.

There was not anymore time for practice, as the soccer match had begun. The scores on both sides would vary by a few points. Trophies would be awarded at the end of this game, as it was the last one of the season.

Janice went onto the field to replace the top kicker, who had sprained her ankle. Janice's team was one point behind and only a few seconds remaining in the game.

The players moved down the field and the ball came to Janice for the last shot. She kicked the ball and it went straight into the net. Everyone was so proud of Janice, as she held up the trophy.

The competition of life will be discouraging at times, but we need to keep our eyes on Jesus. The final effort for us to achieve our goals will be a crown of life in glory.

Fearful of Deep Water
December 4

We cannot stay in shallow water and learn how to swim. Chances of drowning are very slim in shallow areas. Sometimes it takes a catastrophic event to move us into the deeper elements of life.

A young man was fearful of the water. His friends would come by and ask him to go swimming. As much as Jim wanted to go, he was just too fearful.

Several times Jim would walk into the shallow water, but as soon as he got waist deep he would begin to panic. He would calm down when the water was below his knees.

One day he was walking by the riverside, enjoying the scenery when he heard cries for help. A small boy who was swimming alone was having cramps in his leg. He was drowning.

Jim was the only one who could save his life. The cries for help inspire us to leave the peaceful shores and go out into the deep waters to rescue the perishing.

Listen, the cries for help are all around us. Fear will keep us in the shallows when souls are sinking deeper in sin. Let us go a little deeper with prevailing love to bring the perishing to Christ. Shallow waters arc full of regrcts. Dccp watcrs: sins forgiven, souls saved, and lives are blessed.

Faith Comes by Hearing
December 5

When we go to church or Sunday school, we hear some very important things that help us along the pathway of life. Every time we hear a sermon or the

Word of God is read, we receive something very special in our lives.

It is very important that we listen very carefully to the words that are spoken. If we want to go to heaven, we had better pay attention.

Just any old words will not affect us. There are many books in libraries and bookstores that are interesting to read. We buy them to obtain knowledge and for the pleasure of reading them.

It appears to me that we have entered into a mystery of hearing the Word of God. We all would like to know, where does faith come from? I have already given a number of clues.

Let's examine faith a little closer and listen more intently to the words that are spoken. When we have faith, we will trust and believe in God.

We have been in suspense long enough. I want to thank everyone for listening and believing the words that were spoken. Where does faith come from? It "Comes by hearing, and hearing by the Word of God" (Romans 10:17).

Personal Response Required
December 6

Suppose a letter came in the mail sent from the throne room of grace. It should have arrived in the mailboxes around the world. No one was excluded from this personal invitation.

The address of each individual was carefully chosen to ensure no one was left out. There has never been any letter like this before. Read the address and make sure you have the right one: "Whosoever will, come, Love for one and all, anywhere in the world, 24/7."

I believe we are all in agreement that each of us has the correct one. This would be a good time to get acquainted with the Son of God. Some of us have alrcady met Him. We know He is the Christ the Savior of the world.

Since this is a personal letter, Jesus will deal with each person individually. Each of us will have a chance to respond to His salvation plan.

If we choose to live for Him and then for some reason we slip back into sin, He will not turn us away. Notice on the envelope, "Return unto me." We want everyone to have the same privilege of making things right with God.

Send all replies to: Creator of the World, Personal Response Required, Express Delivery, Heaven's St., Love 4u

Trapped in the Mine
December 7

The miners went to work one day unaware of the terrible tragedy that would claim about three hundred lives or more. It was at the beginning of a shift change.

At the last report about one hundred miners are still trapped inside the mine. An electrical unit exploded, causing the accident.

Special equipment is brought in to help in the rescue operation. There is a slim chance that some of the workers are still alive.

Oxygen is pumped inside of the mine to keep the employees alive. The families of the miners wait outside, as the rescue operation continues. There were survivors at the time of the explosion. I do not know how many.

This mine is about a half of a mile underground. We are hoping and praying that there is another entrance to the shaft. Rocks and boulders have to be removed.

The excavating team works day and night, drilling holes and trying to make an escape route for those trapped in the mine. We hope that many more lives are rescued from this death trap in Turkey.

There are times in life when we are trapped in the confinements of sin. We cannot get out unless there is divine intervention. An escape route is made possible by the precious blood of Jesus. Death may claim us, but faith in Christ will be life forevermore and a home in heaven.

Daily Inspiration
December 8

My hearts desire is to write words of inspiration to help others along the pathway of life. Grace comes from above and I know what Christ has done for me. He came into my heart many years ago and forgave me of my sins.

I know that time is short and we are just passing through. Life on earth will end and time will be no more. If we can show kindness, others will see Christ and follow Him too.

There are times in life when we all need inspiration to pick us up when we fall, when we stray, or we just need a friend who will stand beside us.

My imaginary and true stories will help others find Jesus as the greatest friend of all. He is the one that will never leave us, no matter how severe the storm.

He will stand beside us and if need be, He will calm our troubled souls, "Peace be Still." Each of my micro stories contains a truthful, spiritual thought.

We might go on an adventure, a journey into the past, or find a lost treasure, but each inspirational page will inspire us to love God with heart, soul, and mind.

As God inspired me to write, I hope He will also inspire you to accept Christ and live for Him. "Be of good courage, and he shall strengthen your heart" (Psalm 31:24).

Special Moments of Prayer
December 9

Time alone with God will give us grace for the day's journey. Fellowship with Him is a relationship of unending mercy. We are bound together by the Holy Spirit.

Take a few minutes to meditate on His goodness, thank Him for His never-ending love. When we take the time to pray, all heaven rejoices when from our hearts we give Him praise.

It just takes a few moments to call upon His name and throughout the day we will have tranquility and peace, all because we took the time to pray.

A good time to meditate, to come into His presence, is in the morning at the beginning of the day. Some people have found that noon is a good time to meet with God in prayer.

Still others have found the evening hours at the closing of the day bring peace and contentment for the presence of God all the way.

Whatever the time or the place of our special moments with our heavenly Father, we will find that grace always abounds with unwavering love.

His love is great toward us and He looks forward to being with us, no matter if it is day or night. We come into His presence in Jesus' name and God welcomes us with a holy embrace. He is never too busy to hear our heart's pleas. Let us pray with Jesus, "Our Father and our God."

Jesus gives us Peace
December 10

An overcast sky is soon covered with dark clouds. A thunderstorm is moving into the area. An outdoor activity is ruined by the terrible weather conditions.

A family having a picnic ran for shelter to escape the drenching rain. They were very fortunate to have a place of refuge so close by.

The storm was becoming more severe as the wind was also picking up. Lightning flashed across the sky and the roll of thunder followed with a voice of anger.

This shelter was in the picnic area and it was built with cobblestones. The rain beat hard on the roof as if it were trying to force its way into the dwelling place.

Strong winds came with a vengeance and they tried to rip the door from the hinges, but there was no breaking into this shelter. The storm was determined to bring misery and sorrow into the lives of this family, but it failed.

We have a gentle reminder that Jesus is always close by. He is never so far away that He cannot shelter us from the storms.

Trust in Him and there will always be peace in our hearts. "My peace I give unto you." Let not your heart be troubled, neither let it be afraid" (John 14: 27). The world did not give us this peace; neither can it take it away.

Peace with God
December 11

I know it will soon be winter with strong winds and snow covering the ground. Sometimes I just like to travel back to the peaceful times in life and meditate on God's love and mercy. A lake is a place of serenity for me.

There is a lake out in the country. It is a favorite place for those who love the great outdoors. This is a wonderful place to get away from the cares of the world and leave the worries and troubles behind.

Take a fishing pole, bait, and enjoy a day of fishing at the lake. Whether the fish or biting or not, it does not matter. We just want to get away for a little while. Enjoy the scenery and take a few pictures.

Occasionally a mother duck will swim by with little ducklings following her. This is a peaceful time that we feel the gentleness of nature.

While enjoying God's wonderful creation, we have peace in our lives that passes all understanding. God's love never dies. His love is the same through all the ages.

It never changes with the weather, even in a harsh winter, or storms of trouble and strife. Spring brings back the memories and God gives us peace throughout the winter, all the days of our lives. We have peace when we make things right with God.

The Choice is ours
December 12

All through life we will make many decisions. The choices will not always be the best for our benefit. Let's all go to the bank this morning.

We will observe some choices in action. There are two people and they both need to make a withdrawal from the bank. Their methods are entirely different.

The first one comes in and holds up the bank. The money is placed in a sack and he runs out the door to escape capture. That didn't work out too good as he was caught by the police and had to go to jail for his crime.

I believe we would all agree his way of withdrawing money was not a good choice. The other man came into the facility and requested a withdrawal and the money was given to him.

He peacefully walked out the door and casually went about his business. He had the same choices as the thief, but we know which one is behind bars.

All of us have a very important decision we need to make about living holy, righteous lives, or continuing down the path of corruption.

Sin takes us to the bank of evil intentions and like the thief we will be punished for our crimes. When we choose Jesus as our Lord and Savior, we go to the bank of salvation and receive life eternal.

Blank Page of Sin
December 13

We are going back in time when the pages of our lives were filled up with sin. The years have gone by and we accumulated many sins.

They were of a variety that contained everything imaginable. Each of us held our own personal collection of favorites in our possession.

There were times when we shared these special attributes with friends and personal contacts of interest. It was not uncommon for us to selfishly yield to temptations request.

Since there were so many varieties and assortments of sins, there was no fear of there ever being a shortage. It seems as though the warehouses were full, an abundant supply of disreputable things.

These pages reveal many dishonorable facts and immoral conditions that pollute the sanctity of life. Lies seem to be the chief aggressor and the leader of the pack.

I don't really know, since the documents were so untruthful and camouflaged with conceit. Sin has deceitfully invaded our personal lives.

A page of special interest has appeared that has caught our attention. This one is blank, what does that mean?

When Jesus comes into our hearts and forgives our sins, all the transgressions are gone and we have a new life in Christ. Sins are white as snow, just like this blank page.

Little Sins and Giant Waves
December 14

There were some people out in a boat and it was pulling two skiers. At first the waves were very small, as the large boat was a long ways from shore.

Small waves are not harmful to anyone, but when they grow in size, they can become extremely dangerous. Two fishermen would soon be struggling for their lives.

It all started one morning when James and Robert put their small fishing boat in the water. They had planned on staying all day at the lake.

The two fishermen cast their lines into the water and were catching some really nice fish. Neither of them noticed the waves were getting larger and their boat was beginning to sway back and forth.

The skiers were on the other boat now, and this vessel was traveling up and down the lake at a high rate of speed. These teenagers were trying to create really strong waves.

Finally they got too close to James and Robert's boat and it flipped over. The teenagers kept going, as they did not know they had caused an accident. A short while later, the two fishermen were safe on shore.

Sins are like the small waves barely influencing our lives. We do not realize the danger until the full impact is forced upon us by stronger sinful waves. A little sin can create a giant wave.

The Blood Trail
December 15

Our imaginary journey today will have us on a blood trail. Each of us needs to be diligent in our search for a man's life is at stake. It has been reported that He was found guilty of certain charges.

The evidence shows that each of us is responsible for the offenses committed and that He is an innocent man. It is best we hurry along; there is no time to waste.

The dark hour of death is quickly approaching. This man will die in our place for our punishment. We are the guilty ones with many transgression and sins committed.

I just hope we arrive in time. Finally we get to the place of His execution. We are too late as Jesus is hanging on a cross, the blood dripping from His wounds.

If we had only arrived earlier, we could have prevented this crucifixion. Saving the Son of God would not save us. Each of us could have died and we would still be in our sins.

Jesus was the only one who was holy and not contaminated with sin. He became our sacrifice, the innocent for the guilty.

The blood trail ends at the cross where Christ gave His life to save us. Life begins for us when we accept Him in our lives.

God's Gift to Mankind
December 16

Let us go back many years ago when Christ was born and laid in a manager. This was a very special time for Joseph and Mary.

Jesus was not born in a hospital, but the place of His birth was in a stable where they kept the livestock. I suppose that lanterns were used for lights and there was no running water.

A stable was His birthplace. This was the beginning of His life. Later as a young man He would go to the cross and die for us.

God has given us the gift of salvation. When we receive Christ into our hearts, we have the greatest gift that has ever been given. When we accept God's gift we receive life eternal through Jesus Christ our Lord.

Please don't turn Him away; a rejected gift will fill each unrepentant heart with sorrow and deep regret. Jesus paid the ultimate price with His life for this gift of salvation.

He gave all He could give. All He asks in return is for us to believe and love God with heart, soul, and mind.

"For unto us a child is born, unto us a Son is given: his name shall be called Wonderful, Counselor, The mighty God, The everlasting Father, Prince of Peace" (Isaiah 9:6).

Give Him our Hearts
December 17

It's that time of year again when we go shopping for a special gift for a loved one or friend. There are a variety of things on the store shelves that interest us.

The toy department is always a good place to take the kids for the holidays. Gifts are special when they are given with love. Children play and family ties are stronger.

The adults have their own special needs and so we walk up and down the isles, looking for those gifts. Sometime we have to make a return trip to the store because our first attempt did not produce good results.

There are a lot of really great things to buy, but the problem is choosing the best one. We are not looking for the most expensive thing.

But we are searching for something that will show our love for those in our families and friends. After several trips to the store, we finally have the gifts that will show our heart's true affection.

There is one more gift that each of us need to give; this is probably the most important one of them all. Please don't worry the shopping is over.

What can we give Jesus, the one who gave all for us? We can love Him with all of our hearts and the tears of grace will bind us together with an everlasting love.

Doorbell is Ringing
December 18

The cold wind blows across the earth and snow is falling from the sky. Winter is a beautiful time of year with landscape scenes that captures the hearts emotions.

Holiday decorations are on lampposts and down city streets. Bright lights are on display to create a joyful mood. Houses in the neighborhood create an atmosphere of peace with colorful lights shining.

My Christmas decorations consist of a life size fiberglass horse that I created. Everyday of the year the horse stands silently in the yard, waiting patiently for this holiday season. Crystal clear lights outline the form of the horse and wagon. Giant snowflakes fall, sparkling in the night.

Christmas is a special time of year with the precious memories of the past and the blessings of the future. Sometimes there is a sad moment of loved ones who has passed on.

We may have sons and daughters or another loved one whom we have not seen for years. Our hope is for them to come home.

It would truly be a wonderful blessing to hear the doorbell ringing and see family members again. Patiently we wait for the glorious day when we can tell our loved ones, sons and daughters how much they are loved. Peace on earth is our heart's prayer.

Joy Comes in the Morning
December 19

The people in the neighborhood were getting ready for Christmas. This was many years ago on a small country farm when horses and wagons traveled the roads.

Paul, a family man who loved his wife and children had to go to town, which was about twenty miles away. This trip was very important to Paul, as he would do all the Christmas shopping today.

It was starting to snow and Paul wanted to get home in time for Christmas Eve. He made it to town ok and he found the gifts that his family wanted him to buy.

While traveling back down the road, the snow was coming down harder and the winds had picked up. Soon there was so much snow on the ground that Paul had to unhook the wagon and ride one of the horses.

His wife and kids were constantly looking out the window at the blizzard conditions. Everyone in the family was worried if Paul was all right and they prayed for his safe return. It was late at night when he got home.

When we are caught out in the blizzards, strong winds of despair slow us down, but they do not stop us from pressing on to the lights of home. It is getting late, but joy comes in the morning.

God's Best Gift
December 20

Many years ago there was a family that lived in a small house just outside of town. Every Sunday they all went to church and worshiped God.

Christmas was a special time of year for this family. They always gave thanks to God for his abundant love and mercy; He gave them a loving embrace.

There were never many gifts under the tree, but that didn't matter as long as they had each other. A couple years ago Bob and Barbara inherited a lot of money. This is when they gradually began to drift away from God.

It seemed as though they wanted the best of everything. Soon they were living in a beautiful house on a hill, and they had the most expensive car, money could buy.

They were not going to church anymore, as there was not enough time. The family was constantly quarreling with one another. A miracle of grace would restore the love.

It was now Christmas Eve and they all held hands and prayed together. Soon the tears were dripping down each one's cheek, as God gave them a loving embrace.

There are times in life when we want the very best money can buy. We fail to realize that God has already given us the best gift in His Son Jesus Christ.

If we want temporal things, we can go to the mall, but if it is spiritual, we had better go to throne room of mercy.

Countdown for Christ
December 21

The days of our lives are coming to an end. Death's dark shadows will soon cross our path. We do not know the day or the hour when the sun will set for the last time.

There is no way of escaping the appointed hour. We cannot reschedule an appointment and come back in a more convenient time.

If it were possible, we would cancel the bereavement process all together and send the gravediggers home. That is a happy thought, but reality shows tombstones on the graves.

Life on earth is a temporary thing. We cannot delay or reset the clock. Death will come as an intruder in the night, without warning or any notices of the final hour.

We cannot control our final journey through the corridors of death. The darkness will surround us, but we can enter the halls of desolation with peace in our hearts and joy in our souls.

Peace with God will keep the light on. No need to fear death if Christ is our Lord and Savior. We have the blessed hope of life eternal.

Our days are numbered that is true. The next ten stories give a countdown for Christ, beginning at number ten. If time allows, decisions will be made to accept or reject Jesus Christ into our hearts.

Ten, Another Opportunity
December 22

Our adventure today will take us out to sea. The cargo is the heavy weight of sin that some of the family members in our group will not let go.

What makes matters even worse is that the yacht is along ways from shore and drifting farther away each day. This family had decided to go on a vacation.

When they were miles away from land, the engine died and they had no communication devices. There was no way to contact other boats and signal for help. As a matter of fact, no boats had been seen in the last hour.

One of the family members became very sick and they laid him in one of the rooms on the yacht. Fred was running a very high fever and he needed immediate attention.

Sally his wife was taking care of him and finally got his temperature to drop. He was feeling some better and a short while later he was sound asleep. Fred was not yet saved as he thought there was plenty of time.

It was getting late as darkness had already covered the earth. The rest of the family members decided to get some sleep and try to get help in the morning.

At the break of dawn everyone woke to a beautiful day. It is a wonderful time in our lives when God gives us another day, another opportunity to make peace with Him.

Nine, Your Choice
December 23

The countdown continues with one day gone and nine remaining. We do not know when death will come our way. When it does our journey will end.

This countdown for Christ will help us to understand that if we only had ten days to make things right with God, would it be enough?

Many years ago I was in a church service. An evangelist was speaking that morning. I had not yet invited Jesus into my heart.

He preached about Jesus dying on a cross and giving His life for us. That morning he had a countdown for Christ. He was going to count from sixty back to zero and then he was going to dismiss the service.

While he was counting back the numbers, the Holy Spirit was dealing with my heart. I don't remember which number he was on, but he said, "Heaven or hell, it's your choice.

I walked down the isle and Jesus saved my soul. We are having a countdown from ten days back to zero because I want you to know the same Jesus, His love and mercy.

We only have nine days to make a decision for Christ. God loves you; Jesus died for you. The days are slowly passing; please don't wait too long. Soon it will be eight.

Eight, Christmas Eve
December 24

Let's return to the family whose boat lost all power. They were drifting farther from shore and Fred became very sick and was in desperate need of a doctor.

This is the third day on the water without any sign of a rescue. The countdown for Christ continues; time is running out.

The first two days are gone; they will never return. There have not been any decisions to accept Christ. Even though one man is barely clinging to life, Jesus is waiting for our response. If we wait too long, it will be too late.

If Fred does not get help soon, he will die. The other family members are trying desperately to save him. All communication devices are disabled because the boat's engine will not start and Fred's chances are slim.

Another terrible incident was taking place on the yacht, as Becky a very poor swimmer fell into the water. Jim dived into the ocean to save her. A rope ladder was extended to help them back on the yacht.

Later a broken wire was discovered and Sammy spliced it back together. This was the miracle they were hoping to find. The engine started and a call was made to a helicopter unit. Fred was flown to the nearest hospital.

It's Christmas Eve and the other family members were back home. This was a time of rejoicing, but it is the bottom of the eighth and no souls saved.

Seven, Christmas Day
December 25

This is a special time of year when we celebrate the birth of Christ. He was born in a stable and laid in a manger. Later as a young man, He died on a cross; He was buried in a grave and resurrected by the mighty power of God.

When He was born the angels proclaimed, "Peace on Earth, glory to God in the highest." The Bible tells us, "For unto you is born this day in the city of David a Saviour, which is Christ the Lord" (Luke 2:11).

Now this family had just survived a life-threatening ordeal at sea. Two of the members had near death experiences and neither of them were Christians.

So far this family has not been able to grasp the true meaning of Christmas. There was still no heavenly peace in their lives and Jesus was not recognized as their Savior.

They did have a certain amount of earthly satisfaction, which gave them a portion of peace and contentment for having survived this life or death situation.

It is time for the Christmas dinner and the family gathered around the table. The doorbell rang and it was Fred. He was released from the hospital and came home.

This family was blessed and they were really thankful, but the seventh day is about over and they have not made peace with God.

Six, No Excuses
December 26

There are not very many days left. This is a really important decision that each of us needs to make in life. Death will not wait on us and life eternal is not automatically granted.

If we want to go to heaven, there is only one way the gates will open for us. Jesus is the way, the truth, and the life. No man cometh to the Father but by Him.

If we try to get into heaven by some other way, we are the same as thieves who breaks into homes. Jesus is the only way. There is no salvation in any other.

This family as of yet had not responded to the gentle urging of the Holy Spirit. I expect there will be all kinds of excuses all through life and they will follow us to the grave.

If we do not accept Jesus as Lord and Savior while we are living, how are we going to do it when we are dead? There is no repentance in the grave.

We are counting the numbers one by one and everyday that passes is one less than before. When the last one is gone, will there be any more?

Not if the sun sets for the last time and funeral arrangements are made for a burial in the cemetery. Soon the last opportunity will be gone. Let's follow the family for the next five days and see if Jesus comes into their lives.

Five, except we Repent
December 27

Sammy was driving down the road, enjoying the scenery. He was on the freeway and there was an awful lot of traffic that day.

He noticed a short distance ahead of him there was a bear cub on the side of the road next to a concrete barrier. The frightened cub was on the verge of crossing the highway.

Sammy was expecting the little bear to be killed, but the mother bear picked the cub up with her teeth and pulled it to the other side of the barrier. Another cub was with the mother, as they went back into the woods.

Along time ago Sammy had raised a little bear cub. When it was old enough he took it to the mountains to live in its natural environment.

While driving, Sammy thought about the time when he first rescued the baby cub. Its mother was killed in a forest fire and this cub was the only one that survived.

Smoke from the fire made it very hard to see the trail. Flames were reaching high into the sky, but the cub was saved that day. It became a faithful follower of Sammy.

If time permits, these two friends will meet again for another rescue operation. We only have four days left in our countdown for Christ. Except we repent, we will die without any hope of making it to heaven. I hope it is not too late!

Four, Unexpected Visit
December 28

Jim was back on His farm working in the field with his tractor. The fence posts were in bad condition and they needed to be replaced.

All morning he worked digging holes with his new excavating equipment. It was getting close to lunchtime so Jim parked the tractor on the side of the hill.

He sat a short distance away on a pile of post. No sooner had he started eating a sandwich when a rumbling sound distracted him.

He quickly turned around, but he could not escape the tractor that was turning over onto him. Jim was injured as he rolled down the hill away from the tractor.

There was no one else on the farm and the cell phone was broken. Jim was lying on the ground and there was no movement. It seemed as though death had made an unexpected visit.

The sun will soon set for the last time on the horizon. I know we were having a countdown for Christ, counting the days when life would be over.

I have to admit I was totally surprised with this accident. It was not my intention to end this story without giving each person a chance to accept Christ as Lord and Savior.

Please don't close the book just yet, as Jim is getting up. He is all right, only a few bruises and cuts. He was temporally knocked unconscious. Only three days remain!

Three, Turn the Herd
December 29

We are getting very close to the deadline. Three days to make a decision for Christ. There is no guarantee that we will make it that far. Today is the day of salvation.

Yesterday is gone and tomorrow may never come. We have already seen several instances where family members almost visited the coroner's office on behalf of loved ones.

The gravediggers are on call, waiting for special appointments to fill unexpected graves with potential residents.

Carpenters have been working overtime, making pine boxes more accessible to the deceased.

Pallbearers have already been chosen and each of them has a backup in case they are unable to carry out their obligations.

I don't like to use such insensitive words to describe death. It is a very personal matter with loved ones dying. Sorrow fills each person's heart.

Even as I write these words, the funeral parlors are open for business and loved ones are taking that final journey through the dark valley.

Please forgive me if I offend, I am just trying to turn the herd from death to life in Christ. Heaven or hell it's your choice. We have two more days if we live that long.

Two, the Fear of Death
December 30

The final two days, I expect there is a lot of trembling going on right now. Every hour that passes brings us a little closer to the grave.

We hope there is a lot of soul searching with more sincere thoughts given to salvation. Our decision for a life in Christ will guarantee us a home in heaven.

The family we have followed for the past eight days are now in a cabin on the mountain. This is their last weekend before they have to go back to work on Monday.

Sammy thought it would be good to go for a walk down a familiar trail next to the creek. This mountain area is where he grew up.

He was casually walking along when he heard the rustling of leaves. A huge bear with two cubs came out of the underbrush.

Sammy was fearful of dying on the trail that day. Immediately he started running from the grizzly bear. The mother of the cubs growled furiously and ran after him through the woods.

Sammy accidently tripped over a fallen tree and was lying on the ground in front of the bear. This seemed to be the final death hour.

The mother bear recognized Sammy as the boy who rescued her from the fire. She spared the life of a friend and went back to her cubs. We have One-day and then the end.

One, Fire Drill
December 31

We have been traveling with a family for ten days. This is the last one as we hope a decision will be made for Christ.

They all decided last night to go to church this morning. When they arrived the pastor greeted them at the door. He told them that today we are having an evangelist speak in the morning service.

While everyone was in the sanctuary, the fire alarm when off and the people walked single file to the outside. Soon the all-clear signal was given and everyone went back inside.

The evangelist, Steve had a special message that he felt the Lord had given him for this service. He did not know they were going to have a fire drill this morning.

After a few moments of meditation, Steve thought that this drill would go right along with his message, "Heaven or Hell." He began his sermon about the fire alert and used the thought, fire get out by the grace of God.

When his message was about over, he decided to have a countdown for Christ. While he was counting, every person in the new family knelt down at the altar and received Jesus Christ as Lord and Savior.

They made things right with God just in time. We do not know when our personal countdown will begin, but we can be saved before the death shadows cross our paths.

Epilogue

My hearts desire is to write words of inspiration to help others along the pathway of life. Grace comes from above and I know what Christ has done for me. He came into my heart many years ago and forgave me of my sins.

I know that time is short and we are just passing through. Life on earth will end and time will be no more. If we can show kindness, others will see Christ and follow Him too.

There are times in life when we all need inspiration to pick us up when we fall, when we stray, or we just need a friend who will stand beside us.

My imaginary and true stories will help others find Jesus as the greatest friend of all. He is the one that will never leave us, no matter how severe the storm.

He will stand beside us and if need be, He will calm our troubled souls, "Peace be Still." Each of my micro stories contains a truthful, spiritual thought.

We might go on an adventure, a journey into the past, or find a lost treasure, but each inspirational page will inspire us to love God with heart, soul, and mind.

As God inspired me to write, I hope He will also inspire you to accept Christ and live for Him.

Praise Ye the Lord

God blesses us with a Daily Inspiration so we will love Him with heart, soul, and mind. We are inspired to follow Jesus on the pathway of life. As we walk the path together, soon we will be in the presence of God the Father, God the Son, and God the Holy Spirit.

The stories in this book were written from my heart. As you join with me, I'm sure the Lord will meet us along the way. For where two or three are gathered together in Christ's name, Jesus is in the midst.

About the Author

David L. Hurst was born in 1949 in Chilhowie, Virginia. He served his country in the military in the years 1969-1971. After his service in Vietnam, he was married and had one son. In the early seventies, David received Jesus Christ into his life.

The Lord has led him into many wonderful places. He shared the gospel with the little children in Sunday school class. Later he worked with youth and brought the good news of salvation to the elderly at a nursing home.

David attends the Dublin Church of God in Dublin, Virginia. In 1982, he received a very special award by the State Layman's Board of Virginia. He was recognized as layman of the year.

The Lord blessed David through his endeavors and gave him a gift of telling recitations. David and the Gospel Lights, a singing group, would go to various churches to magnify the name of Jesus and glorify the Lord God of Heaven.

God has given him a new talent; he has called and anointed him to write micro stories.

David lives in Radford, Virginia. He knows that life is short; he is only passing through. All the good he can do he wants to do now, for he will not pass this way again. Tomorrow will take care of itself.

While he walks with the Lord, David wants to give a little sunshine and a whole lot of love. His heart's desire is to be a faithful servant and a witness for Jesus Christ.